Aquarium

# Aquarium

## YAARA SHEHORI

TRANSLATED FROM THE HEBREW BY
TODD HASAK-LOWY

FARRAR, STRAUS AND GIROUX   NEW YORK

Farrar, Straus and Giroux
120 Broadway, New York 10271

Printed in the United States of America
Originally published in Hebrew in 2016 by Keter, Israel, as אקווריום (*Akvaryom*)
English translation published in the United States by Farrar, Straus and Giroux
First American edition, 2021

Grateful acknowledgment is made for permission to
reprint the following previously published material:
Lines from "My Blue Piano," by Else Lasker-Schüler, from *After Every War:
Twentieth-Century Women Poets*, translated and introduced by Eavan Boland,
copyright © 2004 by Eavan Boland. Used by permission of
Princeton University Press. All rights reserved.

Library of Congress Cataloging-in-Publication Data
Names: Shehori, Ya'arah, author. | Hasak-Lowy, Todd, 1969– translator.
Title: Aquarium : a novel / Yaara Shehori ; translated from the Hebrew
by Todd Hasak-Lowy.
Other titles: Akvaryum. English
Description: First American edition. | New York : Farrar, Straus and
Giroux, 2021. | "Originally published in Hebrew in 2016 by Keter, Israel."
Identifiers: LCCN 2020042920 | ISBN 9780374105921 (hardcover)
Classification: LCC PJ5055.41.E358 A7713 2021 | DDC 892.43/7—dc23
LC record available at https://lccn.loc.gov/2020042920

Designed by Abby Kagan

Our books may be purchased in bulk for promotional, educational, or business
use. Please contact your local bookseller or the Macmillan Corporate and
Premium Sales Department at 1-800-221-7945, extension 5442, or by email at
MacmillanSpecialMarkets@macmillan.com.

www.fsgbooks.com
www.twitter.com/fsgbooks • www.facebook.com/fsgbooks

1   3   5   7   9   10   8   6   4   2

*To my sister, my dearest friend*

It's been in the shadow of the cellar door
Ever since the world went rotten.
Four starry hands play harmonies.
The Woman in the Moon sang in her boat.
Now only rats dance to the clanks.
The keyboard is in bits.

—ELSE LASKER-SCHÜLER

Aquarium

Suppose I stretched my socks up over the knee. Suppose you saw what fine calves I have; suppose that the skirt above those same fine calves billowed out like a bell. And I'll suppose even that you followed my movements as I rose from the chair and began to walk. Let's suppose. Would you have said something like, *Doesn't that deaf girl have beautiful legs?* Yes, definitely, that's what you would've said, as if I were a grasshopper, with my ears affixed to my legs.

Because in an instant I was the beautiful deaf girl. All at once, a cardboard sign hung around my neck. A sign that couldn't be taken off. For years I got used to seeing and not being seen, like a ghost under a sheet: pull away the sheet and poof, nothing, vacant eyes staring back at you. But when the sheet was finally removed, my sudden new beauty embarrassed everyone. That's how it was, adolescence descended upon me like a wave, soaking me, and all at once I was beautiful. Suddenly the too-wide mouth and the baby fat made others admire me, deaf or not.

Beauty makes a difference. A big one. Like an elevator that takes you up six floors. Say you never wanted it and you're a liar. A deaf liar. And it's still not enough. It's never enough. Not only because I wound up alone. In that moment, as in all the moments that followed, Dori was no more. Even my notebooks piled up just out of habit, because there was no more Dori to read them in secret.

## PART ONE

# NOBODY WHO ARE YOU

*I'm Nobody! Who are you?*
*Are you—Nobody—too?*
—EMILY DICKINSON

# 1

———

Lili and Dori. A light head next to a dark one. Curls and braids. Red mixed with brown. Four narrow eyes. The older has a girl's name and her sister a name they give to boys. At home, they called them Big and Little, a stretched-out hand signaling the height of the taller one and then the height of her sister. Always one in relation to the other, even when they were apart. To the world, they weren't yet Little and Big. They were the disabled girls. They had tanned legs, stung by mosquitoes in the summer. In the winter they wore shorts like boys', without charm, without that blooming sweetness, without whatever shields the soft bones of children—not the flesh but rather that strange, pleasant innocence. That they never had. Mostly they wore oversized straw hats that seemed too adult for their age, the two of them like two black pits.

Hair fell in their eyes, but what was there for them to see—an oil stain on a shirt, a scrape on a knee? They spoke with words unvoiced, but they definitely spoke. They had many words. There was the language. An apple tree stood in the yard and all its fruit had worms. It grew there just as in a legend, and in opposition to all the rules of climate. They threw the apples. They tossed the leaves at one another as if they were two forest girls marrying each other under a green canopy. Lili was brave and Dori a coward, but they climbed the highest branches. They sat on a budding branch and shouted to the moon and the stars. It wasn't pleasant to hear. Quite frightening, actually, like a couple of rabid foxes. The neighbors screamed until they gave up, because what was the point? Ackerman's deaf girls couldn't hear anyway. The neighbors learned and kept quiet. The girls hurled small, hard apples at the cats in the yard. Never hit one.

In truth, the tree belonged to the entire building, eight apartments, each one with lights on in the evening. But only Lili and Dori climbed it. Other than the screaming, the neighbors barely bothered them. Perhaps they left them alone out of pity. Perhaps out of despair. Perhaps they just gave up the sour apple harvest. Not a single child came near them, and they didn't know that was odd.

From Lili and Dori's perspective, the tree in the courtyard was the only thing that made their small apartment bearable. Low ceilings. Warped tiles. A room without a window; the drum rattle of the washing machine and the shaking of the sewing machine that could be felt in the soles of the feet. How cramped they were there. Only on the apple tree were they okay: two daughters of the forest. Two imps. Deaf. Half retarded. Illiterate. Leave them alone.

When their father knocked on the trunk of the tree, they sensed the rising vibrations and hurried home. Sometimes they saw the light in the apartment rhythmically switch on and off, and that was enough. The lighthouse was illuminated. Each of them had worn a key since they were very small, tied to shoelaces around their necks. You need to be responsible, the whole world told them; you're not sweet, and you can't get comfortable with relying on someone else to worry about you. At the entrance to the apartment, each checked the other's appearance. It was hopeless. Lili's collar was torn in two places; Dori's socks were falling off and her braid looked like a mouse's tail. Lili was the big one. When they stood opposite the door, this became clear once again, whether or not they called her that at home. The big one slid a finger wet with spit over the small one's eyebrows, forcefully cleaned a green-black stain above her cheek. It didn't help. The two of them tried to smooth out their wrinkled skirts. Whoever heard of such a thing, climbing in skirts? But that is what they wore that day, over their pants, because the two uncles, their father's brothers, were supposed to arrive for a visit. Their father treated the visit as a necessary evil (and before each visit Dori imagined those words written above the uncles' heads), but the girls were required to look civilized. At least this time.

They certainly could have opened the door; they had keys, after all, but they waited. Finally their mother stood at the threshold with a blank expression on her face and they went in after her. Their father's two brothers sat there. Their discomfort splashed in waves all the way to Dori, who saw four hands that couldn't find a proper task. Uncle Noah interlaced his fingers and then released them. Ari's hands lay dead on his knees. Noah loved to make small, ingenious devices, though this was in no way his line of business. Once he built a tiny bird for her that jumped out from its cage and spread its beak. She looked in amazement at the colorful feathers that had been glued one by one to its small body. Dori never knew when the bird was liable to leave the cage, even though she tried to guess. But his main hobby was children—he built dozens of tiny plaster children who slept in cigarette cases and matchboxes. For days after each of his visits, they found these boxes throughout the small apartment.

It can be assumed that it was only because of their uncles that Lili and Dori learned to read words, the words formed by their uncles' fish lips. Dori was faster than Lili, true, but both of them could understand, if there was enough light and they could clearly see the mouths opening and closing, the tongue rising toward the palate and separating, the rows of teeth. How ugly it was! More than once they trembled in disgust and terror at the sight, with a kind of nausea that had pleasure mixed up in it, like sitting in a monster's mouth without being swallowed. Noah and Ari, for their part, tried hard to absorb something of the language, they kept asking the girls to teach them, but the teaching never went anywhere. Alex asked them firmly, again and again, to let them be; they were girls, after all, not circus animals.

Sometimes it appeared to Dori that while her parents were beautiful and slender and ageless, the uncles themselves were immeasurably old. They were like fish that had been eaten and only their shiny fishbones were left on the plate. After one of these visits, which became more and more rare, they found two blue fish with wings stuck between the M and O volumes of *The Complete Encyclopedia for Young Adults*. The fish were precisely the size of their palms and made of thin metal. It was possible to scrape off the coating with a fingernail, but one try proved that it wasn't worth the effort. The fishes' wings shimmered as if they had been smeared with nail polish.

They were briefly alarmed by the thought that Noah knew the girls called them the fish uncles. "His toys are too sad," Lili proclaimed as her open hand descended in front of her face, her expression conveying deep sadness, and then, in the blink of an eye, both hands, with fingers clenched, moved frenetically back and forth before her chest. Then she pointed to the uncle. But Dori knew that despite Lili's conviction, her sister kept the boxes of sleeping children in the back of her bedside table; she even kept the fish (whereas Dori, despite her best efforts, lost hers). That was how they were then, like two open books in which almost the same thing was written.

If, despite everything, there was something special about Noah—fine hands, in any case—their father's other brother, Ari, was small and withered. He had always been that way, straggling and slow, a mechanical engineer without a drop of spirit in him, as their father once told them. "The living fish and the dead fish,"

Lili giggled when they were a bit bigger, and Dori joined in the giggling, mouth open wide like a dog learning to smile from its owner, without catching the joke. Still, they pitied him. But now, as he relaxed on the padded plaid armchair, she didn't pity him at all.

The large notebook was placed on the table and the brothers took turns writing in it. The brothers had disposable pens, the kind that broke quickly, and their father had a heavy, cumbersome pen from which only he could manage to extract ink and letters. Each one added his words and at their end affixed a period or a question mark. More question marks, in the cases of Noah and Ari. Their father inserted periods but never, ever exclamation marks. And after the periods, silence. If you looked on from the sidelines you would say, mistakenly, *Three brothers are writing together*, but in fact the notebook belonged to their father, Alex Ackerman, the oldest. The other two were just along for the ride. They had nothing of their father's grand, terrible power. Dori tried to imagine them as children and still saw only a giant and two dwarfs, a fisherman and fishes. The two of them were born well after he was. They didn't endure what he had endured, the two girls knew vaguely, without knowing the nature of the valleys he had traversed and the rivers he had crossed. Their father's hands rested in the center of the notebook like a ship in a sea of paper. A moment later he was pressing the pen to the page and writing with quick movements. His brothers read upside down what he wrote. Dori and Lili knew that they were forbidden to interrupt. From the narrowed gaze their father sent them, they understood that their appearance alone was an outrage.

Dori identified a sign of amusement in Noah's eyes, and she knew that Lili saw it as well. But Ari was actually the one who addressed them by name, before their father dismissed his brother's words with one decisive wave of his arm, and they went to their room, which they'd painted in shades of orange after the two of them agreed that nothing in the world was as beautiful as the sunset. Dori had already regretted this more than once. She would continue to regret it but would never paint the room another color.

Their mother waited for them there, sitting on Lili's made bed, with the stretched-tight cover and the teddy bear Lili never hugged. The bear sat and stared at them with glass eyes. On Dori's bed were six dolls, crayons, and a math book, an apple core and pencil shavings and God knew what else. This was all before Dori learned to behave like a human being, when her bed was the last unrestricted zone. So Dori sat down on her bed among the stuff and Lili remained standing and their mother didn't move. They understood that she intended to reprimand them and then cry. This was how she always looked. Her nose was always red at its tip. Despite this, she was an attractive woman and had once been a real beauty. More beautiful than the two of them together—otherwise their father wouldn't have married her. But instead of crying, she said to them in the language that she had a present for them. She was clumsy. Her hands were pretty but heavy and slow when asked to sign.

And she truly did give them a present. A blue coat for Lili and a red one for Dori. They almost never had money for new clothes. They were poor, but—no. Not exactly poor. It was simply that when there was money, they invested it in more important things, in long-term goals. Their mother had a sewing machine and good enough hands, and usually that was sufficient.

"What's this all about?" Lili asked, surprised, but Dori didn't want to see the answer. She was happy. Their mother smiled.

From the front her smile was perfect, but Dori knew that in the back, on the left side, she was missing a lower tooth. A thousand years would have to pass before she'd get it repaired. This was the smile that Dori loved most in the whole world. Her mother suggested, almost without anger, that she shouldn't wear the jacket when she was so dirty. She sadly left it in the silk wrapping paper on the bed. They went to wash their hands. Lili drank water from the toothbrush cup because she insisted that it tasted good to her, and Dori laughed so hard that water came out of her nose. Afterward they helped their mother bake oatmeal cookies. Two minutes of work, their mother announced to them happily. They served their father cookies because his brothers were already on their way out. Lili crossed the distance and put cookies in Noah's pockets. One cookie, crumbling, she placed in Ari's palm. Dori knew that their father saw, he saw everything, but he didn't say a word. After Ari and Noah left, the four of them sat and nibbled on healthy cookies. "Two minutes it took," their mother repeated joyfully, and for a moment her hands appeared to dance. This was one of the good days. One of the best.

That night they lay in bed and made shadows on the wall. They spoke like this many nights, in shadows, until they got caught. Dori asked Lili to tell her about the baby. Every time, Lili resisted a bit and then told her about the most beautiful baby ever born. "She was so small, we found her inside a sack of sugar," Lili said, and Dori laughed. The previous time it was a sack of cotton. This was the story that Lili began telling her a while ago, after their mother recalled a memory from her childhood, that when she was a girl she thought that babies were born from cabbage. Which meant they were found in a cabbage patch, folded up among the leaves. The two of them understood, because they weren't always slow-witted like people said, that apparently people grew cabbage wherever she came from. Dori imagined fields packed with heads of cabbage and two baby legs poking out from each head.

Lili laughed at their mother, but sometimes Dori believed her a bit. Sometimes she thought that she herself had really been born like those children Noah made, that they had found her too in a pack of cigarettes or in a medicine jar, but she, unlike all the others, had opened her eyes. Lili continued telling, the shadows she made with her quick fingers running along the wall. She signs even faster than Father, Dori thought. She looked at the shadows on the wall until her eyes hurt, but she didn't plan to miss a thing. "You were the most beautiful baby anyone ever saw. You had eyes that were almost purple. A nose like a dot. I loved you so much and I believed you were mine. I argued about that with Mother like you wouldn't believe. Who knew that you'd turn out to be such a witch?" The word "baby" was signed as a rocking motion and a finger catching the lobe, as if to signify an earring, and the witch was signed as an imaginary crooked nose and after that a quick rub of the real nose. She knew that Lili didn't mean what she signed, not really, but now her eyes were brown, not purple, and nothing remained in her of the sweet baby she had been nine years before, the baby that someone indeed had rocked, the baby that she had forgotten, but Lili remembered for her. Dori hugged the box that Noah had left her. Inside there was a boy with hair the color of sand. She fell asleep.

So they didn't speak at your house? Anton asked.

Dori looked at him. He looked like a boy made of gold, his pretty head resting on his shoulders as if in another moment it would be removed. Of course they spoke, I already told you. Aren't you listening?

He sat on the windowsill in his mother's old house, which was painted white. She wasn't really reprimanding him, but she could have.

We spoke in the language, do you understand?

He didn't understand, or pretended he didn't.

With your hands, you mean?

Dori rolled with laughter. Yes, idiot, with our hands. What'd you think, that we used Morse code?

# 2

Imagine another world. It moves in parallel with yours, like twin planets creating a figure eight with their revolutions. But its time is different. It has another rhythm. In the other world, one hears different things; foods have a more pronounced taste. Try standing up on your two legs there and eating a strawberry, a lollipop, grilled toast—you can't do it.

In those days the morning star wasn't yet the evening star, but the two of them uttered an identical sound—that is, no sound. Not a rustle was heard. Objects fell noiselessly. Rocks were tossed. Water flowed in silence. The village was still distant and hidden, and what came after it was truly the end of the world, a place reached by sailors whose routes were drawn on ancient maps and who fell with their ships into nothingness. There the mermaids sang to one another and drowned whoever heard their voice or dared to dip a toe in the sea. That's how it was at the time, when Lili and Dori were still alike. There were indeed differences: in temperament; in the shape of the eyes; in the one body that began to lengthen while the other insisted on remaining small for its age; in an expression that was amused on one face, while on the other, the joke might be the backdrop for tears. Because Dori always looked as if she'd be quick to cry, even though she wasn't. So yes, there were differences. But both the little one and the big one lifted hands up in order to speak; the two of them contorted their faces; the two of them were sentenced to be precisely what they were. But their ears, if you were wondering, weren't altogether without use. Because the big one, for instance, to their parents' dismay, would still insist on adorning them with earrings, and she returned home one day with two gold earrings stuck in her lobes, piercing her for eternity. Whereas the little one liked to insert things into her ear, soft things like cotton, bothering no one. Perhaps in another home it would be just the opposite: they would scold the little one to remove right away whatever she'd stuffed in her ears, and the big one they'd take by the hand to the nearby city to punch two holes and choose a first pair of earrings. But not in this home. Their father looked at Lili with a severe gaze and asked her if she knew whom they used to impale by the ear to the doorframe of the house. She didn't know. And Dori just jammed the wad in deeper and felt how the soft became hard and the hard, soft.

If you looked at them from the outside, it would have been easy and simple, and best, in fact, to see them as a single unit. The deaf sisters: nocturnal demons, mythological creatures who were doomed to make a little noise and then sink to watery depths. It was tempting to throw a rock at the two of them, although most didn't bother, because Lili would pick it up and throw it right back.

The Building Association brought them in for a conversation. They sat there. They joined hands. They didn't hear. After some time, the two were declared a lost cause. As it was with the girls, so must it be with the parents; as everyone knows, it always starts at home. They couldn't be reached. They were inaccessible. Severe retardation, whispered whoever whispered it, and the rumor spread all the way to deaf ears.

Maybe they laughed in the committee members' faces. It depends on who is telling the story. Maybe their laughter was insane, impetuous, the laughter of one who cannot hear herself. Because time is a thread one can tie in a knot and suddenly what was and what will be are nearly the same. But that evening, they continued sitting in the tree, hanging from it with surprisingly strong legs, hair dangling down, Lili's red mixed with Dori's brown, a screen through which they saw all there was. Which wasn't much.

They enjoyed scaring everyone; what can you do? Casting their terror down on the residents of the building, who gave the tree a wide berth. They would conquer and rule. Queens without a crown. They could have gone up to the city on elephants and torched it all if they weren't scared of fire. A few months had passed since Uncle Noah built them a platform of equal-sized beams fastened with long nails to the forking branches. Their hold on the tree was complete. This is the world under the moon, Lili declared, and Dori agreed, even though only on rare occasions did they remain among the branches until it was late enough to see a pale moon reflecting down on them. From their perch they stuck out their tongues at whoever dared to draw near. And perhaps spat on them as well. One way or another, they were the stuff of the neighborhood's nightmares. And they knew what was said about them.

Children know. Girls know, even if they're deaf as a rock. If someone objected to the spectacle of two girls up in a tree and many children taunting them from down below, these with stones and those sticking out their tongues, someone would be found to appease him; someone would be quick to pull out the triumphant, circular argument: "Children will be children." And someone would add, "This is nothing compared with what's coming for them. They won't always be treated so nice." In any case, the girls didn't hear a thing. The silence surrounded them like insulation, like that button on the television that mutes the world.

It was good and easy to float on the surface of this lie, as if on an inflatable mattress in a pool of turquoise water. And whoever drowned, drowned.

Because, yes, they were very bad. But deep in their hearts they were Exemplary Little Girls, just like in the book. They repeated the words to themselves: "They were completely happy, the nice little girls, and their mother loved them fiercely; and all the people who knew them also loved them and sought to bring them pleasure." That is, girls like that did exist. Not them—others, Nicole and Claudette, Mirabelle and Bat-El, that kind. With a mother who loved them completely, with all love's strength. Right behind the girls who hurled apples, near the girls with the dirty legs and the barbaric habits and the birth defect—because that's what was said about them, they knew—there resided two girls with fine habits and table manners. Girls on whom the world waited to serve delights on a silver platter and who would say in the language of humans, pinkish tongues rising up and brushing the palate, *merci merci* and *ooh la la*. They hailed from somewhere in France, with noble titles and lace napkins, with servants and coachmen and tales of tragedy in which the poor were the only ones to die. Like Cosette from *Les Misérables*, who actually, Dori recalled, ended up alive and well. Perhaps only Dori saw them this way, and Lili had given up on the old game some time ago, but Dori never forgot: the two of them were exemplary little girls. And therefore maybe they were happy too. But no happiness was to be seen in them, unfortunately. "I beg of you," Dori practiced, trying to form the actual words with the aid of her lips, as the hearing do. "Oh, please, good sir. If you could please forgive me." She knew how to bow, to let a handkerchief drop, to look out with a courageous gaze toward the horizon that was nothing but the hallway leading to the den, without the need of smelling salts. One day, she believed, her knowledge would be put to use.

Because in her heart (the heart swelling with blood, the heart working nonstop, emptying and filling, as hearts must), she could choose to ignore their two sticky faces, which they always forgot to wash; the hair they didn't comb, with knot after knot instead of smooth, silky tresses; the books they left bloated with water in the bath. In her heart, the resolutely stuck-out tongues melted away, and so did the eyes that rolled up in their sockets at the sight of them. They could abandon the faces they wore, like empty masks, frightening the world before it could frighten them. She could set aside the lousy game of hopscotch they played by themselves, inventing rules until darkness fell and they had to go back. Kittens wouldn't go dying on them because it was impossible to bring them home and they shook inside the cardboard box in the backyard until they didn't. In her heart, all was very refined. The cats were well cared for and groomed and blue ribbons were tied around their necks, and the two of them were Dora and Lilith, clean and puffy-cheeked, round-eyed like the dolls they didn't play with, with perfect manners and foreign names that finally suited them. Who would have believed that inside those two disturbed girls, the ones all the parents warned their children about (as they knew, they always knew), there waited two good, polite, likable girls, drinking tea from delicate cups? Even if people thought that they were crazy and defective, they knew their own true natures. And this, of course, is the most precious knowledge of all.

There were other children on their street. What kind of street doesn't have children? A sad street, and their street definitely wasn't sad. They were the sadness in it, yes, that was true. A negligible statistical deviation on a street with children who were otherwise bright-eyed and exceptionally skilled at sports. Nourished entirely by cream and fruit. Children who played games that involved chalk drawings on the street, sticks, and rocks.

Clean and dirty children, disturbed and good children. Children who gathered under a tree until apples and rocks were thrown down at them. Children who were shown with the movement of two fingers how easy it was to cut off wings, ears—everything, actually. Clipping and cutting. Dividing and conquering. And that bit above, that no one bothered the girls? That was a nice little lie. Yes, most preferred not to get mixed up with them, but that doesn't mean that no one did. It doesn't mean a thing.

No one remembers childhood as it was, bad and hard and strewn with teeth poking up out of the ground. You forget that childhood is a time with more monsters than heroes. It really seems to you that it was pleasant: the colors were strong, the smells sweet. Adventures waited around every corner, and oh, how many corners there were! You saw frogs and toads, hedgehogs and cats, and all this even if you grew up in the city, in an apartment block near a puddle that dried up in summer and teemed with life in winter. And the grass and the apples gave off such a good smell and the earth had a good smell and Mother too, and in those years it seemed that this would be enough. You played detective; you caught a thief; you acted honestly and courageously. You earned your just rewards, and this seemed fair enough to you. Because even if you didn't dare venture to the puddle when the others were there, and even if the breeze carried stories about children who drowned in the puddle, you didn't drown. Allow me to bless you—how lucky you were!

After you fall, it seems very easy to get back up. So you fall and get up and forget that you fell, or at least you shake off the dirt and the teeny stones from your knee and know, because they taught you, that it's nonsense, there's nothing to be done about it, everyone falls. I fell, and here I am today. And they did too, because this is their story, after all, not yours. Dori and Lili fell and got back up so often it appeared to be their regular mode of walking. They say that deaf people have balance problems, but that's not true. If they throw stones at you, you fall, until you get used to falling. But not from the tree. Never from the tree.

In Dori's eyes, the other children were a cluster, like a bunch of grapes. Everyone grew on the same stalk, close together and quite similar, waiting to ripen and explode from too much juicy sweetness. Usually she didn't think about them—too bad, because if you don't think, how will you learn? Perhaps Lili thought on her behalf and reached her own conclusions. They didn't need anyone but themselves. They would make progress. They had books and finger puppets and notebooks and the language. So Dori didn't think about the others. She feared only wolves, and Lili told her they were just kids; they'd never be wolves. And Lili opened her mouth wide to show her younger sister that her teeth were actually pretty sharp, even though half of them were still baby teeth. "If there's a wolf here, it's me," she announced.

But Dori didn't believe Lili any more than Lili believed herself. Dori knew that her sister was a bird, at most, definitely not a wolf, and that her teeth weren't as sharp as she hoped. Because the marks that Lili left in the world were quite faint. A long time ago, when Dori was still small, like a peanut with hands, like a baby kangaroo that must climb into its mother's pouch or die, Lili came home with a split lip and a torn collar. A whole lock of hair was missing from the middle of her head, leaving a smooth, round patch like a coin. And there were unexplained scratches on her arms. And there was also a doll, its eyes suddenly gouged out, and then abandoned; there was the repeated bed-wetting at night that dragged with it scoldings about immaturity, a rubber sheet stretched tight. There were signs, if not from Lili's hands. But she would write all this down one day, and Dori would read it.

When they asked her, and of course they asked, she said

something about a dog with stripes. A dog that wanted a cake. But Dori's blood inside her body told her that it was the hearing kids. If anyone ate cake, it was them, and not some stray dog. Because Lili was never scared of dogs, not even after all that. Ever since, their parents had stopped making her go outside to make friends, to breathe the fresh air. There was enough air up in the tree, "perfect for photosynthesis," as their father admitted. In any case, their parents didn't understand the desperate human need for company. The girls invented new ways to speak; they hung upside down like bats, like pendulums in old clocks, as two who went forth to learn what fear was. They both feared the women they would turn into when they got older, women without a voice, without a single unique quality. Like the little mermaid who lost both her tail and her voice, whose best option was to turn into a statue.

Sadly, neither of them resembled Anna, who was beautiful. They always knew they didn't resemble their parents at all, neither Anna nor Alex. They didn't inherit anything important from them, not the impressive lines of their father's face, not their mother's freckles or profile or turbulent tears. When Dori stood in profile, Lili examined her and pronounced that, yes, Dori resembled Noah a bit. But even if the two of them were born from a cabbage or found in a box of matches or in a bottle of baby shampoo, they couldn't imagine not having been, or no longer being, Ackerman's deaf girls. And to a large extent they always would be.

**Anton looked at Dori, who was again startled by how handsome he was. Handsome and lazy. She saw the wealth that ran in his blood, the obvious pedigree. It was like being handed a doll that was too beautiful and fearing it would be taken away, even hurrying to lose it on her own, breaking an arm or nose as if to ward off bad luck. As he always did at this time, he asked her about her childhood, his**

hands resting behind his back, quite perfect. His nose was perfect. He looked as if there was no more comfortable and relaxing position in the world, and Dori was amazed again at how he did this. It was a talent, she decided. Dori had learned that he felt comfortable anywhere, even if he chose to display open disgust.

He wasn't the first who'd asked to hear about her and Lili (though he called her Lilith, with an almost-whistling *th* at the end of her name, and Dori didn't really correct him). Dori knew that he too was searching for a hidden truth, one attached not to biography but to something deeper, to the bones. A vein of gold. When he expressed interest in her, her advantage stood like a sword drawn from stone. All at once she had something that he wanted from her other than her body (beneath the formless clothes, exceeding the low expectations he bothered to display, her body impressed him time after time).

Dori was small, very small. From a distance one might think that she was still a girl. She dressed like a child who had stumbled into an unfamiliar wardrobe and wrapped herself up in an abundance of colorful outfits, geometrical patterns, clashing colors; it was always a mishmash. Spotted stockings enveloped thin legs inside high boots the color of spilled wine. Not to mention the chewed nails, painted like springtime beetles. She cut her bangs herself and spread a black line above each eyelid. The impression she made was extravagant but not jovial. She was tiny but not sweet. From the age of nine, she knew her face wouldn't allow it.

And in the meantime they learned to be careful and to look. As in the ancient maps, their tree was the center of the world. Sometimes they still referred to the city they built in its branches as the world under the moon. Sometimes they forgot about it, the way one forgets a doll from early childhood: almost entirely. Forgetting on purpose. And if the moon was up above, white and indifferent like a third uncle, illuminated in borrowed light, to the south of them was the Sea of Mockery that spilled onto the faces watching them. They knew. To the west was home. To the north they saw the lands of Adi and Adi, bright-haired girls, fast-moving and tanned from all those hours in the sun. Of course they knew what people called them; how couldn't they know? One can understand the world even without the help of ears. In any case, they knew that Adi and Adi, pug-nosed and straight-haired, hated them with a burning hatred, just as they knew that on the eastern side of the map, at the end of the street, there lived Uriel Savyon. He was a year younger than Lili and a year older than Dori. Uriel Savyon: he'd been sent to blend in. They put hearing aids on him. His arms moved mechanically as if they were made from metal, and their father nodded at him: "The boy is a lost cause. They made him a robot." They looked at him from the tree as he walked to the side of the street, his nose running and his ears covered in earmuffs that somehow only accentuated the hearing aids. Each and every day, Uriel Savyon dragged his feet to the school that the two of them saw from the inside only once. Dori recalled the old illustration that showed every man, woman, child, and cat carrying bundles and bundles of air on their backs, an unseen weight pulling them earthward. That was gravitational pull. Or maybe just gravity. Either way, with Uriel Savyon it was clear as day. Clear as night. "He suffers under the burden of the worst expectations one could imagine." Dori repeated the things their father had said, and each nodded to the other like a person whose fate is looking up, like someone whose hands are empty and free, ready only to sign.

In those years, Dori knew for certain what Lili wanted and what she didn't. What this meant was that she could reach her hand into Lili's throat and retrieve the desire, like a surgeon who removes an internal organ and then puts it back in place, all polished. The desire was primarily something she didn't want: not to be like Uriel Savyon; not to be like the other girls; not to be like Mother. In the future it would be simpler. Lili would want to write, and Dori to read, and maybe the opposite. But then the desires would still make their own demands. They were two greedy girls who sucked the sugar from everything, who saved candy wrappers, who would lick tree bark if they thought it was sweet. And even if they had been raised differently, even if they straightened their backs on a board at night and refrained from luxuries, the two of them would have wanted and wanted and wanted. And Dori, as much as she wanted, instinctively knew that the world was only what it could be. And in this world, moving a toothpick required the strength of a thousand horses and a hundred elephants. Better to suck on another candy. But no, they didn't have to move a toothpick from here to there—they had a role, a mission that was given to them like heads on a golden platter. Only, by chance, the heads were theirs.

And for a long time, longer than you might suppose, they were left alone. The Ackerman family existed like weeds by the main road. They lived off the good hands and the good eyes of Alex Ackerman, off the residual savings of their mother, Anna Ackerman. After all, they didn't need much. Their father collected metal throughout the city and knew how to sell it to the right man. He had a talent for finding half-precious metal sparkling in the sun, glittering inside a pile of nothing. But he had nothing against simple metal either. So he dragged the rusty skeleton of a bed from the edge of a field and Dori and Lili ran after him, moving their hands too much while running, like eager cats after the butcher for scraps. They always hoped they'd encounter one of the golden metals, the names of which they recalled from legends and lands beyond the sea. Their father never got rich—after all, he was just an Ackerman, not a Rothschild—but he didn't collect junk, like they'd say afterward. Only metal. The letters on the back of his van spelled two words, without a telephone number: THE DEAF. Better that they know in advance, he explained, and they understood. The two of them believed that their father really saw pieces of metal hiding in the ground, just as he could tell with one look if the man facing him was a lecher, a coward, an exploiter feeding off the weakness of others, or just an idiot. For years, Dori kept an old catalog of metals her father gave her; the edges of the pages were already starting to bend back then. She never was good at protecting the things that were dear to her heart.

Perhaps this could have continued for eternity. One eternity after another. But of course it didn't. Time seemed endless only to Dori. She didn't connect the dots: the many days they spent unsupervised. Not to mention the weeks that piled up into months and years. The neighbors' complaints. Their parents ignoring the letters that arrived from the city and the school. Pink and yellow pages fell from them, carrying the names of the students Lilith Ackerman and Dora Ackerman. But most of the envelopes remained closed. Dori built them into a tower and then forgot about them. Their mother exhaled. Their father chuckled and Lili waited. In the end they announced, in a letter tacked to the door, that they were coming. "Like the theses of Martin Luther," their father said, and Dori laughed, as was expected of her, even though she didn't understand, and their mother frowned, and a lone tear slid down to hang from the end of her nose. As beautiful as a diamond.

But when the test came, Dori believed that from that moment on, everything would only get better and better. It's true, she was only looking at the scenery, but it would be hard to blame her for that; after all, they had finally transformed into magnificent versions of themselves. The house was cleaned down to its foundation. They tied butterfly ribbons into Dori's and Lili's hair, put them in plaid dresses that, their mother announced, were sewn in London and flown to Israel by plane (the plane didn't fly for them alone, but what did that matter). If you didn't know them you might believe that the two of them were almost sweet, except for Dori's concerned expression and Lili's sneer, which absolutely could not be erased. Try, their mother commanded them, and stuck strawberry-flavored sucking candies under their tongues, where they last longer. And that helped. Sugar helps. Maybe because deaf people have highly developed senses as a compensation for what's absent. Maybe because it's always easy to comfort children with candy.

Their father wore an ironed shirt (Dori couldn't believe they'd had an iron this whole time) and trimmed his tangled beard with nail clippers. But without a doubt this was their mother's show. She removed the old hearing aid from the secretary, which was the only nice piece of furniture in their home, and placed it on her right ear. It was the color of vomit. Like a witch's ear, a prosthetic ear. Hide it, Dori thought, come on. But, in fact, she gathered up her hair so that the device would remain visible to the eye. Dori sat and saw how in an instant their mother transformed into Anna Ackerman-Cohen, as they called her once, who smeared her lips with colored lipstick and sewed dresses with collars and hems on the sewing machine, dresses that she never wore. She looked like another woman, put together, happy. Perhaps she too buried a strawberry candy under her tongue—who knows.

Workbooks were piled up on the girls' table, which was usually loaded with Dori's finger puppets. The dried leaves that served as dresses for the dolls were tossed into the yard—show's over. And everything was waiting. Even the cake in the oven opened its smiling mouth and waited. *Tap tap tap*, tapped a seagull who mistakenly arrived at the window. Who heard him? They didn't open up. His crooked beak met only glass. His round eye stared at its own reflection. *Tick tock tick tock*, tocked the clock urgently. The legs of the table moved and squeaked. Furniture was dragged aside. Drapes were laundered. The house waited.

The night before the visit, a storm of thunder and lightning raged and Dori woke up in the middle of the night and opened the window in their room, above the low bookcase, and saw a sky full of light. The wind blew incessantly and slammed against the blinds that Dori had opened with some effort, and Dori tried to wake Lili by shaking her, but Lili grabbed the blankets that were too thin for weather like this and wouldn't wake up, and Dori crawled in with Lili, who hated when she did that, but she who can sleep through anything has no right to object. And in the morning Lili quickly told how she'd found her in her narrow bed, covered in the somewhat dusty covers, and Dori said that the light of the lightning was definitely what woke her, and Lili agreed. A soft light flooded the street and the two of them went down to see the tree, two branches of which had broken off and lay in the yard like two broken hands, and the leaves blew in their multitudes, but nevertheless it had withstood that nocturnal storm, and the two of them rushed upstairs to get ready because there was no time to lose, and besides, the soft light that flooded the washed-out street was a good omen, so their parents said, as if they suddenly believed in omens, and the four of them knocked on anything in their house made of wood.

If they had knocked on the door, who would have heard? When they rang the bell and a red lamp flickered, the dresses were straightened, the backs were tensed on the tall chairs without touching the backrest. As much as they tried, they did not look especially cheerful, but what could be done? The reference and diagnosis team passed through the door. Two people entered the living room. The supervisor was sent from the neighborhood school with a social worker who called himself Arad (strange, they were sure that it would be a woman, and suddenly: a man). Each of the girls held a slice of cake in her hand and nibbled on it fastidiously. Dori tried to smile like Lili, whose smile spread out over her teeth. She squeezed Lili's hand; finally, they had their chance to be exemplary little girls. Their mother was prepared to present the advantages of homeschooling. Dori waited to see the admiration spread over the supervisor's face, her mother reflected in the pupils of the social worker. But Lili was pale and blood dripped from her nose onto the napkin, the chin, the dress, the smile. Dori looked at her and their mother apologized aloud; she really spoke their language and said that this was because of the changing seasons, even though no season was changing, and the night's rain couldn't explain a thing, and she took Lili to wash her face. Now there was no one to speak. The social worker and supervisor, who were very friendly, had papers and pens. Folders and files that rested on their knees. The social worker took a slice of cake and didn't eat. Dori liked him. But time was passing. The blood apparently continued to gush. Perhaps not only from the nose. Perhaps from every hole. Time ground to a halt. But the crumbs continued to pile up.

Dori ate the cake in her hand in two quick bites and ran to bring the finger puppets from their room. She bowed and waved her arms forward. In the bathroom their mother kept cleaning Lili, the water flowing like the blood. Dori spread out her hands and performed for them the show of the little mermaid whose legs hurt like pins. The index finger on her right hand was the mermaid. The left hand's middle finger was the prince. Arad, the social worker, smiled. The supervisor smiled as well. The puppets danced on Dori's hands and she continued dancing with them, whirling around the room, not touching anything, her feet no longer clumsy, until the palm came to rest on her shoulder, and Dori was like a light unplugged (or perhaps it's better to say: like a finger puppet that no longer has a finger in it. Entirely emptied). But despite her mother's hand signaling to her, Enough with that now, grasping Dori's face and turning it to her, and despite Father's anger, which was placed around her in heavy straps, she knew, she simply knew, that she had impressed them. That this time she was at the heart of things—she, and not Lili. And thanks to her, all was saved. They needed to thank her, even if they never would. There you have it: you're welcome.

So you saved your family? Anton asked with appreciation. You think? Dori laughed. I was awful. From my mother's perspective, I ruined everything. She trained us to behave nicely and smile, and I came in with my act. And my dad completely refused to look at me after that. But they looked at me and saw exactly what they'd been told I was, a little autistic girl. Environmentally delayed. So yes, that saved them. I saved them not because I continued my mother's act, but because I proved to them what they already knew—that I was completely cut off.

And how did that help? Anton looked at her, confused, and what was there to say? Dori enjoyed this confusion, the power in the old story that could finally be precisely that, just a story. When the old shame crept in, strangling her like a hot scarf, Dori ignored it. She also took off her socks and got under the blanket. You're right, she told him. Clearly, it wasn't supposed to help. But you never know what will happen next and what you're afraid of is never the right thing.

She closed her eyes, as she always did when she told him these stories, which made her feel as if she truly had something to give him. Like a girl from a broken home who shows her iron-burned back to the prime minister's son. Dori remembered herself as if she had crawled into the body of the girl she had been back then. As if she truly had the chance to go back to being who she had been, to see, from the slits of those eyes, as through peepholes opened wide in an old painting, the world of then.

# 3

---

nd perhaps there is just one way for things to happen. Like water that's always diverted into the same channel. Like dolls cut from a single sheet, so only simple features need be added: A strict father following his own rules. A beautiful, exhausted mother. An opinionated sister. An absent-minded sister. One who will write and one who will read. One who sticks to the facts and another who will ask, *And what if?* A family. A quiet family.

And perhaps because of this, and perhaps for other reasons, they left everything. That visit from the reference and diagnosis staff ended well, but nevertheless, it was decided that they would leave. At once. They traveled to a village in the south, a hot, dry place with exposed roots and broken glass worn down by the sun; small, low houses, stems clinging to and hanging from their walls, and wild, scruffy animals that came out only at night, their eyes gleaming in the dark. A village of immigrants who were themselves the last of the immigrants to get there, even if they hadn't crossed a desert in order to arrive.

In the village, so it was decided, they would have a place. Life would be simpler. And their decisions, or rather his decisions, would have force. The force of words you couldn't just dismiss. "The force of Alex Ackerman," as they would say—not the family, but others. "We move and life moves with us," they announced to the two girls before they left, and they gave their parents a look and an hour later scratched the door in the old house like cats. For the most part they scratched surreptitiously, at the door of the room and their pillows, but they scratched until they caused real damage to their room, the cost of the repair for which would come out of their allowance, if only they were entitled to an allowance. They saw that Mother couldn't believe those two scratchers were hers. Dori saw her tightly closed lips, the stone-faced expression, and understood that if she could, she'd get rid of them at once and go through the world a childless woman. But not without Alex; with him around, she'd stay.

Their father delivered a brief report on their future life in the village, a life that was supposed to fit their hand like a glove, or at least one finger of a glove. The village was like a blurry slide stuck in the projector. Beautiful at first, then frightening. Because what was in a village? Lili asked with the adolescent scorn she had already acquired by the age of eleven. "Sheep and cows, fields, cousins getting married." And, Dori would be able to add later: bread in the oven, sex behind the chicken coop, stray dogs, impoverished workers brought in shipping containers to pick whatever needed picking at the time, and babbling tongues. "We should get a gun," Lili announced, but Dori could tell that she was kidding. No gun would be fired there. Dori was Lili's perma-nent audience. She was her only audience, long before Lili started talking to sheets and pillowcases in that hotel in Austin or New York.

Lili's sharpened senses caused her to recoil, while Dori felt that the village was drawing her toward it. In contrast with her regular cowardice, she wasn't frightened of the village, and in fact fell in love with it, her hands wrapped around an invisible orange that signaled the orchards of their new destination. In the beginning she was afraid, yes—like Lili, or as a result of Lili, if the order of things matters at all. But bit by bit the love nestled inside her, sleepy and content. Love for the village raised its head in her like a mole coming up through the earth.

Their parents took them there in the peeling blue truck on the back of which the letters THE DEAF stood out like they were written in fire. All their possessions were loaded inside, hidden in crates or tied in bundles, and whatever was left behind deserved to be forgotten. The two of them were tucked in among artfully bent iron. An ornamental metal coat hanger poked into Dori's back. She could feel each and every hand-forged spring, but she didn't complain. You can't complain about everything.

Weeks passed in the village. The nights were black and the days almost too bright to bear, and their father still treated it like the perfect solution. As if each thing that fell onto them from the sky had been designed in detail. "Village life called to us," Father announced as he sat them down in an abandoned cotton field to watch the twilight approach. The field belonged to someone, as did the adjacent orchard. Nothing was in fact abandoned, but to Alex Ackerman this didn't matter. They'd come there, he explained with restraint to an angry Lili, because there were places where, when you're different, you stick out like a dislocated bone no one can put back in place. Their mother bit her bottom lip with her teeth until it looked as if she had no lips at all. The few freckles that had survived over the years suddenly stuck out. Dori was shocked by how ugly she appeared, their beautiful mother, and Lili, who knew what her sister was thinking, pinched her on the arm to make her stop. But this was what they were supposed to do, not blend in but stick out. Not to be two more girls on bikes. And the prominent freckles were a good start. They would make the villagers think the most awful, terrible things about them. They'd dress them in their own nightmares. They'll see yet, their father explained, and they looked at the low houses. In a village they'll have use for nightmare makers like the Ackerman family. If they don't throw us down a well, they'll let us live in peace.

Their mother announced that from now on she would grow

vegetables herself. The two of them giggled to each other. Their father could continue his metal-collecting business there too. Four senses told him that success awaited him there, of all places. And not much more was demanded of the girls than coming down from the apple tree.

Lili found a pile of jute sacks in one of the sheds teeming with mice. They couldn't decide if they should wear them or if it was enough to sew patches out of them, because they had already learned to sew and the sewing machine stood unused anyway. When their mother caught them with a pile of sacks in their arms, she burst into tears, but they were no longer moved. This time the crying stopped quickly and she gave them a concrete task: to take apart two crates and straighten up the room that was supposed to be theirs, because the visitor was on his way.

Arad, the social worker they met in the previous home, was supposed to arrive for a first visit in the village. He was the foot that the establishment insisted on wedging in the door. They knew that their parents had decided that he was the lesser of two evils. Dori thought that he had a nice smile; Lili didn't say anything, but Dori was quite certain that she thought the same thing. Before he came they baked a cinnamon cake. Lili said, "Turns out that cake is the solution to everything," but their mother managed to ignore her. And when he came and stood in the door and then sat down on the least damaged chair in the house, just as before, their mother was the primary spokesperson; a smile stretched out across her beautiful lips, as if she hadn't spent her days drenched in tears. The ugly, repulsive prosthetic device, which gave off a diseased smell, was again placed in her ear, and Lili and Dori tried not to stare. She sliced the cake and served him, warning the girls with a single glance to behave as they should. This time Dori observed the details: he had a mane of black hair that was combed back; he had thick glasses and a diamond-patterned sweater, with an ironed white shirt peeking out. He told them he had studied film before switching to social work. Their mother moved the coiled space heater toward him and said something about Buster Keaton. When Arad protested that the heater was pointing only at him, but nevertheless spread his hands out in front of the red-hot coils, she explained that they barely felt the cold. "We are hot-blooded," she said, as if Arad the social worker was a cold lizard warming himself on a rock.

Lili and Dori looked at him so they wouldn't miss a single word. They were required to sit and solve problems when he came. They had pages of homework that were prepared in advance. Nevertheless Dori couldn't control herself and smiled at him the wide smile of an exemplary girl. Lili signed to her that she looked like an idiot, but she didn't care. Let them say what they would say; she knew that he came for her.

The two of them learned that day about Columbus's egg, and Dori tried to concentrate on the arrogant Spaniards who thought they could do what Columbus did. She wondered if it didn't make sense to break the top of the egg so that it would stand up straight. She knew that if her father sat around the table with Columbus when he returned from his travels, he would find his own way to stand an egg on its head. She knew that this foundation, which their father called healthy logic, drew near and evaded her again. She continued to read until Arad came and sat down beside her and asked her about the village and her dolls and Dori didn't know how to answer. He suggested that she write the answers down. "Like some sort of Pocahontas," Lili would say later on. But Dori knew that was wrong. That she was Columbus and Arad was the Spaniard who needed to be shown how to stand an egg on its head. Dori smiled at Arad and wrote in his notebook almost everything he wanted to know.

What did you tell him? Anton asked her.

I told you. What he wanted to know.

It seemed to her that Anton was jealous of her first listener, even though she didn't utter a single word into Arad's ears, just wrote and wrote. And as if to console Anton, she finally told him that Arad was interested in her only because he was writing a thesis that focused on "The Advantages of Homeschooling in Difficult Cases."

Afterward he published it as a book, and I was the difficult case. One of them, anyway. The girl D., the deaf girl with Columbus's egg. For years the book was quite popular, she said, like someone with a stake in the matter. She didn't look at him as she spoke. I read his thesis a few years ago, she added, and meant the research itself, and not the book, which was much less detailed and drifted into other stories, and she resisted telling him about the day she spent in the library reading the description of her, which was made up of lies and a strange truth and gave her hot and cold stabbing sensations. And later on, when they found out? Anton asked, leaning, interested, on his elbows. Ah, it was already too late then. And probably for him too, Dori answered, as if she didn't really know what happened to him.

Their mother was the one who told them, while she was still battling the spiderwebs that had set up shop in every corner during the long years in which the house had been abandoned. And they said—not their mother, someone else—they said that the man who lived there before had shot himself after his lover went back to her husband. That was why the house was so cheap. Or maybe it was actually the deserted lover who took her life. But

Anna Ackerman refused to elaborate; the two of them had their doubts whether she knew anything at all. But they knew.

Girls know things. Even the deaf ones. Vibrations pass through the earth. Winds blow. The winds blowing through the village undoubtedly whispered into their deaf ears, those evil winds that tore away laundry, laundered and stretched out again, dirtied by the village's holy soil, adorned with marks that said it all. But their mother couldn't hear anything or read any marks. Definitely not then. As if she were blind in addition to everything else. Approaching a certain holy status. The two of them pondered between themselves how long it would take for blood to pool on the cement floor. And who had found the dead lover (they decided that it was actually she who died, and not the man with the rifle; that way it was more romantic) and if her eyes were open or closed. Dori imagined that she was very beautiful, with folded hands and a long, beautiful name, but as much as she tried she couldn't link letter to letter or picture her right before her eyes, perhaps only her palms, which were definitely white as snow or sugar, loaded with rings given to her by the living or dead lover. No one had an inkling of what they knew about the case. There were more urgent items on the agenda.

The Ackerman family, understand, had plenty of its own to deal with and had no need for village fables, as Anna Ackerman would announce at every opportunity: "We have more than enough on our plate." Once, she admitted that this was what her mother, the grandmother whom Lili and Dori never met, used to say. Lili argued that at least that stupid saying of their mother's pointed to Anglo-Saxon ancestry. Maybe their grandmother was the queen of England. They had no other evidence.

Another week passed. "Put out your hand," their father instructed them. The smell of whitewash no longer wafted from the main room, the only room that was ever whitewashed, but its walls were still very white, like sugar or snow. Seven boxes still stood there, one on top of another, and it didn't seem that anyone would ever tear the packing tape and remove from their innards the kitchen utensils, or the winter clothes and boots and toys that could be used by much smaller children. Dori thought that perhaps they would keep on living like this forever, and in the end no one would remember what was in the boxes, and only in a thousand years would researchers come and, thanks to the boxes, come to understand something about their ancient culture. Instead the boxes were eventually opened and everything more or less found its place and children's toys kept rolling around the house, as if the two of them had any interest in a smiley phone on four wheels. Their father smiled and each girl obediently raised her right hand, which in a single moment transformed from a simple speaking appendage into an actual hand. "The thumb is the king," he explained. "Or the queen," Lili added, and he agreed, with a smile. "The whole royal family, in Buckingham Palace. But as a shortcut, the king. Next to him, the pointer, she's the merchant whose task it is to finance the king's wars." "And the palace too," Lili added, and their father said, "Yes."

"And the middle finger, she's the soldier who will fight for him in the wars. And next to her is the worker whose labor they steal." By this stage they no longer understood a thing, but they smiled the rest of the way through. This was no longer a story about a king and a queen, as they'd hoped, but the two of them noticed that only the pinky hadn't been given a role. When Lili finally mentioned this, their father didn't get mad. His eyes lit up, and they understood that they had gotten to the point. "The pinky is us—the artist. The beggar. The fool. The deaf. That's us. We'll begin as fools and beggars and in the end we will become their saints. This way, with our finger, we can overpower the entire hand. Thus kingdoms fall. Thus they rise. Remember."

In the village, the Ackerman family flourished like couch grass, which flowers beautifully when left untended. Suddenly it seemed that the unwelcome weed was a sumptuous bloom. So, in fact, when the village's welcoming committee arrived, they didn't know that they were at the door and didn't let them in. The braided challah and the small container of salt were left in the doorway, and only two days later did Dori bring them inside. No one ate them. Their mother went out for air again and again, to turn over the beds, to battle the pests with teeth bared. To the nearby houses, one after the other, came their father's followers—"*les misérables*," they called them, "the beggars." Dori and Lili laughed so hard they had to hold their stomachs. With a discerning eye, Lili looked at Salman and Gita and declared them "ducks," and so they were: quacking away, unable to fly. This especially suited Gita, whose speech always reminded them of wings flapping, and, in fact, when Gita caught Dori in the shade of the house, she explained that when she was a "little-little girl, littler than Dori," they didn't let her sign their language, and tied her hands behind her back, here, like this: she demonstrated a rope's imaginary grip on her wrists, and Dori noticed that her arms couldn't meet behind her back. But now no one could tell her to be quiet, and they'd show them what was what. "She made it up," Lili ruled when Dori told her, "it's a fairy tale." But about this, of all things, Dori wasn't so sure.

In the plot of land behind the house, Lili and Dori used a kitchen knife to cut a perfect circle in the soil, with just the two of them inside, much less odd than whoever might come to join them. A circle drawn with dirty bare feet, the perfect diameter of which signaled to all who came near: we are not like you.

Because in the beginning these were the original simpletons: Gita and Lotti, Salman, Ezra, Uri, Hundar, and that other one, you know. Their innocence was a label affixed to the lining of their clothes if they got lost. But despite everything, they never got lost. They looked at Alex with admiration, as if they were seeing the moon in all its fullness. Salman would often squeeze his hands, really shaking them. Lotti would giggle and her round eyes would open wide with pleasure every time she saw him. "I think she's bowing down," Dori said to Lili, but her sister didn't believe her until she herself saw the slight bending motion that Lotti adopted and that spread among the rest of the simpletons. Yet it appeared that Alex didn't notice; he adjusted easily to the people who took to following him, waiting for the slight flick of his hands that would direct them to their task.

It was a long summer, and the two of them learned that in the village there are a lot of dead hours. One tree more or less didn't matter to anyone. The trees grew on their own, and were it not for the parasites, thought Dori, the trees would rise up and take over the village, twisting through the windows, splitting the roofs. But in the meantime the trees presented no real danger, even though most of them grew and flourished and, when the time came, produced fruit and flowers. The trees in the village had a clearer purpose than the apple tree in the old house, making it hard to believe that it was once their entire world.

Village life, which they were only beginning to adjust to, caused a new busyness to sprout in all of them. Anna hoed the earth and fashioned beds, which blossomed. Everything she planted grew. Lone seedlings and afterward plump plants. Their mother really did have green thumbs. Amazingly enough, she could make anything grow; when the tears weren't falling, that was what she did. Dori recalled the old story about the cabbage and was happy that, all things considered, she hadn't chosen to plant cabbage. And while their mother tended to a vegetable garden, with beautiful tomatoes and other vegetables for which she needed to invent new names, Lili sat on the best-maintained stretch of the green couch and wrote down in her notebooks everything that happened. She had already taken control of their father's notebook, which had stood neglected since they moved to the village, and she filled another notebook and a half with dense handwriting. Their father, in addition to the metal collecting, which was, after all, their main livelihood, submerged himself in the business of being holy. Which, he said, would work "in any kind of situation, and even better when the winds rage and the flesh of the land is torn." And there were those who gathered around to listen to him. "Unbelievable," Lili said to Dori. "He really had a plan."

And as for their tree, a few days after the Ackermans left, the city quickly chopped it down. An unequivocal hazard, a danger to the public, the entire trunk was rotten, mortal danger; who would plant an apple tree here? Lili knew exactly what they said even if she didn't hear a word. In its place the municipality planted something useful, something suitable for the local climate, not just for stories. Telling all of this to Dori, Lili knew that such was the fate of the world under the moon, a history composed only by its end, signaled by a period, after which, only empty space. But she didn't write so much as a word about this. What could be the point of writing that there was a world there, with forks and scratched plates and glasses with the lenses fallen out? The ones who chopped the tree down were definitely glad to be rid of the whole business. Maybe they let their little girls play with the tableware, the abandoned glasses, but probably not. Probably they didn't want to touch anything that remained.

Dori knew that she was supposed to save it. She'd had one

tree to save and she had failed. She didn't discuss this with Lili, even in silhouettes at night. Because in truth she wasn't an exemplary little girl, a girl with hair tied up in a ribbon and tears of determination in her eyes, a girl everyone praises for her strength of spirit and who, when the crucial hour comes, hugs the trunk and doesn't let them chop it down. Nope, Dori was exactly what they said she was: difficult. A biter. A demon. A nuisance. An Ackerman. She knew all this and she didn't care one bit.

Anton wasn't interested in the tree, but the tree was there. He asked for the entire story and this was what she had to offer. She spoke as if everything would have been very different if, for instance, the tree produced different fruit, apricots or pears, instead of those hard apples. Even though she saw that Anton's eyelids were lowering, that his patience was waning and that her advantage was dwindling too, and she guessed that in a bit he would stand up, shake off the imagined dust that never touched him, and be lost to her—nevertheless, her mouth never grew weary of speaking. When she spoke about the tree it was the truth: it grew leaves and shade all at once. But when she spoke about who they had been, about Lili and Dori from back then, the two of them only became less real. Two girls from an old story. And she wanted to tell him, Wait, it'll get better soon. Soon something will happen. But in the meantime she didn't have a thing to tell him.

# 4

Inside the world a clock ticked. Dori heard it even though she wasn't supposed to hear at all. But that's how it is; there are people hard of hearing who hear background noises, just as there are deaf people who hear sounds that aren't there at all, that exist mainly inside their heads, and who knows if it's heard like a sound at all. Maybe it's like those sounds that only dogs hear. Maybe it's like underwater sounds. Those deaf from birth have nothing to compare their sounds to—and it's not that they don't try. Quite a few deaf people have a piano at home for this very reason. And that's a fact, said Lili, who had looked into it. Fact.

But Dori heard a clock, not a piano. This occurred in the second month of their life in the village. The uncles came for a visit and Lili received the clock and notebooks, while Dori received a doll with long eyelashes and a bag of candy. She lost the doll within a day. At the age of nine, Dori was clearly too mature for dolls, not that her uncles knew this. She thought that perhaps the dead lover, the one who died in their house, had taken the doll for herself and now the two of them were winking at each other with their long eyelashes—but no, of course not. She waited for Noah's strange presents, which were always the real treasures. Only months later did she discover the gift bearing a tiny tag on which "Dori" was written: a gold cage with a bell inside. She placed it on the windowsill until it disappeared like her things always did.

So in the end, or perhaps from the beginning, Dori had nothing and Lili had notebooks and a clock. Nevertheless, Dori was the one who actually heard the ticking. Dori smelled and tasted time like Captain Hook, who heard the clock everywhere, reminding him that time was running out. But not exactly, because time is infinite, after all. The days had no boundaries at all and they blended into each other until they couldn't remember when they got up and when they went to sleep, and again there was geography class, with a globe from which half of Africa had been erased and which had gin bottles hidden inside. Only Lili and Dori drank from them sometimes, and laughed at their mother, who had no idea that the globe she'd been given for teaching lessons to two ignorant girls was, in fact, a home for such bottles.

And so while Lili wrote and wrote and their mother brought shoots to the garden, Dori had an abundance of time that passed in waves of nothingness, time in which nothing occurred except for a second continental drift. It ticked even in her dreams, which were all set in the same place. She walked on a bridge that stretched in a circle above a blue land, crowned with trees and homes of many stories that stretched out in curved lines, a world that was an oval dome. The air was thin but she recognized every bit of it. The clock hung in the sky, a large object that looked about to drop like an apple, though she knew it never would.

In her sleep she could see it too, a red wristwatch with images of clowns. Lili kept it safe and already closed it using two different holes in the rubber strap. White stripes signaled that Lili's hand was growing, all the while writing and writing. They were already ten and twelve years old. Because time moved, despite everything, and someone bothered to count the days, to give a sign, in a world of nothing but a surprised lizard in the cracks of the house, a single fish, and piles of metal that accumulated around the house, confronting strangers with impenetrable islands.

Old plaster fell bit by bit. Again they painted their room

sunset-colored and again they soon came to hate the color. The fish swam in a round aquarium and Dori looked at it. They had received it as a pet, a present in honor of the new home. They fed it on and off and didn't give it a name. "Why would a guard dog help?" their father asked them when they begged for a dog. "What good is a barking dog if no one hears him? For us, a fish is better." This was supposed to be a joke, and Dori smiled and Lili didn't. But that was how it was. They didn't tell him that they didn't want a dog tied to a chain but a dog that would sleep in bed with them, one night in Lili's bed and then one night in Dori's. Lili wrote it down. Back then, at least, she wrote down almost everything. Not what could happen and not what she wanted to happen (because Lili was used to wanting only in the negative— not to leave the house, not to chop down the tree, not to move to the village. Even wanting a dog wasn't her want but Dori's, and it didn't do much for her). Lili Ackerman wrote down only what did happen.

And perhaps, here, the rift finally opened between the two. Because until then, the space between them was very narrow, like, say, the space between two front teeth. Even if someone, it doesn't matter who, already broke her front teeth. Maybe as a result of running into a pole after which the two teeth fell into the palm of her hand. Luckily they were baby teeth and sit nicely Dori and don't move and new ones will grow in.

When the front teeth grew in, adult ones, not baby, they were straight and close-set. "Very beautiful teeth," someone once marveled; Dori paid attention as if he had signed this in front of her face, when the sun was behind him. She acted as if she never had other teeth. Lili examined Dori's new teeth up close and tapped them with her nail. Nothing was said between them, but the rift that had opened grew wider (as if Lili had banged Dori's head into the pole, as if the teeth fell out only because of her, which of course isn't what happened, though it seemed, all the same, that something had).

The two of them still regarded their father with some admiration, because they didn't have a choice, and ignored their mother, because they definitely did have a choice. And the more they ignored her, the more weeping there was. A weeping willow the stream was about to sweep away. She spent her days in the garden and tried to teach them there, she really dragged them with her, setting up two chairs opposite the sunflowers that grew there (what an idea!) and calling this "outdoor lessons." She acted as if this were some special treat, math exercises and questions of general knowledge coated in sugar, until one of them, that is, Lili, said to their mother, "What's the point? We're going to read what we want anyway. I think, and Dori runs around in the marsh. Anyway, you teach us geography from your bar. Better that we don't do anything, and you stay here," Lili said, and looked at the garden flowering in yellow. "And we won't tell Dad."

Dori couldn't believe her sister's audacity and waited for a cruel and terrible punishment. She waited with a pounding heart, mixed also with excitement because her sister would be locked up in the closet, there being no basement in the house, and she imagined a bird thrashing its wings over and over against the door until Dori, Dori alone of all people, could open it up and save her. But their mother simply turned around and knelt next to one of the sunflowers to aerate the soil.

A year passed almost without incident. On Wednesdays the two of them joined in collecting the metal, until the iron wagon gradually resembled the ship of Theseus, the deck and mast long since replaced (in the village the enormous metal wheels were replaced with actual tires from tractors no one drove anymore); nevertheless, its fame spread far and wide. Almost every week, their father found metal wires no one needed. In the village, the metal practically collected itself. A thin strip of scrap metal began to stretch around the house like the glimmering lines of mucus a snail leaves behind. On one of those Wednesdays he brought them to the same field where they'd sat during their first days in the village. They again crossed property lines, although it appeared that even the land's owner had lost interest in them; after it became clear to him who Alex was, and the nature of their family, he let them be. The sun descended like a bomber and shone in strange, washed-out colors, and this they really needed to see, their father stated solemnly, behaving like a magician who has revealed something behind the curtain, something even more miraculous than what was displayed onstage. And when the last light fell, Alex turned on a flashlight that illuminated his mouth and hands and he explained to them that what they were seeing was the result of a volcanic explosion that had occurred on the other side of the world. In a land where the mountains were high and the people quiet like their beasts of burden. Dori wanted to see these beasts, carrying on their backs boiling cubes of lava, the follicles of their hair standing up straight like flower stamens, while they looked with blinded blue eyes into the infinite and eternal. Because that was what Lili saw, she knew. She looked at the dim pink connected to the orange on the distant horizon and saw only colors. Nevertheless, when Lili pinched her, she immediately pinched her back, because that was how they did it, in order to remember this moment when they observed a beautiful, distant explosion, when the danger transformed into pure beauty and Alex showed it to them.

And also in the years to come they would remember, the two of them, the cold of the wintry evening hour and the wind that moved the air. If they were different girls, perhaps they would have held hands, but no, not these two, because what were they? Two cold fish facing a red sun.

Except for Wednesdays with their father, time's grip on the week was very loose, and the days, as we've already said, blended inextricably into each other. Again and again Dori was encouraged to adopt a hobby. She loved to roam at the edges of the village. If she saw children in the distance she made herself not see. If they spoke to her she didn't hear. Every day she wandered to the big puddle that filled up with tadpoles in winter and in summer dried up completely. She searched for tiny clams, crabs, and creatures with bulging eyes. When she found them she rarely dug them out. She knew that mermaids can't live in puddles that dry up every summer. She no longer searched at all for mermaids that turn mute on dry land. And despite everything she still thought about that tree sometimes. When she thought about it she also thought about Lili, who in the meantime was already thinking her own separate thoughts, and Dori could only guess that her sister's thoughts weren't similar to hers at all. Not even how apples and oranges are similar, but rather, say, apples and bicycles, or, if you insist, fish and mermaids. At night Lili was tired and her stories grew shorter. There were nights she didn't tell Dori a thing and the beam of light was cast onto the wall in vain, like a moon without a sun. But maybe they were finally happy. Finally they were a family of four half-full glasses.

By the second year in the village they no longer resembled each other much. Maybe they never had resembled each other. Maybe it was just that the two grew up together, their hair combed into the same braid from which it always slipped free, even if one had red curls and the other nearly straight hair; that the two wore the same clothes and in fact traded clothes (the skirt that they wore over the pants; the shirt with the defective snaps; the corduroy jackets, red and blue), maybe all that was enough to affirm that they were twins. Because despite everything they still called them Ackerman. They were Ackerman's daughters, the deaf couple's girls. Even though the range of deaf people expanded in the meantime, and others came along (lame and blind, amputees and lunatics, all of them found a place even if they had next to nothing in common) from whom the others in the community averted their gaze. It was no longer possible to actually single out the four of them. The trailers in which these new characters resided were placed near the Ackermans' house. The infrastructure was late in arriving but nevertheless, after one month and another two months passed, technicians in orange overalls arrived and the trailers were connected to electricity and water. In some of them, wallpaper resembling a forest landscape or a library packed with books was stuck to the walls. Someone grew potted plants on their front steps. Dori could look into the houses because the doors always stood open, except during torrential downpours, since they were always a bit stuffy inside, as she knew. She tried to pass by them without looking. She looked but without stopping and didn't respond to any pair of strange eyes that grabbed her. She and Lili rolled on the ground with laughter when they saw them walking around like defeated ducks, though they couldn't explain what was funny even as the tears fell from their eyes.

The two of them grew taller and taller and the marks made on the doorpost showed that Lili was now, believe it or not, a head taller than Dori. But even if the sidewalk under their feet had switched to soil, and the two of them had abandoned their habit of climbing trees, and even if the trailers filled with characters stranger than these two neglected girls, no great changes occurred. They were who they were. Big and Little.

Sometimes their father sat them down on the rattling chairs and threw all the usual accusations in their faces, because this was a fatherly practice. They embittered their mother's life. They shortened her days. They had to be her right and left hand. Help her. Lili always rolled her eyes, because these demands weren't connected to anything in particular and even their father once admitted that the girls both had two left hands, and Mother had fine hands, green thumbs, while he himself had hands of gold. This was the permanent order, which he suddenly wanted to upset. He moved his gaze between the two of them and explained: the blood presses down on the arteries and the heart is a pump that's liable to fail. Her heart is weak, after all, they know, they must remember. All this he said ostensibly with calm, and his fingers too signed soft angles as if he wasn't angry, seething. And this confused Dori, who cried bitterly because of the difference between the words and what they truly signaled, but Lili, more stubborn, just looked past him. Her hair was combed back with water. Her mouth was soft and large and her nose sharp and angular. From certain angles she resembled a handsome boy. A rebellious youth. It would be reasonable to suppose that their father hated this.

About their mother people said, "When you get hurt, she bleeds." About their father people said, "They don't make them like that anymore." Not many said this, but it was said. But after he left, the window remained open and banged against the frame again and again until Dori got up to close it, and she didn't dare draw nearer to Lili, who cried and pushed her sister, who beyond being curious truly wanted to help. She brought Lili juice from the kitchen and placed it on the floor next to her. For three days the glass stood there with a white film floating on top until someone got rid of it. Dori didn't know who.

They knew that he was preparing them for the great war. When it broke out they would not be confused. He said again and again: "One day we'll leave here. But until then, don't believe a word of theirs," as if they had any chance of hearing those words. Dori wanted to answer and explain that they knew, they'd never be so stupid as to trust the hearing, but Lili pushed her with her elbow; it wasn't the time. Their father continued, "You mustn't be indifferent like them. And if you're lucky, you'll see the fire trails and escape." When he signed "lucky" he meant "intelligent," and also "industrious" and sometimes "instinctive." Because what appeared to be a disadvantage would yet be revealed to be the opposite. And whoever stops to look will falter, and whoever relies only on his ears will miss the most important detail. And maybe no underwater piano plays for the mice that flee first, but they survive. They recognized these words; they weren't insulted to be called mice. Their mother sat to the side and ran thin fingers through her long hair, hair black as a crow that went gray like a crow, hair that unfortunately neither of them had inherited. But one day there would be a war and it wouldn't matter if they were beautiful or not, hearing or not. And their mother, the beautiful and the fragile, would always be hopeless. It was clear to the other three that without them, she wouldn't survive.

Anton and Dori lay on the pale carpet in his mother's house. Only the marks engraved on the corner of the massive writing table confirmed that he too had lived there once. Even though this was their regular place, she always felt lucky that he took her there, to the house of the woman she saw only once, from a distance, and she knew that try as hard as she might she'd never be able to acquire her elegance, the old money and the tart candies, like the one that rested in her mouth just then. Dori closed her eyes. She tried to impress the details of the room onto her memory, as always, to transform their elusive and fragile present into something one could grasp, write about, hold like an object. She thought about what she would tell Lili, but knew that this time the words would be lacking. She knew that it didn't matter if Lili would answer; sometimes the facts aren't important.

Anton hung his old jacket on the back of the chair and Dori imagined him sitting there in his youth, handsome and angry and silent, solving geometry problems and engraving perfect lines onto the doorpost, and it seemed to her that she could see the band of sun that fell on his face then, and him trying to drive it away with a young hand, and she knew it was a false memory. Suddenly he appeared innocent and soft as a boy to her, lacking tools for life except for the money he always had. In piles. Rolled-up bills that rested in his pockets and drawers. As if he'd suddenly have the urgent need to buy a yacht with cash. She held on to this precious knowledge that was given to her like a silkworm in a box, something very soft that, at least under a certain kind of care, might transform into something else. The tea he poured her got colder and colder. It had a mound of sugar in it that slowly dissolved. They didn't have teaspoons because his mother had gotten rid of most of the things in the house during her minimalist period.

When he asked her with genuine interest about their survival training, about the lonely nights in the field, she was silent. He asked the wrong questions. They heard cars passing by, outrageously slow, because below his mother's apartment a busy and somewhat dangerous street was being paved, a street that unfortunately lowered the value of the apartment. Anton referred to this only once, his concern regarding the actual value of the structure and the land, the future construction plans. This didn't suit the anarchist he proclaimed himself to be, but, as Lili would say, the rich will be rich.

And in the days to come they behaved as if the lessons were proceeding in orderly fashion. As if there was an order. Lili abandoned her notebooks, where she'd written God knows what, probably nothing, and Dori didn't go to the puddle. Their mother looked more happy than surprised, as if she had scored a certain victory, as if she had waited all that time for the rebellious girls to return from their evil ways so things could once again unfold according to a correct and proper arrangement. She announced that they would study geography and geometry and they nodded. The two of them put forth an effort in the geography lesson and their mother bought an actual atlas, a hardcover book with colorful maps of countries and conquests, minerals and precipitation. The globe of drinks disappeared as if it never had been. In the geometry lesson she gave, the shapes matched each other too, triangles and polygons and all the rest. They differentiated between the polygons in boredom as they calculated acute and obtuse angles, but boredom was good. Boredom was a sign that no one was crying, at least not right then.

And Lili didn't rebuke Anna at all, and their mother seemed encouraged; the redness climbed up her white cheeks. She told them about the explorers of the world, without whom they would have no geography at all, without whom they might think that the world was flat or looked like a portable bar with a zipper cutting it in half between North and South America. She spoke about Vasco da Gama and the Cape of Good Hope and the two of them traced the boats' paths with their fingers. This was the most normal of days, or at least it pretended to be—the label of normality poked out through its clothes. After all, it was only normal at first sight, because almost a year had passed since the three of them last sat down together and memorized a chapter of something. And on this day of all days, Lili began writing down the time. The present, itself. It is hard to believe that it began then, that this was the opening chord, because certainly she wrote a lot before then; she was already used to filling notebooks with dense script. But this time she added a date and an hour and that was enough. Because immediately afterward came the next hour and it too required words. The notebooks were set in time; the clock met the pen. And there was morning and there was evening. One Lili.

# 5

"What are you actually writing?" Dori asked her once under the blanket, as meager light illuminated her fingers, and her sister spelled out a long word for her. "Chronicles." And when she saw that she didn't understand, she added, "The history."

Lili wrote down everything, reported on everything, events and facts, no reflections, no feelings, without fantasizing at all. Above the words the time was noted, the hour was fixed, and lucky for her she had a watch that displayed the date. And even if the watch was standing still, Lili would never have been wrong.

"Lili writes and Dori climbs the walls." So their mother summarized the state of affairs. Exactly so. Lili no longer hid anything from them, not after their mother snatched a notebook out from under a pen. Lili looked straight at Dori then, forcing her to get involved. "What do you know? There are no secrets today." And then she looked at her mother and, without averting her gaze from her for a moment: "You really want to read? Then read." While Lili stood with hands folded, their mother solemnly sat down at the kitchen table and read, without getting worked up by her daughter's new toughness. She knew that underneath, the yolk and the egg white rested in their delicate membrane. Slowly and gently she browsed through the notebook, like someone looking at an album of photos taken in another land.

And what their mother read (and Dori stood a bit behind her shoulder, because if there was nothing to hide then there was nothing to hide) was everything that had happened to them. As if the world had changed places with the notebook. Today was spread out in all its details, as well as the day before.

*At three thirty the mailman arrived no longer wearing a uniform dragging a grocery cart an electric bill in our box.*

"What's interesting about the mailman arriving?" their mother inquired, and Dori waited for an answer that would explain everything. Lili shrugged her shoulders. "I'm writing chronicles."

"She's writing the history," Dori explained to her mother, and for the first time in days Lili looked at Dori without anger. Perhaps she even smiled at her. Who knows. And Dori smiled at Lili like she was catching her sister's pen as it fell.

Their mother looked at her two daughters. Her hands were empty. Dori looked at her as she dropped them to her side without knowing what to do with them. She smelled like slightly moldy cinnamon and sweat. She smelled like tea. Lili's notebook rested on the green Formica as if Lili would never walk the necessary three steps to take it. Their mother went out to the garden, to the beet bed, without looking at them; you don't always have to look, they too knew what she looked like without seeing her. After all, the world was steady, and they themselves were like a sound played again and again, day after day, and if you live under the bell tower you're liable to go mad. That is, if you can hear it. Regardless, this is what Anna Ackerman looked like at that moment (and perhaps at all moments): the stained skirt flapping around her legs, the hair gathered into a braid of gray mixed with black, the feet in comfortable sandals; she had square toes that the sandals accentuated. Lili once said to Dori that she was already starting to try to be ugly and Dori didn't understand that at all, as there was no logic to it. While Anna Ackerman went to aerate the soil around the beets, because the sunflowers had been uprooted the year before for the sake of the ugly vegetables, all understanding between Lili and Dori was instantly erased. As if it had only been written on water. Lili took the notebook as if nothing had happened and began to write, and Dori didn't know what to do with all that water.

Their father wasn't present whatsoever. If they told her that he flew through the window with the wild geese and went off on hair-raising adventures, Dori would almost believe it. Of course Lili wouldn't, but that's already another story. They knew that he lived a tempestuous life, separate from theirs, that his dream was coming true all around him. But Lili also remembered what happened before this, their previous, ancient life, with greater clarity than her sister. And when he returned with a dead goose in his hands, the two of them looked at him. Their father was covered in a thick layer of mud but the dead goose was very beautiful. "Whoever flies with them doesn't kill them," Lili explained to Dori. "This goose, there's no chance that he hunted it. One of his lackeys definitely brought it to him." The goose had a gentle face like a prince from a book of fairy tales. Their mother rinsed away the blood, cooked it, stuffed the feathers into a pillow. They ate goose soup and goose pie and goose omelets. They threw up after every meal. Lili already barely ate meat by then; she bit hard and chewed hard and said enough. In fact she already barely ate anything, and if someone had paid attention to this they would have thought that she was feeding on the air or the plaster in the walls. Only Dori stuffed more and more into herself.

And she learned to cook. Because, as her mother announced, all that wandering to the puddle and daydreaming wouldn't get a person to the grocery store, as if Anna Ackerman ever went to the grocery herself and wasn't satisfied with the monthly supplies their father brought in burlap sacks. And since Dori hadn't yet found her talent, because sighing over the beauty of drowsy princesses from fairy tales is a generic attribute, not a talent, it was best to do something with herself. So Dori began cooking (not geese. The next goose that their father brought home they buried in the yard) and their mother grew them vegetables and Lili ate almost nothing. That's how they were and if their father's followers and lackeys, the miserable ones, hadn't brought them more food, they would have continued living on the burlap sacks and expired crates of food and Dori's attempts at cooking.

When their father returned home in the evening, always bent over a bit in the doorway and standing up straight once inside, he looked like a giant in Dori's eyes. His beard again grew wild and his beautiful eyes glanced around happily. And then, as if according to some agreed-upon sign, the world fell into order. Mother and Lili stopped arguing; Dori took off the black swamp boots and kept herself in rather clean socks. Somehow food was brought to the table, one of Dori's inventions, stuffed eggs for instance, and it didn't matter to their father anyhow. His only need was to have his fill. He always chopped the same big salad, upon which was poured the same pink dressing that they loved only because it was their father's specialty, a dressing that required shaking and waiting and pouring from above. Sometimes the thought occurred to Dori that in fact they were presenting to their father the same performance that they had given the reference staff in the previous house. Nevertheless she believed that he was happy because of them and smiled because of them, pleased that they were flourishing like Mother's plump beets (because it was impossible to deny that she was mainly getting fatter while Lili was mainly growing more beautiful), and she didn't want to upset him by saying that their days were stuck together like eyelids, that they slept hour after hour and weren't learning a thing. Dori understood without being told: if you don't have anything nice to say, just lie.

# 6

"Today bring me the envelopes."

"What envelopes?" Dori tried to get out of it, as if she didn't know. That day, like almost all days, Lili smelled of milk and soap. She lacked patience.

"C'mon already, the envelopes from the mailbox." Lili hated leaving the house. She preferred to remain in her room as much as possible, with the notebooks or God knew what. But there were still things that Lili needed from the outside, such as envelopes.

This started with the announcements on the central bulletin board. Announcements for the transportation times into the city, the movie club, the knitting club, the swimming club. They passed by there with their mother, who in a moment of resolve instructed them to come with her to the hairdresser. Until that day Alex had always cut their hair at home with his black metal scissors, if they had their hair cut at all. Dori loved long hair even if hers looked like mouse tails, even if their father wanted her to cut it so it would grow back stronger, as everything does after it's cut. Lili had long, knotted red hair that she gathered close to her head. But this time their mother decided to go to the hairdresser's, which was located in a low house on the other side of the village. They didn't even know there was a hairdresser there. Dori looked at Lili and said, "Maybe she wanted us to go to the library?" and Lili burst out in her doglike laugh, a glimpse of how Lili used to be.

The door was open and they entered one after the other and only then discovered that the place was empty. The hairdresser was standing outside and smoking and looking at them. Their mother gave her a note that she'd written in advance. The hairdresser had fiery red hair, a bit like Lili's but not exactly. Her eyebrows were red as well. She caught Dori looking. "You'll see when you grow up, today everyone gets it from a tube. Except maybe your sister, who probably got it from some redheaded uncle," she said, and winked. Dori didn't wink back. Their mother sat down in a chair and the hairdresser walked behind dragging wooden clogs. "Maybe we rinse the gray out of your hair?" she suggested, and Anna Ackerman's lips narrowed with resentment.

The hairdresser's fingers stirred through her hair and undid the braid. "You actually have a beautiful face," she said with emphasis and surprise. Lili and Dori were angry, as if it weren't known to all that their mother was pretty, that even when she was ugly she was pretty. Their mother paid no attention and removed a few sheets of paper from her pocketbook. Dori couldn't see what was written there and the hairdresser raised her hands, wrapped an apron around their mother's neck, and began cutting. "So, what's new with you?" she asked as her hands were busy with their mother's hair, hinting at the coming motion of the scissors. She added, "Young women need to be well put together." Dori deliberated over whether or not she was being serious. The hairdresser's face was reflected in the mirror, almost floating over the hairdresser's robe she was wearing, and her mouth brought to mind a dead fish. It expressed horrible things, and across their mother's beautiful face spread silent agreement. If they could hear maybe it would have been possible to listen to how the hairdresser cut the empty space, a moment before the black scissors swooped down and cut the hair for real. But they didn't hear.

When they left there, their mother with her hair cut and the girls as before, the hairdresser removed her robe and swept up all the hair clippings into the garbage. She swept up the notes as well, those that Anna Ackerman wrote: "I would like to have my hair cut." "I can pay." And the note on which was written in French the word *bob*. "Such poor souls," the hairdresser whispered to the scissors and the brushes, to the nearly professional blow-dryer, because in truth no one was there to hear.

Dori made a request that normally wouldn't have much of a chance, but maybe the French bob had raised their mother's spirits and she agreed to stop by the store, which had no sign above it. They waited for her outside, Dori swaying to and fro. They saw her clogs through the crack in the door, standing last in line to buy them phosphorescent candies as if they were six years old. Lili was the first. The first to notice the announcements. And Dori looked as well and saw that the tacks pinning them to the cork bulletin board were all different. Their rounded heads were engraved with a club, a flower, a droplet, a star. The two of them looked. The tacks were different shades of gold. They glowed. Lili quickly removed the four tacks from the notice and gave them to Dori. She took the flyer "Swim Club Starting" from the board and folded it up. Dori put the tacks in her pocket; they poked her as she walked. She thought that Lili would get angry but her sister nodded. It's good to destroy evidence. As they walked to the house behind their mother, phosphorescent candies illuminating the darkness of their mouths, Dori asked Lili under their mother's line of sight: "Are you crazy? You want to learn to swim? They'll never ever let you." Lili answered, "Who cares about swimming? Didn't you see what was weird about that flyer?" Dori took the flyer from her hand and tried to understand, like a riddle. She guessed, "The club's at six in the morning? Probably no one will go."

"No, look at the letters. You saw the flyers for crochet and the movie club; only this one was handwritten."

"Who wrote it?" Dori asked, and Lili closed her eyes and elaborated: "Someone whose stomach hurts. Someone who misses their son. Someone who chews gum."

"Three people?"

"No, the same one."

In their room, Lili asked Dori to help her remove her boots. They were small on her, but Lili said she didn't feel it because her toes froze after a while. She didn't ask where the boots were from—they were blue, beautiful, made from soft leather, not appropriate for the village—just as she didn't show her that she placed the four tacks in Uncle Noah's miniature child's bed with the rectangular headboard.

The next day she said that she needed envelopes. There was a reason for all this, because a talent you don't cultivate is worth nothing, and Lili had found her talent. More than the chronicles, even, she needed to practice analyzing handwriting, understanding the writer deeply, what troubled him, what he loved. Because it turned out she had a sense for this—a talent, that is. She told Dori that she could learn everything about the writer from their writing. This information too was a kind of fact. A fact out there in the world just waiting to be found. In a few more years she'd be a detective and solve murders using only handwriting. So Dori wandered around the village looking for handwriting for her to practice with, and returned to the bulletin board, but there really wasn't much there other than a note about lost keys, which she took; then she passed by the post office and took two envelopes sticking out of mailboxes.

Lili was pleased, even though Dori said that she'd never in her life do that again. Lili actually kissed her on the forehead in thanks and opened up the first letter. It was in English. Lili read and explained, "This woman is in terrible mourning, I see that she lost everything she had." "Let me read," demanded Dori, who was certain that this was written there. She looked at the page of thin lines but didn't understand a thing. All the letters were connected one to the other in loops of ink and the only words she managed to decipher concerned a vacation and the seashore. "You're just making it up," she said, and returned the letter to Lili. "You know I'm not making it up," Lili said, and glued the letter to her notebook as evidence. "When I read someone's handwriting I know everything about him. Where he's been and where he's going, what he likes to eat and what makes him sick."

"Well, even if you know everything about him," said their mother, who had forced her way into the conversation, "then you'll still have no idea about what he sounds like." She smiled a wide smile, and Dori could have sworn that she was pleased by Lili's shock, because she had made fun of her in a way that mothers are never supposed to make fun of their daughters.

**You never told me this, Anton said with obvious appreciation. So I'm telling you now, Dori said. And could she really do that, your sister? I'm just telling the story, she said, and slipped away from him. Because she knew that this was a test, that there was no way he believed the fabrications of a thirteen-year-old girl. Even she didn't exactly believe them, and in those days she would believe three impossible things well before breakfast.**

This lasted as long as it lasted. Until the day their father returned home, his hands rust-stained, ignoring their mother as he had since she'd gotten her hair done, and went straight up to the two of them where they sat staring into space on the green couch that had already started to rip. "So Lotti needs to come and tell me that you're thieves?"

"We didn't steal anything," Lili said.

"From mailboxes! No less! What's my genius daughters' next move? Robbing a store?"

The anger darkened his face until it seemed to Dori that in a moment his fury was liable to turn into laughter, because it wasn't possible that this black fury was real. In a parallel world, he would praise them for their subversiveness. He would say that they were starting to fulfill their role, the role assigned to them; finally they were the fifth finger. But none of this was said. The hands fell silent and Lili was all white. White as milk.

"We were only fishing," Dori explained. That's what they called it, fishing for envelopes.

"Your sister is a little girl." He faced Lili and ignored Dori, as if Dori wasn't there at all, not in the room and not in the world. "But you had to know. Running around the village like two criminals. They saw you, you understand? You want them to take you away? To an institution? Do you understand what you've ruined?"

Nothing could be said. Maybe they were the fastest signers in the west, maybe their hands spoke quick and precise, but their father's hands swallowed up all time and place. They left a desert behind.

"Return all the letters you stole and write a letter of apology for the bulletin board. As for your punishments, we will have to see." He said "we" and meant "I." They had already started to learn something about the punishments that rained down on him in his childhood, and he, unlike them, had never stolen.

"We don't have the letters, and Dori's not to blame. I did it."

"I had no doubt. So tell me, where are the letters?"

"I burned them."

She was ready for the slap Lili would receive, for the cheek that would burn with her too. But she didn't know that it would actually be her mother who would land it on the two of them, one for Lili and one for Dori. There was a deep, infinite justice in this. Because it didn't matter what they would say, what Lili would say, what their hands would sing, Dori knew: the two of them were guilty.

# 7

While they were together, she thought he didn't resemble anyone she knew. Anton was a memento from a separate world, a beautiful, stubborn thing she didn't quite understand. A wormhole leading to a world where they eat caviar and discuss Goethe and bonds. Surprisingly, the world in her imagination resembled an old movie house, like the one that she and Lili, all washed and bundled up, were once taken to from the village: "Because even if you don't hear, you'll at least enjoy what's happening on the screen." As if they were two orphans, their cheeks blue from the cold, taken in by philanthropists in a carriage. She still remembers how marvelous the velvet seats and velvet curtain were, and the darkness that fell on all the children who sat there, even the two girls sitting up straight in the fifth row. And when the movie started it shocked her body; she thought, This is what electricity feels like when it passes through you, and she had to leave, quickly. She tugged Lili's hand, but Lili stayed.

Their mother had two leather-bound albums with her old name, "Anna Cohen," imprinted in the center of their binding. When their hands were clean they were allowed to browse through them. Lately, though, only Dori looked at the pictures and sighed over their beauty. A freckled girl with a pug nose and a thick black braid appeared in most of the pictures. When she wasn't holding a parasol at Purim or leaning on a hollow wooden horse decorated in festive colors, she sat at a long Passover table, her hands crossed, her back straightened, her face glowing with a smile. There were pictures that showed her playing sports, lithe and flexible, qualities that neither of her daughters inherited. She, or someone who very much resembled her anyway, jumped over a hurdle, hung from rings, grasped a pole. They didn't know what most of these activities were called. And didn't remember if the leather cylinder with legs that she jumped over was called a horse or a donkey. They had no one to ask; their mother wouldn't agree to look at the albums. I have no time for that, she declared, but the two of them remembered that once she would sit next to them and explain every little thing.

On the last page of the album were two glue marks without photos. "What happened to the pictures?" Dori asked the last time she looked at the album; it was a mellow afternoon, the light filtered in and rested on the couch with the flower cloth that Dori had found and placed there to make it pretty. In that mellow light you almost didn't notice that the cloth did no such thing, that the room remained as it was, just with a covering of roses. Specks of dust stood flickering in the air, living their tiny, strange lives. Their mother boiled like a kettle with a black bottom. She hurled the pan with the signs of soot and the burnt oil into the sink, frightening Dori. "Nothing happened. There were never any pictures." At night she and Lili spoke opposite the glow that the night-light gave off (because sometimes Lili didn't just turn over to the other side and pretend she was sleeping, sometimes she gave in and they spoke almost like before). Lili said there were definitely pictures of the boyfriend she had before Father. "But she didn't have a boyfriend before Father," Dori protested in surprise. Nonetheless Lili was certain about what was in those pictures once glued to the pages. A tall, handsome man with a square jaw and hair the color of apricots. A man who rode horses and motorcycles and shot moving targets. Dori didn't believe her.

Actually, she remembered that there used to be something else there, a group of girls with arched eyebrows and round mouths. "You mean the class picture," Lili declared. "She has a ton of those." "No," insisted Dori, who had already seen their mother's other class pictures, with the X that always marked Anna Cohen's spot, even though there was no need for it. They always knew it was her. She tried hard to remember, and very slowly, details of the pictures or at least one of the pictures appeared. She recalled that her mother stood in the center, hands folded, her round mouth smeared with pink lipstick, her braid to the right. "I think they were singing," she said suddenly. Lili sat up in her bed and with her right hand pointed the light away from Dori's finger and toward her own face. "What are you talking about, singing? She's deaf, our mother's deaf," she explained slowly, as if Dori had suddenly gotten mixed up. "She was always deaf. How would she sing?"

"So what," Dori said with her old stubbornness, which popped up all at once, like it used to, before she started trying to please everyone and signed "excuse me" and "please" even to the furniture she bumped into. Because Dori was sure that their mother, well before she was their mother, stood and sang with a rounded mouth. Lili turned off the light. Neither of them fell asleep, at least not right away.

Indeed Mother had two albums that were no longer taken down from the high shelf, because enough was enough, really, but their father had no photos from before they knew him, from before he met Anna. What there was, they knew by heart. One photograph of Alex and Anna from their wedding, standing under the chuppah, young, their father's hair cut short down to the skull, their hands not touching, and behind them a view of tall buildings. The next pictures were of a tiny Lili in hospital pajamas in their mother's arms, with wild red hair, and afterward pictures of Lili and Dori together, as if they were twins even though they weren't, not at all. Their father had a memory like an elephant, so he didn't need pictures. Absolutely not. And Alex Ackerman's No List extended almost without end: No father and no mother. No history. No past. History started, they always knew, with him. True, there were the uncles, yes, his two younger brothers, but the two of them evaded any questions they were asked. Regardless, what was there to say, there was nothing to say, not about what was, at least. And if you dug with a teaspoon you'd hit a wall. There was no address where their father and brothers were raised, no door to knock on and find out. Nothing. He was what was. Other than him, what had been, all that was, had died.

"There was a miserable boy." This was him, who else—Alex Ackerman. The two of them were already old enough to hear. This happened a short time after their mother's albums disappeared. Almost as if they were receiving something in exchange, which wasn't logical, because such bartering never interested them. They got the story about the boy. The others brought him, the boy, down to the cellar. They had strong hands, they had a grip you couldn't escape. They carried him with the kind of ease with which they would carry a wet kitten. They didn't even have to win his trust like Dori and Lili did when they tried to catch small animals they could raise in a box. He trusted them from the beginning. "Who would he trust, if not them? They were his parents." Their mother told them the details. Their father confirmed them. Dori and Lili sat close together, like girls, on two mismatched chairs, as if they were really girls and not two complicated mechanisms of black thoughts inside girls' skin. They saw how the old covenant between their parents tightened again.

Alex and Anna were like two hands: one speaks and the other sings (no, no); one tells what was and the other tightens into a fist. Their mother narrated as if she herself had been there, and maybe she had been. Anger bubbled up in them, and after it, astonishment. He had parents. This meant they had a grandfather and a grandmother. But they couldn't delve into it. Because whoever delved died. Truly died.

They tried hard to think about that cellar. Perhaps they always suspected its existence. Perhaps it was always waiting for them out of the corner of their eyes. They tried hard until they felt four black walls rising up around them and a low black ceiling. Dori felt her tailbone, the spot from which she would sprout a tail if she were, for example, a monkey, grow warm. And in the room it was suddenly hot, very hot. Burning. The chair burned. The bone was forcing her to get up and walk around the room, but Dori remained seated and so did Lili. Their father was the boy from the cellar. This was the period at the end of the sentence, the stain that darkened every view they saw. Once they realized that, it became the one and only true measure for all that had happened.

And that time their father returned and his face was green and he lay on the couch in his work clothes (by this stage not much remained of the dark rose fabric, the stained and torn cloth; who remembered that once, unnaturally large flowers had bloomed on it?). He puked into a pot without handles that Lili brought him and the two of them squatted around him and attended to him with concern. His vomit was foamy. Blood pooled in the corners of his eyes. Lili grabbed Dori's hand and signed to her, "Don't worry, it's from the metal." This was one of the side effects of the secure livelihood, their wise livelihood, and the time had arrived for Dori too to know about it, because the last time this happened Dori was just a baby.

It was heavy metal poisoning, the kind that's life-threatening, even if that life is as unusual as their father's, their father who seemed in that moment to transform into an antique oil painting of a deathly ill person in the corner of the room, the shadows falling on him and Dori and Lili standing above him dressed in white, holding oil lamps. The pot was filled with thick vomit that gave off a smell of death and it was clear that a doctor wouldn't be summoned. But Salman was once a medic, one of them recalled. And perhaps he, the father, had called on them from within the painting, whatever it showed. A father lying horizontally and two daughters squatting, wringing their hands and pulling out their hair with worry.

Dori ran to Salman and knocked on his door even though there was clearly no point, but still she wasted almost no time waiting and burst inside, waking him from sleep even though it was only seven in the evening. But when he understood he rose, and without changing his clothes, which were as full of holes as if he had intentionally burned them himself with a cigarette, he began walking, and Dori wanted to remind him that he was wearing oversized white pajamas filled with holes, but she didn't know how. He walked in front of her with long steps, like a giant woken from his slumber, a mountain that suddenly decided to reveal its legs. He opened the windows in the house and instructed their father to drink milk and luckily there was milk there, almost half a carton, and he cooked a few weeds in a different pot, and their father drank and Salman checked his pulse and they waited.

Alex Ackerman, it turned out, would go on living. No need for an ambulance or to fall into the hands of the butchers of the establishment. Dori knew then that it was the cellar drawing him back to itself like a poisoned mushroom, that the cellar wanted its boy, had sent him poisoned metals from the earth. She told Lili, who shrugged her shoulders because "metal poisoning is metal poisoning, not witchcraft and not mushrooms and not underground arms that reach out from below the earth and grab you." And the time had come for Dori to know the difference. She preached to her as if she were many years older, as if she were tired of Dori straggling after her like a rag doll after a real girl. Suddenly Lili very much resembled their mother. And this did not please Dori. Lili would have hated it too if she only knew what Dori was thinking.

Lili sat down and opened one of her notebooks and Dori guessed that she would write about the metal poisoning. Lili didn't show her what she wrote, even though she asked her to. "You'll read it later," she explained, because there was no point in hiding it. The two of them knew this. Dori always knew where Lili kept her notebooks. There was no chance she'd do something that Dori didn't know about. Even when Lili disappeared for entire days, Dori knew that if she only tried very hard, she'd be able to find out where she was. Because that was their way, like conjoined twins who share a single pair of ears.

Lili explained, as she always did, that she couldn't read it now, that she should come back later, when the ink could no longer be smeared. And once Dori had flipped through the notebook she asked, "Where did you write about the cellar?" and Lili said that she hadn't. "But why not?" Dori really didn't understand and her sister winked, and who even knew that Lili knew how to wink? But it turned out she did. It's possible that Dori also knew how to wink, only she never tried. She squinted the corner of her eye, and Lili said, "I only write chronicles, you know that. You can read whatever you want but I only write the truth," she signed. "Nothing but the truth."

This family is a lone tree falling in the woods, Dori concluded for Anton. And he didn't even notice that she said "this family" and not "my family." Because Anton himself would never touch the walls of a cellar and think: these are the roots, this is the trunk.

# 8

Picture for yourselves a world made entirely of crystal. Golden and amber. You are the fly trapped inside it. Suddenly you too are beautiful and arouse admiration, like the resin you are trapped in, which over the years grew so valuable, or at least respected. If you don't arouse admiration, then your six legs, your netlike eyes, your body forever fixed, it will at least get people choked up. That's how it was then. All at once Dori was the fly. The only problem was that when she learned she was the fly, the amber started shifting around her in golden ripples, the firm became liquid, and suddenly she heard every whisper. Every word. Commas, periods. And she had no way back. It was no longer worth it to be the fly.

Because the official letter finally arrived and the injunction arrived and the establishment arrived. The real establishment, not friendly meetings with Arad when she wrote deformed, plotless fairy tales for him and sometimes also reminded him of their role as the village fools, because she sensed that this would interest him and that stories like this would cause him to come back. But they didn't see Arad again. Arad who would write the book, who would build up his career on its success, and who'd drown like a man who up to that moment was sure he could walk on water. The establishment itself, square and gray and windowless, replaced him. When it arrives, nothing can stop it. Not even Alex Ackerman, who, perhaps for the first time in his life, didn't think to escape in time.

**I don't understand, Anton said. Was the boarding school because of that? And Dori confirmed, it was truly impossible to understand.**

"Dori Ackerrrmmman," the teacher said in a scolding voice. She called out a name whose syllables spread out and moved through the room like electric shocks, Dooo-rrriiii, again and again roused her from her reverie as if this was the proof, as if answering aloud—*Yes, present, the answer is, the moon is a rock floating in space, the formula for water is $H_2O$ and on this side of the zero there is a row of negative numbers*—was the point. She had to pronounce everything aloud. If she wanted to stay, that is, because there were much worse places and she was lucky that she wound up there out of everywhere. She at least had to say her name. To say, Me. To open her mouth wide. Do-ri.

Strange that they were strict with her like that, scolded her, spoke about last chances. Dori looked at them in astonishment; did they really not know that she had no choice? There was an injunction from the court. It was in the best interests of the child, the girl, her own best interests. There was the old mermaid, with the soft eyes, who accompanied her since the days when she was taken to the white room, a room with a soft rug and not one picture; there was the researcher sent on behalf of the Ministry of Welfare, who continued coming for regular visits; there was a man in a suit who wore glasses. All of them extended cool hands and along this bridge of hands she walked until she arrived here, at the wooden chair facing the green writing desk, on which Dori didn't leave a single mark even after months had passed. The writing desk was spotless. She didn't intend to be seen. She didn't intend to speak, nor, if possible, to hear. She preferred not to.

The house was somewhere. The entire world, the world she was taken from, was somewhere. She was the victim of a kidnapping even if no one treated her like one. Dori was planted with her head in the ground and her feet up on a strange, distant planet with odd customs, where the air was thin and no one needed to carry the globe on one's shoulder or back, where there was no way of knowing which side to tap the egg on, how to hold a fork or a knife, how to fall asleep at night. Everyone she saw, down to the last person, made shapes with their mouth, insisting aggressively on the click of the tongue, the friction of the palate, the grinding of teeth. Each and every one of them insisted on Dori waking up and admitting the facts.

They waited. They demonstrated patience. They waited for her to begin speaking. Because hearing, they decided, this girl had always been able to do. Years of calculated pretending (so it was said), of hysterical contagion (as the minority opinion put it), finally had to reach their end. After all, deaf doesn't mean mute and moreover this girl—the girl named D in the semiofficial documents, which flowed in their roundabout way to the curious—this girl could hear. A simple examination was enough to verify this, and the fact that it had taken so long to carry out such a simple and necessary step testified to nothing but negligence.

In some ways she's really like a baby, they said, her development so delayed that this was a case of late, almost endless infancy. They invalidated the reports by Arad the social worker, who had concluded that the girl was very intelligent, and who had been fooled for so long. The assessment was that this was a case of a family that had deceived the system, and that the girl, who sat facing them on a low chair and didn't respond to a word, had been but its plaything.

Dori knew little of this at the time. Not the assumptions or the facts or even the stories that they composed between the former and the latter. The words *negligence* and *abandonment* were stretched out in arches over her head and she absorbed whatever she absorbed. Dust and shards. The only story that fit together in her head was that she would not be returning home. Rooms were painted in shadowy hues as if colors were gone from the world. They called her name so many times it became stranger than ever, the spoken letters and syllables falling like metal plates onto the floor. More than anything she would remember the smell. The thick smell of the whitewashed room, the smell of mopped floors, the smell of the heavy cologne and perfume that surrounded the men and women who sat across from her, with one leg over the other or planted apart and hands folded between them. The brighter smell of the mermaid, the sharp smell of the man in the suit and glasses, the smell of sweat in the room where she slept, beneath the smell of the liquid disinfectant used on faucets, railings, and plates, a slight smell of urine that was preserved in the dolls they put in her lap so she'd play with them and that perhaps arose from her own self.

Dori's hair was combed daily and they assisted her in dressing and undressing, in placing the folded clothes on a chair, in brushing the top and bottom teeth. Sometimes it appeared that she couldn't learn a thing. Each and every day she required the same help she had needed the day before. And their patience definitely could have run out here—all that, just for Dori to spend the day slumped on a chair with crusty eyes and no expression on her face. Only patience was needed, someone opined, so that one syllable might cling to another and you'd have a word, a sentence, an entire conversation. The mermaid sat and smiled and cut her meat for her. Another week passed and she herself separated the rice from the meatballs. The carrots from the rice. The food tasted like sand. She chewed and swallowed.

No, the others said. She's not like a baby. They identified the rebelliousness in the averted gaze and later in the eyes that just stared off into space or directly at them, empty and glazed over. This girl, they argued, she's seriously stubborn. "What's your name?" they asked as if they didn't know, as if they really wanted to know. "Say your name." Facing her low wooden chair, they sat on the edge of a metal chair and said Do-ri. Dori. They were many, but afterward Dori remembered one man with an un-formed face, a suit, and glasses. What did he demand of her? Very, very little. She only had to repeat after him, to let her voice climb up and out. Sometimes she nearly loved him when he left, he had such white hands.

Time passed (how much? Who knew. Not her. She only knew that time covered her, heavy as a blanket), and the man who wore a suit and glasses continued to come. She barely saw the old mer-maid anymore. In one of the meetings she signed her name. The hand formed a sign in the air, open and horizontal; she signed "little one" because that's what they called her. And then the hand started spelling out the four-letter "D. O. R. I." She wasn't stubborn. Understand that, at least, she always wanted to please. She wanted to be a good example; she wanted the man to love her. But she knew that he didn't see and wouldn't see and the hand fell slack and went back to sleep.

They agreed on one matter only. They'd truly saved her at the last moment; a moment later and it would have been too late. She was a girl raised by wolves, and the wolves were driven out at the right time. At the last moment Dori Ackerman was removed from the wolf's jaws, if not from its stomach. The mermaid stuck to her explanation that Dori was still holding on to a single strand from her parents' straw broom and that she must be allowed to let go of it on her own accord (wolves and witches, yes, many images buzzed about among the people who dealt with her case. Each one grasped whatever he grasped and wrote whatever he wrote).

But alongside the relative restraint with which the institution's educational staff treated her, the children adopted surer means. These were very accomplished children and they wanted to prove she could hear, who was she kidding? If the whispers and screams didn't work, the pinches, shoves, and notes buried in her clothes would. In truth this was quite banal but nevertheless, as is the way with these things, effective. It was not for nothing that the educators believed in the healing power of the company of other children, in the power of the flock to awaken the failures, in that power, as of the students of the great sages, to toughen each other up with suffering, to sharpen knives against their thighs or however that saying goes. So without announcing it, by some turning of a blind eye that did the trick, they let the children be. And the children saw her.

**Anton looked at her as if she were suddenly transparent and he could see through her to the expensive drawing that was hung up behind her. She saw how his eyes wandered along the thin sketched lines suggesting two pregnant women. She guessed that he had already identified himself with those other children. But Dori herself knew that this couldn't be. There are things that permit no reason to doubt. The very paleness that spread across his face was evidence that Anton would never have joined them.**

And one day a bird sang outside her window:

> *Soon little Dori Ackerman*
> *will finally*
> *open her mouth.*

> *It will be a beautiful day*
> *when Dori Ackerman*
> *admits it all.*

The bird was right, of course. It was a fact that Dori heard it singing even though the window to her room was sealed shut. Because on that day, which would certainly be a spring day, the flowers would be blooming in the garden of the institution, the birds would be singing, and all the measures that had been taken would retroactively be deemed to have been necessary. Clearly it would have been better if she had given up and surrendered on her own. Clearly that would have been easier, and things would have played out in her favor. Many would even have agreed with the bird's speech, if only they had managed to hear its voice.

But Dori Ackerman was a loyal soldier in a different army. Despite everything, she knew the children didn't and wouldn't see anything about her. She was Columbus's egg and they were foolish Spaniards who would never reach America and would never discover a thing.

Sometimes she saw the three of them in the house in the village, without her, but less and less over time. Their house teetered like a nutshell, like a paper cutout in which everyone's likeness would dwell for eternity. Her mother's paper doll was a crying figure. The tears ran from her eyes in two long white strips that fell to the earth. Her father stood on a small hill, his hands in his pockets, but the paper clouds of smoke that were cut from his pipe signaled to her that everything was temporary, everything precarious, and that she must remember who they were, she must remember the pinky finger. Whereas Lili, Lili was folded up like a boy in a box of matches. She missed her, Dori did, as she would a hand cut off with a knife.

## PART TWO

---

## OTHER SISTERS

*I would like more sisters, that the taking out of one, might not leave such stillness.*

—EMILY DICKINSON

## LILI

Alex and Anna left me alone like generals giving up on a lost battle in an ongoing war. Because Father and Mother went back to being who they always were, Alex and Anna Ackerman, without any extra add-ons, getting along better without offspring around. Behind Father went his regular pack: Aharon the deaf, who made wooden sculptures that always looked like broken ships, smiling with his wide lips to show how harmless he was; Lotti, who was fat and dimpled, and looked warm even though she showed no warmth to anyone other than my father; Uri, who wore an ironed blue uniform every day and never did anything; Ogden, who since meeting my father had removed the devices from his two ears and felt twenty years younger; and Salman, who remained as he was. They followed him, a line of motherless ducks. They loyally carried out my mother's longtime task, quacking yes and yep. My mother, who during that year stopped crying and went on longer and longer trips and returned from them glowing, eyes torn open, as if she had seen an exceptional natural phenomenon. A glacier or a fjord or a sperm whale washed up on the shore. But I already understood that since there were very few natural phenomena where we lived, she was apparently seeing something else.

We didn't talk about Dori. Dori was even more hopeless than I was. I was the touch of a finger away, even if no one around us touched anyone. In the beginning they told me the country was small, I could visit her, but we never did. "Didn't you once have a sister?" they asked me at the regional school. "Weren't there two of you?" I wagged my tangle of hair, orange as sun-drenched apricots, and pretended I didn't hear. Perhaps I really didn't; sometimes deafness is very useful. If my parents had long since accepted my flimsy cooperation, my passive belonging, Father's pack was in despair over the situation. The hard core (because there also was a softer layer around it, like a cloud of busy electrons) nevertheless tried to convert me. Lotti especially was determined to baptize me into the covenant of the innocents. The ceremonies she thought up always included a water motif and the smashing of hearing aids with a sledgehammer. She was easy to avoid, but her fervor impressed me. I understood that she was trying to like me even though she never succeeded. The five of them tried really hard to win my father's affection, the kiss that always remained on his lips and that no one earned, like in *Peter Pan*.

More than anything, the quackers saw the aids I wore to school as their personal failure. When they saw me they shook their heads and Lotti rocked her whole body for emphasis, how sad, Alex's daughter of all people. I could have told them that their Alex wasn't much of a father, but they wouldn't have listened to me. Turns out that they too discovered the advantage of deafness, probably even before I did.

And I actually loved our language. No, it was deeper than love. That's like saying you love your internal organs. They are the words that spell the world, the words with which I said "I" and "sun" and "home" and "Dori." Like in that Russian song that Mikala insisted on playing for me on repeat when I moved to New York, and that she translated loosely, because being exact is never possible: "I wish there would always be sun, I wish there would always be sky, I wish there would always be mother, there would always be me." She sang along to the recording in her broken voice, which didn't fit her at all, and said that roots were important, and I told her that those weren't my roots. And she insisted on translating it into English and claimed with emotion that mother is the source of the world and I agreed and sang *sky* and *mother* and *sun*.

But beneath that I said, Dori. I signed onto my hand her name and my name, but only that and only there. Because from the time I decided to stop speaking our language, I preferred to be silent. This began at the regional school, where the more silent I was the more popular I became. I got excellent grades, even though I didn't make a sound in class. Perhaps it was actually because of that. I was silent as a stone, like a mermaid whose voice has been taken. That's what Dori would have said; between us she was the one stuck on fairy tales. Silence, I thought then, is the only thing that will save me. When I was left alone I was no longer willing to be mocked. There are things that two can absorb that one cannot.

And at home as well, it was as if everything had changed. The establishment was watching Alex and Anna through a magnifying glass, this we knew; they were waiting for another mistake on their part, for more neglect and foolishness, but the focused gaze made Alex hold his head up straight, root up weeds, give Lotti and Ogden and all the rest the rules of the current management, the tedious detail work. Even the scenery around us changed. Our empty flowerpots filled up with plants that were supposed to last in all weather, even in the desert; the envelopes from the regional council were opened, the letters read and arranged in a pile; Lotti took on cleaning duties and Ogden was in charge of upkeep. Uri walked around and around like a guard, dressed in blue and clutching a crooked branch to defend against potential enemies. These were the foundations of Alex's kingdom, even though I didn't know it yet. Around then, Salman planted the first apple tree saplings. Perhaps because the apple was Anna's favorite fruit or maybe Dori's. I always hated apples. Anyway, I think the saplings were given to Salman as a gift, but this, of all memories, I doubt. The world gave my father's people nothing but obvious flaws.

In the beginning they came for weekly meetings and afterward they showed up twice a week and quite quickly the empty units once occupied by immigrants were in use. They lived around us like small, hardworking mice, but they still resembled ducks most of all. Alex's followers were characters organized around a single attribute, flat as a pancake or a parable. And with all their one-dimensional might, they settled among us and announced that they had no intention of leaving.

Father's quacking ducks would come up to me with eyes ablaze and hands shaking. They said to me with heavy mouths, in a language that a few of them spoke with an impressive stammer, that there was no man as marvelous as my father. My mother's few friends, whom she assembled from God only knows where, admired her and despised my father. They said that she was wasted and meant that she was wasted on us, on the husband and the daughter. Her garden won one prize and then another. Her friends took her out to coffee and cake. Perhaps it wasn't the friends but someone else. I learned to nod like a bobblehead dog by the windshield and then, as in an old trick, I came to resemble the windshield itself. I became transparent. And not even this changed anything. I was a weight around their necks. I was the tree planted in the wrong soil. The branches obstructed their view, they saw through me.

Father and Mother and I, still living at one address. If we had a dog, the picture would have been complete. No one spoke about

Dori. Because from the time that everything was decided and agreed upon, with swift legal and social work intervention from the regional council, the die was cast. Due to the charges, which were later dropped, my father was in custody for almost a week. He returned with his beard shaven and his eyes sparkling. He was thin and happy. Someone said that his lawyer slid him out of there like an envelope under the door. "They had no reason to arrest your father," the lawyer said to me, of all people, when he returned him to our house. "To be disabled is not a crime." I didn't tell him that there was no point in addressing me, I didn't tell him that he should revise the dictionary when addressing Father's quacking followers. He sat on the edge of the porch and when Father entered he called after him, "Mr. Ackerman!" But Father went right past the lawyer, walked right past me too like I wasn't there. Father didn't hear.

I counted the changes to myself, reluctantly interested in them. He, Alex Ackerman, began smoking again but went from a prisoner's cheap cigarettes to a pipe that Uri carved for him, engraving in it his initials, "A.A.," and my mother sat silent for many days. Finally she offered to braid my hair into two braids. I refused, and not only because my loose hair hid the aids I wore. Afterward she didn't offer me anything again. Had I known that it would be this way, perhaps I would have said yes, okay, you can groom me like a ten-year-old girl. But I doubt it.

The hearing aids arrived via special delivery. My mother threw out the first shipment. The second accidentally fell under the tires of our pickup, and when the third arrived the deliveryman stood next to me, waiting as I put them on, then adjusted the volume and left. When I wrote about this to Dori I described the deliveryman in a blue uniform carrying the box like a cake tray. I didn't send the letter.

This too could be told differently, because the deliveryman, due to his medical training (real or imagined), appeared calm and content. His thoughts flickered across his face like the letters on a neon sign. He'd heard my sad story and was certain that in his hand was the gift of the gods and modern medicine. He expected an outbreak of joy, a reward for the good deed, additional affirmation that science can fix everything. The lame shall walk; the deaf shall hear. The aid was removed from the box. The instruction manual was glued to the top. He put them on, he left, I shrieked. I stuck around to hear.

When I was sent to the regional school the teachers assumed that I was deaf and dumb. They saw what they saw and heard what they heard and nobody bothered to correct them. I certainly wasn't going to be the one to whisper the truth in anyone's ear (ha!) and tell them that deaf-mutes are an invention. This was also an invention of mine, the mistake I took hold of throughout my first months at school; I rode on its back like I would hang on skates behind my dad's pickup, something Dori and I almost never did except that one time.

Maybe I wasn't mute, but I knew how to be quiet. When someone said he knew one way to make me scream and moan, they quickly shushed him. It was like I was stepping down the long and deserted corridors of eternity, touching the sides, and suddenly encountering a stretch of damp wall where paint refused to dry. A piece of eternity. And I touched it.

Within a year I acquired what my father always wanted, everyday holiness. The art teacher claimed I had an Etruscan smile. The little girls stood in line in order to brush my hair. Even the big boys looked at me with eyes full of emotion. I reminded them of something they had been robbed of without noticing. And I only sat and smiled, gazing out at a nonexistent horizon. No one knew a thing about me and whoever knew preferred to forget. They loved sitting by me, as if I were an oak tree or a goddess from Atlantis; they told one another that they achieved calm next to me, discovered the correct answer, that I had this quality. And perhaps I would have been tempted to believe them had I known the truth. But even the truth wasn't important. I was what I was. A sea where every wave erased the one before. A beautiful silence.

Strange how sweet that period is to me. A period sewn out of empty hours. A period in which thought receded from me like a cloud dumping its rain in another place. I put down the notebooks. The famous notebooks, the notebooks in which I wrote everything that happened as long as it changed. But that didn't matter anymore. Because there was no Dori to read while I pretended that I didn't care and that it didn't matter to me and that her eyes, running over the lines, weren't saying anything to me as I sat opposite the notebook with nothing to write. In that place I heard everything. At night I heard even the insects that spread out across the nearby field; I heard gates slamming, illicit love (wife of, husband of, son of, all of them sucking at each other's flesh with a deep, dark lust). I heard children running away from home and being brought back with a reprimand; I heard the dog barking and the dog that wouldn't bark again.

In art I made birds full of glue, in literature I memorized tragedies. I liked Ismene more than Antigone. Ismene the appeaser, the persuader, the beautiful, the lukewarm, neither fire nor ice. The sister who stays behind. Whose lines are especially boring. Of all characters, she was the one whose lines I memorized during long, colorless afternoons, when Alex and Anna were Alex and Anna. And there was actually no point to this, because in the end I appeared in the role of Antigone, dressed in a well-stitched sheet with my hair gathered in a braid on my head like a Russian farmer. The drama teacher worked with me on diction. He made me practice breathing in order to produce a voice. My articulation, heavy mouth and jaw, sounded artificial in his ears: "And now, Ismene, you can prove what you are: a true sister, or a traitor to your family."

This was a very ambitious school and somehow these aspirations suited me. Like those hand puppets that have the wolf on one side and the grandma on the other. I was Antigone on the outside and deep inside I was a supporting player who doesn't drive the plot—because I read, and that's what they write about Ismene, that's what they always write about her.

I've since lost patience for Greek tragedies. You can find more logic in a phone book, and probably more dysfunctional families as well. With regard to the deep truth of my life, I prefer sticking to clear principles over ancient sins and capricious gods. Yes, even alphabetical order and area codes. Facts are preferable to fiction.

Alex and Anna looked at me and saw the one who remained. I was the big one without the little one, without a relation or a growth chart. Although I secretly thought otherwise then, I wasn't the right daughter. Sometimes, when Anna and I suddenly found ourselves in another long, slow afternoon, yellow as a lemon cake we didn't eat, it seemed to me that she wanted to sign something to me. She'd begin saying something, then the hand would drop down. Sometimes she asked, "Did you eat?" and I'd nod. Sometimes she asked if I'd slept, if I'd done my homework, as though imitating a reasonable family in which a dialogue like this was conceivable. Only once did she ask me, "What happened to your notebooks?" But perhaps it only seemed to me that she asked, perhaps all of this never happened. Because her war against my notebooks succeeded, and since when does a warlord take interest in his slain enemy? Again, Dori interferes with my images.

Anna didn't ask if I was writing. If I read. And if she had asked, I wouldn't have known what to answer. The words hovered midair. The facts drowned in the sea. I was empty and shiny like the shell of an egg that had been emptied with a thin needle.

So this continued until Uriel Savyon arrived from the old neighborhood. Uriel had been stretched upward by time, which had also spread an enthusiastic look across his face. Despite everything he still looked pinkish, freckled, and fresh, like a strange character from an animated movie, like he was only a basic sketch that someone had intended to finish but had set aside, half there and half blurred. But there was enough to point at him and say, "That one." It was him, the boy who Dori and I pitied from up in the tree and down below, the boy who dragged along a bag that was heavier than he was and limped on one leg.

Uriel Savyon, ladies and gentlemen, didn't know a thing. He didn't know who I had become. He didn't even know that by means of the aids I'd heard more than a few things in the world. Those ugly aids definitely did the job if I didn't turn them down all the way. Maybe I didn't hear everything, but when I wore them, if I wore them, I understood that this din that seized my body from within, that this assault was what people called hearing. Perhaps you might expect that this was wonderful; you can hear, and it seems to you that this is a wonderful attribute. You pity the deaf, after all. You've seen those videos of the deaf people who begin to hear and joy washes over their faces. I've seen too. They spread like viruses. The baby smiles, the grown man cries, the girl covers her face with her hands. But I, when I could think about something other than the pain, understood that Alex, my father, was right. It was terrible.

When they first put the aids on me I felt as if someone had cut me in two and there was nothing holding me together. I felt ravaged, but I didn't have the words for this. My friend Jenna told me that when she started to hear it was magical. They played her a Beatles song. It's always the Beatles. Paul and John sang in harmony and her parents cried. She cried too. From joy, what else.

She smiled when she said this, like she was aware that the story was in bad taste but nevertheless wasn't willing to wrinkle her nose at it. After all, we were about to be therapists, to reflect like a silver spoon the feelings of whoever stood before us, to slowly undo the knots. To listen. I held my opinion about this propaganda from her. As if all the deaf were surrounded by a world of pain and silence until technology came along and saved them. But I turned up my nose; yes, that was obviously my role. The wrinkles of the nose, and the sarcasm, and the unnecessary cigarettes and so on and so forth. She told me things that were utterly foreign to what I knew. Her parents spoke to her so that their voices would be the first things she heard, after the Beatles. And she was happy and even if the happiness was temporary and fleeting she held on to it. Because that's how she told it to me, without her regular giggle, in what was suddenly a little girl's voice. I believed her when she spoke. I still do believe, like the Italians Marco Polo told about China, bringing with him a noodle as proof. Wonders and miracles, an unbelievable land.

But if you want to know, I signed "hurts." I signed "enough" and "stop." Maybe I shrieked. They turned the aid off. When they turned it on again, apparently no one spoke. Someone played music. Something repulsive. Something I haven't heard since. Not on purpose. My mother spoke first. I knew that it was her although I hadn't heard her voice before. My father looked at me. No matter what, Alex spoke only in our language.

When Uriel Savyon saw me in the eleventh-grade hallway, under the "Young Leadership" poster, he gave me an ignorant, stupid hug. A hug that wasn't acceptable between boys and girls, contact that was uncommon even between us at home. I stood there and waited for him to stop; I counted the flakes of dandruff that had fallen onto his collar. Students began gathering around us; two of the smaller girls who I couldn't always tell apart opened their eyes wide as he spoke excitedly about me and about Dori, and how he always wanted to be our friend and how nothing was the same since we left. He spoke loudly and fluently, but from time to time signed in order to emphasize what he was saying. I don't know if any of them noticed this. I tried to get away from him, but he wouldn't stop talking about Dori and the whispers were rising all around us so I had no choice and said in a voice lower than usual that he should come over that afternoon. He was the first person I ever invited home. I said to him, "Meet me next to the back gate." It was a half-hour walk from the main road, I figured, maybe forty minutes with all his hand-waving. It might cool him off a bit.

He really was waiting next to the gate, smiling. Optimistic and kindhearted like a sheep at pasture. I saw that he was trying hard not to run to me, forcefully sticking his feet in the ground. A pocket had been revealed to the world and it held my entire past, but I wasn't hurrying to open it. As if Dori herself was liable to fall out of it. When we turned onto the dirt path Uriel again said something about her, how funny she is, even though there was no chance he ever really spoke to her, even though Dori isn't funny at all. He spoke formally every time: "Dori Ackerman." After the fifth or five-hundredth time I said to him, "She's dead."

The moments stretched out on the path until his whistle broke the silence. Even in the days to come he didn't ask about Dori; weeks passed and he didn't ask how she died, under what circumstances. Had he asked, maybe I would have said. Maybe I would have told him everything. But the first time we walked home together he just whistled. He whistled a kind of intricate melody, not something he could have come up with himself. Months without rain and our shoes kicked up small clouds of dust. He whistled and I listened, and suddenly we were like two people listening to Beethoven's *Emperor* Concerto. Two people who became emperors themselves while listening. Of all things to remember, as if the thing lodged itself in my actual childhood memory and wasn't taken from some educational story for girls. I almost told him about the hero of that story, a girl who tries to pretend that she's someone else and secretly listens to records until someone, a boy, say, joins her and they listen to Beethoven on an old, scratchy record.

When I read this story for the first time, I hoped that my ears would cease being just two pieces of flesh stuck to the sides of my head. I had a complete list of things I had only read about and meant to hear. I knew that one day I'd hear everything. Beethoven's Concerto no. 5, the *Emperor*, was entry number thirty-four on the list. I planned on listening to it, hugging my knees from all that beauty, like that American girl from the story, who, I imagined, was all elbows and knees.

And suddenly it was clear to me that this is what he was whistling, that he was walking and whistling the *Emperor*. I asked him and he said, "What are you talking about, it's Tchaikovsky," and then he added, "No, just kidding, it's a gum ad. I'm crazy about it, you?" I admitted that I was, that I was kind of crazy about it. It really was pretty.

His hair was already cut short and didn't cover his ears like the funny haircut he had when he was nine or ten years old. When the dirt path turned into a shiny black road he said to me, "They cut down the tree."

"I know," I said to him. "I've known since it happened. It's like they waited for us to go to get rid of it." I waited for him to deny it. When I got rides to the old house I saw with my own eyes the notice in the stairwell announcing that parasites had been found in the tree, the fruits had worms, the tree didn't suit the climate, it wasn't planted in the intended place. Even then it sounded to me like a bunch of fabrications from the municipal sanitation department. But in those days I couldn't have put that in words. "That's right," Uriel said, "that's exactly what they did. My mom said so too. She complained to the city, but the tree was the responsibility of the building, not the street, so there wasn't anything to do. They didn't plant anything in its place. It just stayed there, a stump." I told him that I knew that too, though I didn't.

When we got close to the house, Lotti, one of the head ducks, welcomed us. She signed to me in our language, "Welcome back." "Lotti," I said to her, "I hear with the aids and you've heard from birth. Maybe you can tell me what you have to say." But Lotti, whose eczema had spread from the neck on up by then, just looked at me with the obsequious smile reserved for the leader's rebellious daughter and stepped aside. "There's food," I explained to him without looking back; I knew he was walking behind me. "They cook here all the time, even though my dad doesn't eat a thing. The refrigerator is full, see for yourself," I said, and opened up our domestic horn of plenty. In a pan I warmed up two pieces of lasagna though I debated whether or not this was the proper way to heat them. The lasagna was delicious and the two of us focused on eating.

"I mourned when you left." There was something strange in the way he pronounced *t*, but other than that, to my ears his pronunciation sounded almost perfect, in its way. Almost the pronunciation of a hearing person.

"I went searching for your things like some junkie."

"And what did you find?"

"Not too much," he said, and then I knew that he was lying. I remembered what we left there. "Us too," I said to him, "we mourned too." And I didn't know if it was the truth this time. The facts were no longer identical to the truth and anyway even when they rolled right under my feet like pebbles I didn't pick them up. Uriel talked about the model airplane club and the amateur theater group and it became clear to me that he had turned into one of the people with hobbies. The dandruff was actually bits of model airplane glue. His enthusiasm for the world stuck to him like a second skin. And after describing the special glue for the airplanes, which he revealed could be made at home, he went on to tell me about the transplant, about the cochlea he got when he was ten years old. About the surgery and the special fit, close to perfect, "even though nothing is perfect," he said with satisfaction, as if repeating someone else's words. He wanted to expound upon the exercises they taught him, but this wasn't the place to talk about that. Our house, even after adding window boxes and a doormat, was an implant-free zone.

"You're not normal," I whispered to him. "How could you let them do that to you? You're really a robot." I didn't care that he looked at me with astonishment, that according to all logic I was the one who should have been astonished. I could see, after all. Had I looked at him I would have seen. "Do you understand the power over you that you gave to them? They can insert whatever they want into you. Implanting fibers in your brain. You have no control at all. You—you're like an android. It's not normal."

He smiled. That boy of model airplanes and drama, who once walked with a limp, Uriel Savyon the miserable, smiled. "Lili," he said. "What are you talking about?"

"I don't believe it," I said again, and got up from my place. I cleared the table and put the dishes in the sink. The salt shaker too. I turned on the water that sprayed straight onto the clear plates where cracks had formed along the edges. I didn't want to imagine what Father would say if he knew what I had brought home. The water washed away the mess in every direction. I stood and looked at the waterfall that I made myself, in the sink, with water. Uriel left, I knew he had left, but the water continued flowing. At that moment Alex Ackerman, like a dog with a highly developed sense of smell, entered the kitchen. Unlike normal, he stroked my hair. "Dad," I said to him, speaking with my lips while my hands remained under the stream. "Dad," the lips pronounced, unaccustomed to this nickname being uttered aloud. "You must remember Uriel, that poor kid from the old house? You won't believe it, he got an implant. They gave him an implant, the little traitor." I finished speaking and turned around to him. I signed to him "hello" and "everything's fine" and "there's food in the fridge." The words I spoke were absorbed only by the walls. No tragedy had occurred. And we met again, of course. At a certain age there's nothing to be done. The system demands that you meet each morning. Sit and listen to a Bible lesson. Or meet in art class and dunk gauze into plaster. During that time everyone made a cast for everyone, hollow casts hung all over, in classrooms and public places, the art department at school was at its peak then. For most of the creations I served as a model. I would walk down corridors and see five Lilis, skillfully made this way or that, painted according to their owners' talent, looking back at me with their plastered gaze. Some of them raised a hand in the air. Some had hair added to them and others looked on bald and smiled at nothing. Perhaps it would have been better to fill them with candy and smash them open under the right circumstances, but it seemed that everyone, truly everyone, was impressed. I loved the feel of plaster hardening on the skin, and sitting under the gauze, which was my only contribution to art class, earning me a perfect grade. Outstanding model. Uriel Savyon actually didn't get caught up in the cast craze, but instead toiled over a statue made of gum. I admit it sounds quite disgusting, but somehow it wasn't. I meant to be mad at him, but when I saw him again, enthusiastic and full of anticipation, I didn't have the energy. He moved aside the leaning columns of gum and I cleared away a spot for him next to me. My right hand was full of gauze as well as my neck to my chest. Two industrious girls were now working on a cast for my feet and were making their way up in the direction of my calves. Achilles' heels covered in white.

Dori would say, "Look at you, what did they do to you, you look like all your limbs broke at once." Perhaps she would have signed this to me in hidden writing on my back, over the shirt. But Uriel didn't say a thing. When the plaster hardened and was detached from my body, and only a grayish dust remained on me that didn't hint at what had happened there, I rolled down the ends of my pants and put my shirt back on and he asked me to come with him. Of all places, he wanted us to go to his parents' house. Strange, as if my imagination and his had been restricted to those of good children whose hair is combed to the side and who hurry back home after school.

I felt as if I was walking in a dream. And, as in a dream, when you know that there's no significance to anything you do, you can actually do anything without bearing the consequences. Like for example visiting the well-kept Savyon family home in a nearby affluent suburb. The house was large and made of simple forms, without any special decorations. The light fell perfectly there; this is what he told me and I was uncertain if he was being sincere or ironic. But it appeared that Uriel was proud of his parents and their well-kept home, as he already was, for some reason, proud of me. He appeared truly happy when his parents hugged me one after the other. They were a family of huggers and they remembered me. His father hummed in agreement when his mother said how beautiful I was, how beautiful I had grown. She wiped her eyes and blamed the tears on an eye infection. A bright blue stripe stretched out under each eye. And after she put in a few drops from a bottle pulled from a pocket of her blue silk shirt, she wiped her hands on a kitchen towel. In this way she departed from the regular custom of the house, according to which each object had a clear role. Eyes were wiped with a handkerchief, and the towel served only to polish wineglasses. And even Uriel himself, who looked to me as if he were constantly standing on the tips of his toes, trying hard to reach higher, appeared calm and relaxed as well. As if finally his toes and tensed muscles (tensed cheerfully, yes, but still) had quieted down a bit. Because he himself wanted so much, but his parents, I understood quickly, had already stretched out to their full height.

I didn't plan for us to become friends. It seems I didn't plan any of what happened. But in those days plans weren't my top priority. Everything was so sticky anyway, and each morning it seemed that the sun had moved a bit. Our beautiful world tilted over, slightly bent, as if an earthquake no one felt had taken place and all of us continued walking along the earth's crust, ignoring the valleys and gorges, the new furrows that had been formed.

In my eyes the world sometimes resembled those leaves that fall spinning from the branch and all that remains of them in autumn is their skeleton. And inside that larger rotation Uriel and I also began to spin, airy and weightless, stuck to each other because of proximity.

We spent the afternoon hours at his parents' house. His father tended to work in the adjacent home office. His mother was a judge in the juvenile court and in the evenings would tell us briefly about the cases over which she presided. She spoke about them as if they were archeological findings she dug up in the garden, with the excitement of someone who unexpectedly finds a statue under the petunias. I quickly came to understand that her tears were primarily a result of seasonal allergies. Even when she told us about the kids who burned down a garage, who tied cats' tails and worse, the tears that flowed were thanks to these allergies. I nodded along to keep from revealing how much I resembled the kids brought before her, even if I still hadn't committed a crime, not a single one you could be tried for. I assumed that this was how it was among women of a certain age, that their tears begin to spill out for some reason. Time after time, Uriel Savyon's mother talked as if these were comical misfits on trial. Sometimes I felt that they expected me to say something, share my opinion. But it wasn't my plan to be ground up under the wheels of water or justice, like Max and Moritz in the stories. And they never asked me what it was I didn't want to say. The Savyon family let me be a clean and reduced version of myself, a feathery version of Lili, fluttering about innocently in a world where the light fell equally and naturally upon every illuminated room.

After some time he introduced me to Dima. They met in one of the classes for advanced youth or advanced thought, classes that Uriel always quit before long, but before he quit they managed to see each other, and seeing means identifying. Dima believed only in substance, in structures and what one could touch. Uriel believed in everything else. Dima put his faith in the perpetual revolution, and with us the revolutions dwindled in our grasp. One day they'd stand people like us before the wall. This we knew. We were people for whom there was no use. But still we also knew that the one who would save us from the wall was Dima. For now we were a trio. Uriel the hard of hearing, Dima the deaf, and me. They stuck us together with carpenter's glue, deaf glue. If they gave us nicknames, we didn't hear them. Our routine was set in place quickly, with nails, until it was easy to forget the days when the two weren't by my side. Dima would escort me to school on his bike and continue on to the factory. Uriel would sit down next to me in class.

Uriel was quite brilliant and they bumped him up a grade. In class he spoke nonstop, but to my surprise he didn't earn constant ridicule, the usual lot of the enthusiastic at an age when no one wants to be enthused. The others left him alone and I told myself it was because of me. Dima was stormy and irate, like the first page of a wintry novel. At the steel factory he had already advanced to line manager and to the best of our knowledge performed this job with the diligence and anger that characterized him. In the evening he guarded building sites and read books on physics and Marxism. I did the math and found that the two of them together were like three-fourths of a Dori at most. We were simple shards that didn't exactly combine to make a whole.

The constant sound of the aids was soft and unremitting even when no one spoke, when Dima didn't scrape his shoes and Uriel didn't cough. When no car honked. When Dima caught me gargling water, my head bent back, I explained to him that this was something I'd started doing since the aids. Sometimes the water overwhelmed the brain; my throat filled up with water and the world was forgotten. Dima told me to empty my mouth and dried my face. He explained to me that gargling was a well-known method, a method that was once considered an effective means for teaching the deaf to speak. He told me, slowly and seriously, that during the brief time he wore aids it seemed to him as if he were diving underwater. This was one of the reasons he decided to get rid of them; actually, the most important reason. And in truth, this was how the sounds reached me, slow and submerged, rising to the water's surface. He said to me, signing the words in his characteristic wooden manner, "You so badly want to be like the hearing that you gargle. But that's not what they hear."

I shrugged my shoulders again. Maybe he was right. "Nevertheless," he said to me, "nevertheless there were worse methods to teach us to speak their language. If one is allowed to choose torture devices, gargling water is at least preferable to the tongue they used to install in deaf children's mouths. You understand, this was how they hoped to develop our sensitivity for manufacturing sounds." This was one of the longer conversations we had. Dima looked at me as if this had happened yesterday morning, as if they had forced Dima himself to grow a new tongue in his mouth. Only when I had the time to read for myself did I discover that he was telling me about good intentions that had led to all kinds of hell, about terrible acts that took place hundreds of years ago.

A bit after this, the three of us went to the beach. None of us had a bathing suit, but this didn't make any difference. It was as if my ear grew all at once and took in the entire sea. As if the aid absorbed and finally broadcasted the sound of the world. The two of them looked at me happily, knowing they had done a good deed. That they'd succeeded. I remembered Dori's tales about mermaids and I wondered if those fish girls lived in fresh or salt water. I knew that somewhere they still sang to her their horrible songs, which I could never hear.

I smoked my first cigarettes with Uriel and Dima. Perhaps this is the main thing that remains with me of them, the intensity of these habits—the morning cigarettes, the sea, the gargling. Dima predicted a revolution. He had a very clear estimate of when it would happen. The superpowers would collapse, the tectonic plates would quake, and even in our small corner we'd see tanks in the street. He said the time had come for the deaf to establish territory for themselves, that no one would voluntarily give us a thing. At these moments he reminded me of Alex, even though they were so different; Alex was rotten and Dima was fresh and therefore

I couldn't hate him. I couldn't tell him that I wouldn't find a place in this republic of his. With an almost identical fervor, Uriel believed in the theater and nanotechnology. He planned to establish a theater company. He believed that this was the purest of all arts.

Each of them despised the other's dream. Uriel and Dima were such characters, so concentrated, like mercury or heavy water, that sometimes it seemed to me that I invented them. Perhaps I invented them because I didn't have a dream of my own, at least not an all-embracing dream like theirs. I just was and it seemed that this was enough. No one knew that I wrote once, that again and again I chose facts over stories, because the difference between the two already appeared to me slimmer than slim. Sometimes I let them caress my hair, but not more than this. If someone had asked I would have explained that they were my brothers. But no one asked.

So it continued until Uriel came to the two of us and said he had visited Dori. It was a Saturday morning. Dima and I were eating pancakes with sugar in the Savyon family's back garden. I knew his parents weren't crazy about Dima, but they accepted our presence there. We were their son's first friends and they had no intention to object to this aloud. This wasn't the first time we were there without Uriel. We had also gotten used to coming there when Uriel stayed late at theater club or working on one of his model aircraft carriers. In contrast to the two of us, who always woke up at the same time, as if the bed had pushed us out, Uriel prolonged his mornings to their very end. Just before eleven he joined us, his hair disheveled as always, his front teeth seeming to stick out more, the crust still covering his eyes. I restrained myself from sending him to wash his face. He looked as if he was about to explode; he never knew how to keep news or secrets to himself. "I visited Dori," he said.

He said that she didn't look at him or ask him anything. That her hair was short. That her buttons skipped a hole. As if he had stood in front of the mirror for an hour and was describing only himself. He said that she didn't answer a single question but didn't tell him to leave either, and when she talked it was only about outer space. About planets and dying stars. About Saturn, which is the Jews' sun. I cut the pancake into thin triangles, into crosshatches. Everything he said sounded like secondhand impressions. Dima looked at me. He never knew about Dori, not from me anyway. I tried to read something from Dima's expression but I read nothing there. Uriel still stood in front of us, leaning a bit on the glass table. We were still sitting. Perhaps we could have been frozen like this forever, on the edge of an explanation, though I knew it wouldn't end there. I waited for him to produce all the doves from his top hat already. "She made a drawing of stars," he added. "At least I think they're stars. So I asked her if I could take it. I brought it for you, you want to see?"

For the first time in ages my sister and I resembled each other again; at least we shared a single silence. I didn't intend to answer him, just as I didn't intend to look at the sketch that Dori drew instead of listening to him. I drank from the glass of milk that was in front of me. It had a fatty taste. I thought of all the good girls who drink milk, of all the little sisters whose hair is pinned back. I forgot all of them. Their names were erased and after this the lines of their faces as well. Glasses of milk were emptied into unseen mouths. There's no way she's interested in stars, I thought, no way. But maybe she really did start to draw.

Uriel too gave the power of silence a try. But after a few minutes, after his face reddened and paled, he returned to words. "You know, Lili, I just wanted to help."

Now I spoke. "Help? Help with what? Did I ask for your help?"

"But you didn't know where she was. You thought she died.

And now I found her. And it wasn't easy, you should know, I had to check on my mom's computer, to connect to court records, to her files. After I found out, I went to her on Friday evening and said I was her brother. They bought it really easily. They were happy that someone from her family finally came to her, you get it? Look, I can take you to her. Maybe we'll take her out for the weekend." Everything had already come together for him in his head, the facts and the stories, the long trip in the car his parents bought him, too bad it didn't have a sun roof, Dori becoming part of our gang, her face glowing with joy. I'm sure he had already selected a soundtrack for the journey. Maybe he would also want to replant the tree.

"I just wanted to show you that she's still alive," he said again, a bit defeated. "But she wasn't at all who I thought she'd be. She wasn't like what I remembered either. And you two, you're not alike at all." Dima was still silent. The two of us knew it was my turn to speak. I ate the rest of the pancake. It had no taste.

"There's a reason for that," I said to him. "The reason is that Dori died and you'll never understand anything."

But I forgave him; his mother intervened with her judicial temperament, she mentioned how rash her son is sometimes, quick to be impressed, quick to act. She explained and I forgave him. His mother was also the one who said, "Lili will be a psychologist someday," and signed me up for evening classes at the open university. I didn't know where this confidence, which quickly became certitude, came from. Perhaps from my habit of being quiet, of nodding when she spoke. Like everyone, she too fancied Lili the silent. It looked as if I held on to every word spoken to me. If only she knew that as she spoke to me I was counting backward. Sometimes from one hundred. Sometimes from a thousand. Maybe that's what all psychologists do. Maybe that's the essence of attention.

His father didn't actually believe much in psychology, but he too considered it a promising career path. Though his office was attached to the house, he was seldom seen, since decisions could be made and finalized in invisible ink without him. I liked him, I really liked him. I knew that he had once been excitable and enthusiastic, just like his son, until his wife centered him. They hoped that I would do this for Uriel, be the compass point, the leg that stands firm while the other spins around in hasty circles. I suspect that this was supposed to be flattering. She insisted on seeing potential in me, and I let her praise fall on my shoulders like snowflakes that would melt in a moment. When she talked about me, it was as if she was referring to a different person.

When Uriel and I traveled, he to study theater in New York and me to the different courses his mother signed me up for, my most important goodbye was with Dima. He was about to volunteer for the army, alone among the three of us. I hadn't supposed that this would happen, but in fact it did. I could imagine him as a soldier, inciting the battalion, mining entire streets and attacking the capital. Teaching them our language. My parents actually accepted my leaving with indifference. My mother even looked pleased, and just then my father was occupied with his own inner journey alongside his pack of quacking fools.

His mother thought that I was interesting, that I was talented, that there was promise buried inside me. She clearly thought that I had more imagination and ability than her son, whose lack of hearing was the main thing that made him unique. I said to her again, "You don't see him." I should have added "love him," but there was no point. What I had nevertheless dared to say she attributed to my natural generosity, which actually wasn't that generous. "Yes," she said, "he really tries hard to be special, our boy. But there are things one must accept as they are." She paid for both of our studies and ignited the flame on my tail like a guided missile. I didn't ask her the obvious: Who would want a deaf psychologist? Maybe because I was no longer deaf, not entirely, but instead living in the eternal in-between position of someone who went through a modification to please you, the hearing. Maybe because it turned out I have no interest in psychology. I should have expected this in advance, but the psychology courses were two out of the only three that could fit around the capricious schedule of my job at a hotel. Actually, I would have preferred to take Gardens in Japan, but she never said, "Someday Lili will be a Japanese gardener."

I know what caught your attention, like a butterfly is caught in a net. Like dewdrops that will never fall. The world shimmers, but those are spiderwebs. And I'm the spider. Correct: I can hear. I've been hearing for some time. That is, as they say here, old news—an oxymoron, I'd say, for it is the nature of news to renew itself, but I prefer to clean the corners of the room, to straighten a sheet, to impose order on the mess you left. I know enough about you after cleaning, quite enough. I have no need to hear your idle talk, if you speak at all with your companion, with your wife. Ears are superfluous here. All the same, I know what you did on the bedcover and where you put the peels and the nail clippings. You're on vacation now and you demand that the vacation match all your dreams, all the ornate ribbons you tied and paid for in advance. But you'll go back in a few more days and I'll clean up after you then as well. I'll place a chocolate heart on the pillow. I'll clean the phone's handset with a cloth. I'll gather up the few coins you left as a tip and set them down by the beggar at the entrance. We traveled for one purpose but I was detained by another.

I heard the world's faint tones, the whisper of eggs cooking on the gas, a cat sharpening its nails on an armchair, the rustle of the wind in the Savyon family's garden and wintry gusts in the windy corridors of the city that Uriel and I moved to. I heard voices from the outside, even though I sometimes struggled to decide if the conversation I heard with half an ear took place on television or in the next room. In my ears even the ticktock of clocks sounded uniform and resolute, threatening to overpower the rest of the voices with its monotony. This was the kind of thing that Dori talked about. By the time I heard the clock, it became clear to me how strange it was for so much to hinge on its ticking. I thought about searching for my old watch that Dori loved so much and I never agreed to loan her. I don't know where it wound up, if anywhere. She heard the watch, almost unconsciously, and now it was my turn. But as close as I tried to listen, for me it remained just a stupid ticking that caused things to move and come back. Maybe that's not so strange; Dori and I never liked the same things, except when we had no choice.

I really had the surgery. That's the missing detail. I was operated on even before we left, Uriel and I. Small children are better candidates for the implant, but I convinced them with signs and wonders until they agreed and acquiesced. I received a full subsidization and three days of hospitalization in a room with a standard curtain that gave off a smell of industrial cleaners. I was implanted. I crossed the line. From the hospital I returned to the home of the Savyon family and, five weeks later, when the implant was already working and I had gone through the first training, I showed up at our place. Uriel wanted to come with me. I said to him, no. Even he understood.

I expected the house to look smaller, like a memory from another time, but it was exactly its size. Alex's fencing of crooked metal surrounded the house, as always, sparkling in the sun, impersonating something beautiful. Everything was quiet, the hum of the electric wires almost couldn't be heard, the Ackerman family was a large magnet of silence, and it seemed that the sound of everything in its vicinity had been erased. Suddenly, in opposition to all that my old and new senses were telling me, I wanted to go home. It was a lofty and childish desire, and it threatened to lie down on the floor and not get up until I surrendered before it. I wanted to go to our old room, lie down in bed, sleep, and wake up as a girl again. I wanted to find that watch and wrap it around my wrist. I thought about asking them for it, but when we met, the three of us standing as if the world had forgotten to provide a chair for us, I understood that no watch could be on the agenda. The two of them went together, in lockstep, and stood in the edge of the thick shade cast by the house. I stood opposite them, the light of the sun striking back. The scrap metal I passed on my way to them was the accumulated junk of some factory. I tried to picture the man who sat in the factory, who each day made nuts and bolts. A man replaced by a machine, whose daily production became a pile of junk. I tried to see him but I didn't see a thing. I lifted my caressed mane of red hair, my tiger's tail. It was a co-quettish gesture, but I had planned it in advance. I lifted up my hair with both hands; I let them see.

The same trace of pain appeared on Alex's and Anna's faces, as if the world had interfered and forced them to hear.

Alex Ackerman's palms looked very dark. I thought about this. How much they had darkened, as if they had been dipped in coffee. His fingernails had been trimmed close to the flesh, into square shapes; perhaps he clipped them with metal-cutting pliers. His age was evident there, on his palms, on the knuckles that seemed in constant effort even when they were still. I looked and memorized these details. I already understood then that I'd get no closer to his hands than this. Anna Ackerman looked east-ward even though there was nothing worth seeing there. My de-sire was still lying on the floor, urging me to pass through the opening of their forgiveness even if it was as narrow as the eye of a needle. I again smelled the old neglected scent that blended with the smell of the vanilla candles that Lotti lit in every corner. I could have stood in front of them for another hundred years, but I left.

An additional fact is that I lied before. Because these are the facts: I was the one who betrayed them and not the other way around. Even if they left me nine times for the benefit of the poor and oppressed, for plants that did and didn't flower, the tenth time, it was me leaving. I abandoned everything. I kicked over buckets of milk. I didn't cry. That's how it was.

I didn't see Dima dressed in uniform. During his infrequent leaves he met with other people, not us. He finally understood that the deaf republic would need brothers in the cause, not us, not me. He didn't visit me in the hospital and didn't say goodbye to us at the airport. I knew that from his perspective the surgery had actually made me disabled, a toy with a broken mechanism that you throw to the side of the room. He was very reticent in his first letter. I quickly wrote him back. I didn't say I was sorry. He wrote little, just facts, like someone who was infected by the old Lili. Despite this I understood everything. Between the lines I read the pity beneath his anger, the sorrow accompanied by faint contempt. Something of the old talent remained with me, even if it was only an invention, intended to amuse Dori. To anger Dori. To widen the gap between us that ran deeper than I could have imagined.

I had a happy childhood. If people asked, that's what I'd say. Because happiness isn't interesting. You don't ask about happiness with concern or curiosity. Others' happiness is a door that can be kept locked. Little by little the door transforms into a wall and the wall blends into the nothingness around it. Just like that. I'd say that and fall silent. And perhaps I truly was happy then, aside from the gloom bound up with it. Maybe happiness prevailed in the past, against all odds. Or at least something very similar to happiness. After all, I was once the older sister. I had responsibilities. I once wrote down the whole world for the two of us.

If Dori saw me in the street she wouldn't recognize me. "We changed so much," I say aloud, vouching only for myself. If Dori saw me in the street she would recognize me. Obviously.

But there's no chance we'd walk past each other on the same street.

Uriel's mother brought letters from Dori each time she came to visit. She herself met with her, more than once, I found out. I found out all sorts of things, but I learned that they weren't so important. I didn't respond to the letters she wrote me, not then anyway. Sometimes I sent blank, folded pages back to her, just so Uriel's mother wouldn't be disappointed. They were empty fields of white upon white. Dori could write on them what she wanted. Before her graduation party, when she was about to leave the boarding school for only the god of drama knew where, I asked Dima to see, to check what was going on with Dori. "Tail her?" he asked, with no hard feelings. I was overseas where he couldn't see me, but I nodded yes. A week after the graduation party, I received a toy bird in the mail. From Dima, obviously from Dima. I placed it on the highest window in my tiny new apartment, to remind me of the rhyme about the woman who lived in a shoe. And I had a reason for all this. Because I told only the facts. But it wasn't Dori, it was me who died.

# DORI

Anati and Dori stood in the cafeteria at the zoo. Anati's hair had grown lighter from the summer sun, stripes upon stripes of luster. Two days before, she'd dyed her bangs apricot orange and pulled them to the side with a Hello Kitty barrette. Anyone else would look retarded, Dori thought, but not her, as everything with Anati seemed like a joke at the onlooker's expense. And they looked, sure they did. Dori's hair was always a mousy brown, even when she tried to do something about it. That's what they were, a jaguar and a rat, that said it all, Dori thought—the same thought she'd had the day before as well, maybe even at the same time. Two orders of fries and three servings of egg salad on flat plates next to pickled vegetables, fizzing from being out for too many days. Anati wore a T-shirt with LASSO MY HEART written on it, and Dori knew that it was a joke, but the youngest kids, those who'd just hit puberty, they always stared at her. Maybe they prayed for a lasso. Anati looked at them without seeing them. She was a northern goddess with orange hair in the burning desert. A dignified goddess stained with ketchup, mayonnaise, and saturated fats.

Everything in the cafeteria tasted the same. Greasy and burnt. Dori learned this quite quickly. The two of them didn't eat there. Not that this helped. Dori had already gained a lot of weight since arriving. She no longer felt comfortable in her body, in her clothes. She sometimes dreamt about a plate of fries, but when she was awake she ate only foods that came in a sealed package. Other foods seemed fraught with danger.

"Prepare yourself, the food today will remind you of dead flamingo," Anati told Dori on her second day at the cafeteria, because seven flamingos had died in the small pool the day before, and Anati told her, "You'll see, we'll be serving all of them for lunch here, cut up into thin slices with parsley. And they'll pay for it and eat it and ask for more." Dori nodded.

"That's another twenty-seven," Anati says with a blank face to someone asking for another serving, and Dori learns from her. Not to express emotion and not to get excited. Not to fire a single nerve when a red-faced customer, whose forehead is wet with cold sweat and whose veiny hands show just how sensitive human skin can be, bitches about the exorbitant prices or threatens to complain about her to the management. "Please," Anati says, "call. Do you need their number?" The woman mutters, "What chutzpah," and even then Anati doesn't smile.

"We don't get involved, we're not a part of this whole thing," she explained when the snack bar emptied out and they were left looking at the pictures of the giraffes hanging opposite them. Anati had researched the matter and concluded that the giraffes looked exactly like the women with face-lifts who impatiently arrived at the snack bar, their diamonds sparkling on their wrinkled fingers, with their big, heavy bags and their well-dressed, snotty grandchildren.

It's not what they expected of her, those who had expected anything from her at all. Lili wrote her to get the hell away from there. To come to her. That they'd find her a scholarship to art school. But Dori no longer drew. She didn't even remember a time when she wanted to draw. She finished boarding school with excellent grades. The best in the history of the place, according to her literature teacher, who tended to exaggerate slightly but had already brought her the university registration forms. Her art teacher was angry and surly, but even he couldn't deny Dori's dedication, which obscured very average talent. She excelled even in math, which was rarely true of graduates of the art program. And through it all, nothing but peacefulness, patience, and good intentions emanated from Georgia O'Keeffe, the beautiful face of the establishment—and who would have believed that its face would belong to a well-dressed woman in the prime of her life?

Uncle Noah, who was already connected then to an innovative mobile dialysis machine, arrived for the graduation and gave her a toy bird rocking on glass crutches. The bird could do an entire flip on the crutch and Dori tried to protect it completely. But by the first evening, in the lousy pub that everyone, absolutely *every*one went to (that's what Anati said, waving her hands with her constant irony in order to sign the general, widespread trend, until Dori thought that they wouldn't end up going), the bird had disappeared. Dori thought that the noise there was at a level of at least seventy decibels and overall the place needed to be shut down, but Anati didn't hear her and ran to hug someone she knew. And Anton, whom she had already met then, briefly, or at least someone who very much resembled him in his lazy articulation, his jawline, his eyes that looked ill but were nevertheless beautiful, Anton told her, "Your little bird broke." And she only drank more. She drank what one drinks, beer from greasy glasses, shots of tequila from glasses with rims dipped in salt, and every cheapish item from what they called "The Children's Menu." Cocktails that were doubtless concocted from cough syrup. She hoped that she'd get so drunk she'd need to vomit and someone would hold her hair to the side. She said this to Anati, who told her, "You've seen too many movies," as if they hadn't seen those movies together.

Georgia O'Keeffe, who was responsible for her by the power of the Ministry of Welfare or something like that (maybe the offices that supervised her had changed, but she remained), wasn't pleased. Not about the job that Dori had taken on, and even less about Anati. "I'm a functioning citizen," Dori said to her, sitting on the bright, familiar armchair. "This is more than they ever expected of me." She spoke and felt her pinky grow red hot. But Georgia wasn't buying it, even though she smiled pleasantly. For instance, during the final meetings she again asked her to talk about Lili, as if that wasn't an ancient geological layer. Dori said, "At the zoo there's cultural diversity and camaraderie among the staff, and health insurance. I was lucky to find work there." She was echoing the administrator who'd signed the forms, adorned with pictures of animals in seven different colors. Without noticing, she even imitated his stifling tone. "And there are giraffes too," she added, even though of course she didn't take care of the giraffes herself. Because of all the zoo's corners and paths, she'd found herself in "one of the important pulse points," as the administrator had said. So she stood in the cafeteria and arranged piles of bottled mineral water as if she controlled the nerve center. This amused Anati and Dori so much that all it took was for one of them to say "pulse" and they'd be holding their sides with laughter.

When she relented on the Lili front, Georgia started talking about a scholarship that was possible, very possible, not to mention that her personal story would certainly add weight to her good grades, but Dori didn't plan on attending any university. It was easy following Anati, whose report cards regularly featured seven or eight failing grades. That was how she wound up at the zoo. They got the jobs thanks to Anati's uncle, who had seniority there and first claim to any job opening. Despite being the problematic niece, Anati had been given a chance. No one could fire her, though not everyone knew it yet and she'd already been threatened here and there. In Dori's case the situation was different. She didn't plan on giving them any pretext for firing her.

They weren't allowed to spit in the food, to scatter cigarette ashes on the pickled vegetables, to do all the things that Anati told Dori they used to in the good old days. Not even Dori believed that those were the good old days, though sometimes she was gullible as a goat. In her first month in the place, Lotti and Aharon came to the zoo together, dressed in what Dori assumed was holiday dress. They tapped her shoulder to get her attention, and she looked up at the flickering fluorescent lights. Lotti waved her fat hand opposite her face and Dori gazed at her in amazement, counting the silver and glass rings on her fingers. Lotti and Aharon signed furiously, excitedly, with an emotion that was apparently happiness, but her hands remained silent, crossed in her lap. Perhaps she truly didn't understand them. Aharon went to stand in the entrance, tugging on a thread in his too-long pants, but Lotti stood firm, refusing to leave until Anati threw them out. Days and then weeks passed and Dori waited, partly with dread, partly with expectation fluttering in her like a fish, for her parents to follow them. He scolding and she crying. Dori knew what she'd say. She knew how all of it would proceed. She just knew that she would turn the tables on them once and for all. But they never came.

At the cafeteria, Anati and Dori sold odds and ends from the souvenir shop, pencils in the shape of long-necked animals and pins marking fifty years since the zoo's founding, adorned with the zoo's symbol, a smiling blue bear. "Fucking Disneyland," they said, because it really wasn't clear why and how that bear was selected when there was an abundance of miserable flesh-and-blood animals to choose from. But that's how it was and each of them stuck a round pin with a smiling bear to her T-shirt. At the front of the zoo hung the grandest bear of all, a huge balloon, blue and smiling. He had been stretched out over the zoo gate since the celebrations that took place back when the two of them were still ordinary boarding school girls. They hated him too.

The camera above them, a slab of rectangular metal that clung clumsily to the television arm, continued filming. A watching eye. Anati said that when she was taking care of that little brat during last year's vacation, the girl's parents hid tiny cameras everywhere. In toys and in the bathroom closet and in the pot of the pomegranate tree. Sometimes she thought about torturing the kid a bit just to provoke those two, who kissed her in the air when she arrived each morning, and "every night watched what the security cameras had filmed that day and screwed. Better than porn."

Anati and Dori sometimes saluted the camera, taking care to stand in its blind spot. They almost never made faces because there was a guard who looked at their screen too, in moments of boredom. Anati said that making faces was stupid, and that was the only reason not to do it, not some minimum-wage guard. Dori listened to her and was happy for this excuse even though the two of them earned less than minimum wage themselves and acted stupid day and night.

In the afternoon the cafeteria was empty. Anati turned up the music and danced. Sounds of a hit from the eighties could be heard, one even Dori could identify despite having meaningful gaps in everything tied to popular (and unpopular) music. But this song, in which a line was repeated over and over until even Dori herself wanted to jump out of her skin, she actually recognized. "This way my classical education doesn't go to shit," Anati said, spinning on the floor, and Dori had a hard time understanding if this was a joke; when did Anati have time for a classical education? Sometimes she really was quite slow in these matters. "Everything's a joke," Anati told her, "c'mon, like the clown who cries and they ask him what happened, why's he crying, and he says he's just relaxing." Dori looked at her. "Forget it, it's one of my dad's jokes, I can't believe I told it."

Despite her natural charm, Anati was an awful dancer. "Plié," she said, her hands outstretched. "Jeté. Relevé, arabesque." Dori knew she'd fall in the end, but at that moment she danced and leapt. "You see," Anati shouted at her as if she were very far away, "they told us not to sit, but they didn't say anything about dancing." And yes, around then she fell, one foot tripping up the other and her back banging into the soft-drink cooler. But she stood up relatively fast, five days having passed since the supervisor caught her sitting; the memory of his booming threats still hadn't faded entirely.

Dori took care to arrive for each shift by the rear entrance, to breathe in the chlorine vapor from the small artificial lake where nothing swam, to climb the plastic bridge that was coated in a thin veneer of wood, and to slump into the orange uniform with the zoo's old logo, which was composed of the interwoven silhouettes of a chimpanzee and a pelican. Dori had already run out of pity for the bald lions, the hippopotamus devastated by grief; only the giraffes still seemed too good for this place, like long-legged It Girls sold into slavery, which wasn't so far from their actual situation.

The previous year, before either of them worked there, the

judge's daughter had climbed over the fence. She'd rebelled against her father, who was known for holding feasts of scorched meat in his yard. What he did beyond the yard was no less bad, it was said, and it involved other kinds of flesh. Anyway, the judge's daughter was intent on rebelling. She was in the final moment of youth, just before she would no longer be tried as a minor and deeds like this would transform her from a girl with a conscience into just another crackpot. They knew her—that is, Anati knew her, and said to Dori, "What, you don't remember that she came to visit me?" But Dori didn't remember that, and was well aware that Anati had this habit of inserting herself into the middle of every story. The judge's daughter came to befriend the wild animals, to atone for the deeds of her father. "She deserved it," Anati said to Dori, forgetting that the moment before, she had declared her a friend. "An idiot she was and an idiot she remains." The two of them were glad that the depressed animals still had a bit more energy left, even though they themselves no longer visited their cages and even found ways to avoid them. They said that the attack was quick and clean, teeth were bared, jaws, but fortunately there was a guard on duty who quickly turned on the lights and put to sleep the one that needed to be put to sleep. But the one who stayed asleep in the end was the judge's daughter. She was still hospitalized in a private room somewhere, surrounded by flowers. And the zoo was closed for a month and then opened again. They, like all zoo employees, were required to look out for oddballs. This was the explicit term specified on the purplish form that Dori initialed. In the end, she couldn't escape from this requirement either.

Toward noon they popped popcorn in the old machine. Afterward they fried up hot dogs bursting with chemicals, while before them waited, not patiently, fat, heavy families and skinny, unattractive families. Bleached-blonde moms, dads who woke up tired, kids in matching outfits, everyone waiting for fried potatoes, for anything rescued once or twice from the same oil. They were on the correct side of the counter and everyone else stood on the side of the mistakes, shoving their money forward. The two of them competed over who hated the customers more. They even hated those who were kind to them. Who insisted on saying something about how amazing, how fascinating it must be for someone their age to work at the zoo. But sometimes it seemed to Dori that she envied them. She was even envious of children with a father who pushed them to speak and whose mother was angry and annoyed, pulling out and returning cards to her wallet, certain her membership card was somewhere. She didn't know the meaning of the damp emotion that seized her in the presence of the father hitting his children, the mother with the eating disorder, the children who looked as if they were at the beginning of a growth spurt that would leave them even bigger idiots. But she always saw the sneering glance from Anati, who was familiar with Dori's foolish sentiments, and she'd give her an almost identical sneer in return.

In her first week at the cafeteria, Anati told her that there were dozens of cockroaches in coffee machines like theirs. "I'm not making that up," she said. "They opened it up here once and the cockroaches ran out." Dori looked into the depths of her coffee cup. Until then it seemed like a huge bonus to her, free coffee for the cafeteria employees. "Okay, but maybe something changed," she said, as she wavered over whether she'd keep drinking the coffee. But some things don't change.

Georgia didn't say aloud that she was wasting her time, but she expressed it in every indirect way possible. When she spoke, Dori looked for the thousandth time at her fingernails painted white. Georgia O'Keeffe had already learned that Dori called her by that name. It was an improvement on the name that she'd used for her before, which she also knew about. When they met for the first time, in a different bright room where there hung a massive picture by the American painter that depicted a devoured and devouring flower with enormous stamens, Dori thought that she looked like an old mermaid, even though apparently she wasn't that old. She had since said goodbye to her old affection for mermaids, but the eyes that looked at her with calm concern remained the same eyes. She said, "My mother cried bitterly during my birth, but one star began dancing and under this sign I was born." Georgia smiled. From her perspective, quoting from the Bard signified substantial progress.

Dori didn't know whose idea it was to send the teddy bear airborne, to give him a cross-country flight. Maybe Anton, whom Anati'd met someplace and who joined them that day at the zoo's entrance. Dori looked at Anton and Anati. Their heads were turned upward, like those of hopeful youths on a banner intended to promote something or other. The two of them wore their youth like medals, as if it would never be taken from them and melted down in the free market. So Dori thought, because she still narrated the world to herself with such images, which elevated everything.

In the end, with arms crossed and hands in pockets, the three of them stood and looked at the giant bear, tied blue and smiling to the entrance gate. The slogan "Fifty Years of Zoo" was spread across his stomach in thick letters, as if someone had scribbled on him while he slept. The blue bear popped up as part of the zoo's fiftieth anniversary, which had been celebrated two and a half years earlier, and in addition to him there were smaller decorations scattered in town, a new fountain and flowering snapdragons, blooming and immediately withering on the roadsides. This wasn't the first time that a breath of fresh air could be felt there, that a Technicolor rainbow rose over them in the sky. "It doesn't work if there isn't a sack of dollars at the end of the rainbow," Anton said to them, wise and experienced, and Dori thought how she'd never seen anyone like him. This was the second time that she heard him speak. Sometimes she saw him at one of the clubs that Anati dragged her to, which were dark and thick, loud as a garage. But it looked like Anton didn't recognize her, and maybe didn't see her at all.

She shifted her weight from leg to leg, feeling the hardness of the pavement as if she were stepping on it barefoot. Sometimes Dori and Anati ran along these paving stones at night as they returned from another deafening club, their heels striking loudly. "Don't step on the cats' heads," one called to the other, re-creating the old game that they'd played for the first time when, at age eleven, they first heard this term for the stone tiles in the ghetto. But to them each tile was an actual cat head that yawned and sighed.

The bear continued to look at the three of them with round blue eyes. Dori imagined that he had drifted to them from a different city with a different language and different hopes. They definitely made him in China, she decided, and in her mind's eye she saw the battery of Chinese workers who together made a giant blue bear that would be inflated with foreign, distant air, quite distant from their homeland. Each one laid a sleeping child on her knees and reached out with busy hands. The bear can go to hell, she thought, just when its pronounced lack of charm touched her heart. Enough things have already been sent to hell. Let the bear go too.

Anati drew a simple diagram of the points at which the bear was connected to the gate, and which they had to disconnect one after the other. "There are those who tie a district cop to a brown bear and float them in a lake and there are those who hurl a bear balloon off of scaffolding," someone said, maybe Anton, maybe Anati, but apparently it was Dori herself who spoke, and her voice sounded deep. Anton looked at them with obvious exhaustion and said that he was leaving. It was clear that he was pulling out of the whole business and Dori steadied herself so she wouldn't follow him.

At three in the morning the two of them returned to the gate. It was cold, and they had pliers in their handbags, and, just in case, they were also totally drunk. In the darkness that was diminished by the random streetlight, the giant bear seemed more feeble but somehow solemn as well. Prometheus Bound or something, thought Dori. "What about the guard?" she asked in a whisper, and Anati smiled her glowing rubber smile. "The guard is definitely some toothless poet. Only lousy poets guard construction sites these days."

"Maybe they don't even get paid," Dori said, encouraged. "They need this for their biography, for the day to come when they'll get published and show everyone."

In contrast to their predictions, the bear didn't fly skyward but slumped down, first the stomach, afterward the head, like someone falling into a pool without water. And that was how he remained, in the corner of that ugly street, under the zoo's gate. They heard the roars of the guard and while they ran Dori wondered if that was how a poet would scream or if that was one more bit of Anati's nonsense. Her legs ran to the rhythm of an old march song, skipping over all the cat heads, and the maybe-poet ran after them, but apparently he was asthmatic and short-legged and drunk himself from too many weak lines of poetry. Their breathing was young and easy and he had no chance against them as they ran cheering and waving their bent pliers like rifle butts, like an underground squad of African girls firing Israeli weapons at the neighboring village.

Dori and Anati laughed with cinematic pleasure, and their hair got tangled in their mouths as they ran, and their clothes were crumpled in the night wind and for a moment they were freed from themselves. "Blue bear anarchists," Anton had mocked before he left, as if he had momentarily swelled to the size of a big brother, but they couldn't hear him anymore and in that moment they, the two of them, had won.

*Lili wrote to Dori:*

Each morning I roll up the blinds and each morning the very same city wakes up below. Same street, same green plant store, and same pharmacy that offers its shopper perfumes and body oils and light and hard drugs. Sometimes I drag myself out of bed just to see the women walking to the pharmacy in heels. Imagine I was opening the window and you were peeking out from the window of the building next door. We would definitely wave to each other in English. Afterward we would recognize each other in the courtyard and we would play until darkness fell.

Dori, why do you make me sentimental? Suddenly all my words are coated in powdered sugar. I know that you can't stand this, but what will I do, what?

Do you remember the sugar? We were willing to lick the floor for it. No, you're right, you don't have to say a word. We aren't children. No one here is a little girl anymore. I calculate your age according to my age and vice versa and admit the facts. Maybe you still count rings in that tree that died long ago. Maybe you count stars. But just picture us meeting and suddenly you are my baby. I would put you down to sleep in a baby stroller. Covered in a blue jacket. Falling asleep next to you. Move a bit, Dori, make some room.

*Lili wrote to Dori:*

Tell me, Dori, when a letter arrives from me do you read it immediately or set it aside? Where do you put things in general? On what side? Do you have a side? What things do you have?

I'm trying but your mouth is filled with water, Dori. Perhaps you ripped my words into tiny pieces. Perhaps you fed birds with them.

But I don't think so.

I know this couldn't be.

I'm now practicing what we never did.

Pay attention, Dori,

I'm kissing you goodbye.

Lili.

*Lili wrote to Dori:*

If I remember you remember too. The house was always damp and the plaster crumbled under our beds. Hiding in the tall weeds outside the house there were small bugs that stung us on the legs. We feared snakes more than we hated the bugs. The bulletin board at the entrance to the grocery store smelled of rotting wood even in summer. Opposite that board we divided up the plunder—the announcements for me and the tacks for you. You had an insane collection of tacks that you kept under the bed. Where did those tacks wind up? I bet they disappeared in one of those operations, "Clean the house and put on a nice face for the social workers," the ones who arrived after you left. Perhaps thanks to your collection a tack factory in East Germany flourished and then all at once went bankrupt.

I'm writing to you and Uriel is next to me, working on another outrageous animated movie. It's really magnificently bad. I'll suggest that he switch all the characters for tacks. Maybe you'll see the movie one day and read the subtitle "Special thanks to Lili and Dori," because that's what I'll insist on. You understand: without you I'd never think about tacks.

*Lili wrote to Dori:*

This is my two hundredth letter to you. Obviously I'm counting. I could have baked a cake for the occasion, spread vanilla frosting on top and hurled it into the wall. But instead, imagine me not baking anything.

I still picture your life. If I really concentrate I can also see the idiotic friend that you found for yourself, the colors you have in your hair, the closed-up expression that you stuck to your face. I see you grown up but you're always Dori, the exact same Dori. If you're asking, know that I still haven't received any letters from you. Perhaps all your letters drifted away and were lost at sea. Perhaps you're sick of thinking about the past. So I'll tell you about the present. Here's the present: I'm taking Porgy and Bess on a walk; you won't believe it but those are the names of the dogs I walk, a more lucrative and established business than I ever could have imagined. And here is the future: in the very near future, that is, tomorrow or two days from now at most, I will take a break from my very prestigious studies. Which is a nice way of saying that I'm tossing my future into the garbage. But don't worry. I'll walk dogs full-time. Three times a day I'll take Gilbert and Sullivan out for a walk as well as Porgy and Bess, the stupidest pair of terriers in the world.

I love you, Porgy.

**Lili wrote to Dori:**
Know that I forgive you for being silent. Yes, obviously, you're allowed to be silent. It's your right.

We always said that there are too many words in the world.

But maybe you'd want to write me nevertheless.

Maybe, for example, you'd write: Shut up already, Lili.

**Dori wrote to Lili:**
Shut up already, Lili.

## PART THREE

# THE SAFE PLACE

*The safest place to be
is under the branches.*
—SHIRLEY KAUFMAN

Years passed and Dori was still little. Time doesn't grow everything, not every beanstalk sprouts and climbs to the clouds. Anyone looking at her from a certain distance might think that she was a girl. Her nails were still clipped along a crooked line. Her bangs were held with thin barrettes; her pockets were turned inside out. And nevertheless, Dori. She looked from the side at that which she wanted to regard straight on. The way one looks at the sun to keep tears from flooding one's eyes. She heard what there was to hear, for instance, the rustle his coat made when it rubbed up against the glass case. In the meantime this was all that she did, allowed the senses to go in her place. As in a children's book, Dori Ackerman looked and listened.

Anton, in a stylish raincoat, stood in front of the bulletin board that was closed off behind safety glass and a reinforced lock, as if there was a need to protect the schedule from students' greedy hands and not actually from the lecturers, who used to fritter away its hours, leaving buzzing fluorescent lights on in empty classrooms. It seemed that this was a communal hobby of all the lecturers, the progressive and the conservative, those who stagnated and those yet to bloom: everyone preferred to travel to conferences or be sick with diseases that require bed rest. Often they disappeared without advance notice, like secondary performers in a mystery play. In fact, it was only because of this that she intended to peek over Anton's head and verify which of the morning classes had flown away through the faculty's filthy windows. But Anton was half leaning on the holy board and she couldn't read over his shoulders. In fact, he looked like someone who could lean on air particles and they'd hold him up. The material world, even in a school that extolled the human spirit, was beneath his dignity.

Anton looked at the passersby in the Humanities corridor, his sleepy gaze making their haste even more foolish, their acceleration lacking any value, interest, or purpose. He gazed at them but looked like someone who was meant to be gazed at himself, and Dori actually looked and saw the contempt that enshrouded him like a high-collared coat (though the raincoat he wore had wide lapels and a wrap-around collar). And in fact, when he is portrayed in her memory he will appear mainly like this, wearing an old jacket, grayish-blue in color, which looks like it was once very expensive but is now threadbare. In her eyes he seems like a spoiled housecat that pretends to be an alley cat or perhaps vice versa, like the barefooted man who pretends he owns a shoe factory. She wasn't used to either manner and so had many theories about him, error-riddled all.

She will remember with a certain bitter amusement that no matter how much she investigated in those days, she couldn't tell if he was very poor or very rich. Because amusement is the reward for she who finally has the facts in hand and can knead a story from them. She remembers how they met, how he left them with a light step, even before it turned out that the blue bear's final flight would have fewer actual consequences than they had hoped, other than those very much expected, because in the end they did fire Dori from the cafeteria. Brief coverage in the local news was all they got. In the end, the fall of the zoo's symbol didn't move anyone and, try as they might, they were unable to understand the failure. It seemed that the world they knew spoke only in symbols, but they'd chosen to topple the wrong symbol. Stupid bear, Dori thought once again. Fewer and fewer words passed between her and Anati, and perhaps in the gap that was created a place was made. Because, in fact, a short time later they met Dima, who emerged as the only spectator of their failed bear performance, and in their presence he claimed that it was a beautiful act, a beautiful act indeed. And maybe she wouldn't have recalled any of this at all if not for Anton, because what was the point in remembering gloryless failures like the bear? Dori still looked at Anton and waited for him to recognize her, to say "Hey, it's you, the pretty one from the zoo," even though no one ever said a sentence like that to her and Anton couldn't have said it, because she hadn't worked there long enough and also because at best he would have said "the little one," because Anati, not she, was the pretty one, as everybody knew. He didn't say a word about the night with the bear. And she waited until she couldn't wait anymore and then decided to continue looking, because she knew how to look.

No, he wasn't gorgeous, she concluded. Actually, in those moments he looked to her like the skinniest person she could imagine. His bad qualities jumped out at her, the vanity, the childishness, the coddling that was evident in his heightened, swollen upper lip. Someone who loves himself wholeheartedly, she thought. She meant to hate him, but nevertheless noticed that the skin was white and the eyes brown and adorned with dark lashes, that the hair pointed from the temples toward the crown of his head in a strange haircut that she actually found striking. Fine, she concluded to herself derisively, he's good-looking, in his way. Dori saw his exposed gums because he had an insane, charming smile, and when the gums were exposed the white tips of his fangs suddenly protruded and the smile cut across his face like a declaration of joy that everyone could share, like a joke intended for all, and God, God almighty, and all his armies and all the kingdoms that rose and fell beneath him, that was enough.

If they'd asked her, she'd put it like this: her heart fell from its spot, jiggled in the rib cage, moved. Her heart throbbed and throbbed, filled up and emptied out, didn't know what to do with itself. All of her delighted in the way his smiling lips twisted back into a kind of pout ("Childish," Lili would have said. "Feminine," she would have added, after thinking, and Anati for her part would have announced that there was no point in her wasting time on him, whereas Dori would have shrugged her shoulders, neither looking nor listening). She saw the outlines of his hands shoved behind his head as he leaned on the holy bulletin board. The lapels of his jacket opened like the holy ark, she thought with the same wild hyperbole that characterized her exaggerating heart, and she saw that he was wearing a suit under the jacket. He walks in beauty, like the night, she thought, even though he just stood there without moving, even though it was early in the morning, even though she remembered just the opening line of the poorly translated poem.

Anton had returned from a student exchange program in a cold land, a land where many of the students tended to go, but only he came back wearing a suit and a big jacket, dressed in a northern European manner that he made look even better, ignoring the local weather and the fact that the semester was about to end. He'd returned early, she realized later, and she wasn't alone in noticing that he had suddenly appeared and was everywhere. And Dori, you must understand, Dori nearly lost her mind.

Unusually, she was late for the afternoon class in the big lecture hall. The class dealt with problems in the philosophy of language, and that day they were discussing that whereof they could not speak and thereof must remain silent. Since she was late, she sat near the top of the hall. It seemed that the lecturer, who had already started the flow of words that would be interrupted at intervals by regularly scheduled coughs, raised her eyebrows a bit due to the tardiness and the new place where Dori sat down. She thought to apologize, to explain that this was the first place she found and therefore she was sitting by the stairs and not as always in the far-right chair in the third row, because that seat was already taken. But the lecturer had already moved on, and it wasn't as if anyone really expected Dori to open her mouth.

Sitting there felt like getting off at the wrong floor in your own apartment building, and in her head she quoted a French writer who'd said something similar, perhaps related, and she repeated the French phrase for the benefit of that voice in her head, which for its part nodded imperceptibly and said "good" even though it knew that Dori had never read that book to the end, definitely not in French. The seat back was scratched up and she passed her fingers over the scratches' paths as if it were possible to read a secret code there intended just for her.

As the lecturer spoke she heard that voice, which had no need for a body of its own. It seemed to her that the voice hovered over her swimmers' shoulders, on behalf of which she used to lie for years and say that she was a swimmer or a dancer, even though she did neither, and then it dove down inside and found the self that was a half self at most, and said in a tone rather higher than expected, "Look, Dori, there's a cause, and there's the cause of all causes, and you will yet be able to tie all those questions flying in the air before you into a bow. And all that you don't understand will find its place." Dori relaxed in her new seat, ignoring the obvious—that this was all nonsense.

When she sat down, she knew without looking that Anton was sitting a row behind her. When she stretched a bit she could detect from the corner of her eye his thin fingers, fingers of a left hand, sprouting from a too-long suit sleeve. Thus she also saw the thread that remained in the place where a cuff button had fallen off. He was the only one among the students who regularly wore a suit but still didn't look ridiculous. She sat up taller than ever and her back straightened out in the manner of those who are the object of a gaze, those upon whom words land from every direction, and Dori looked at the dry-erase board on which sentences written in blue steadily accumulated, which said the rain falls or it doesn't fall, and sentences more complex than these, with foreign letters standing in the place of actual words. Her posture in these moments was almost fair.

The shaved-headed lecturer cleared her throat for a long time and Dori felt Anton's womanish mouth come close to her neck and pronounce, "There's no world that isn't in language. Only language creates everything." His lips blew the air onto her skin, and a moment later, the shaved-headed lecturer with the dignified face said those very same words.

Dori froze. Right into her ear, Anton had mocked one of the department's most coveted courses, one with few vacant spaces and not only because the lecturer was never replaced by a note announcing a temporary leave of absence. The students, departing the class for the library, their dorms, their temporary jobs, left her lessons excited, and treated the question of language and being as if it were crucial, and when they weren't laboring over their books, or at least over the parts highlighted by whoever studied them before, they asked why the present eludes words, why language doesn't really manage to capture *this*, and a few of them emphasized the "this," the specific, others the concept itself, whereas others stubbornly interrogated, of all things, the "really." Dori, who didn't contribute one word, felt that the conversation inside her was like a noisy bird looking at its reflection in the mirror, looking and chattering, clattering nonstop, but that one day the bird would say something sensible.

The words that Anton voiced into her neck will yet be accompanied by others. Anton will still say to her that these are just chewed up, recycled ideas, that in northern Europe all this is already a thing of the past and that there's a point in learning from the philosophers and not from teachers of philosophy, because this present of theirs is over and done with, that she should take a look at her lecturers, who insist on flying away from here at every opportunity, and judge for herself. But she nevertheless knew that the present was stretching out around her like a membrane that would sprout limbs.

At the end of the class she hurried to meet Dima. As she went down the narrow stairs she spotted him, not yet aware of her, standing in the entrance to the cafeteria, moving his weight from leg to leg and then peeking at an imaginary watch on his wrist. Students thin and quick as rats squeezed inside through the glass doors blurred from too many passing fingerprints, absentmindedly rubbing up against him, as if his body were nothing but an element of the architecture. The same army jacket with missing buttons decomposed on his clumsy body, the scarf she bound him with one needle was wrapped around a soft, thick neck with an undapper carelessness. He looked like someone even a hopeless guerrilla army wouldn't enlist, but for her, okay, for Dori he was part of the core, exactly like Anati and perhaps even more so. Anati, as they'd always known would happen, had remained at the zoo after the bear incident and was transferred to the department of waterfowl. Despite the change in scenery, no discernible change had occurred in Anati's terms of employment; now, with unconcealed resentment, she sold small bags of birdfeed to the visitors. When Dori visited, Anati bent forward on high heels over bird droppings, all the while sending Dori a glowing smile and perfectly signing in the language the sentence that she'd asked Dori to teach her long ago: "I-want-to-die-they're-all-whores." Her work hours didn't overlap with Dori's almost at all and they barely saw each other. Anati spent her free time with the little brat she babysat who had grown by now and shared Anati's love for short skirts and the theater. Between them they rehearsed scenes from plays and fainted dramatically and Dori found ways not to hear them, as if the two of them were from a silent movie, one smashing glass and the other repairing it, and Dori was looking at them through a window without knowing if it was whole or broken. They grew apart from each other even though they lived in adjacent rooms, but they still shared Dima.

Dima and Dori emptied cups of espresso loaded with sugar in the college cafeteria. In the absence of most of the students, who had already risen with much noise for the next class, tattered ads for student resorts were revealed in all their glory, and Dori wondered for the hundredth time what she would do in a resort town in Turkey and wasn't able to come up with a thing. Dima touched her shoulder, she detached herself from a poster on which the hotel's silhouette was painted in pastel shades, and the two of them hurried to get up. Dori felt the weight of the cards in the bag that swung from one shoulder.

The cards were rectangular and cut out with scissors. Dori had composed the short sentences without much care, but Dima and Anati agreed that they were her best work. Other than the lines printed in a tiny font, which more than once forced a card's recipient to put on glasses, the cards also included sentences spelled out in sign language, sketched out in quick and sloppy hand illustrations. The sloppiness made the words look heartfelt; at least, that was how she explained it to Dima, laughing, and he caressed her hair like a trained bear who caresses a doll or a ball, as if the caress itself was a kind of meaningless accessory, something they stuck in his paw.

As always, they scheduled three hours of café visits in the semi-established area of the city. They never bothered with the really rich, who, as everyone knows, believe in the free market and equal opportunity and thus never give a thing. People had gotten accustomed to their visits as an amusing disturbance in the regular cafés, and there they were allowed to distribute the cards and to gather in their haul with a slight bow. In contrast to some of their competitors ("colleagues," Dori insisted, even though Anati and Dima stuck to calling the other card carriers "competitors" and that was it, and some of them were even very shrewd and organized in ways that are better left unmentioned), they were never kicked out. Perhaps because Dori identified every complaint in time to order their quick retreat. They were a winning team, if it was at all possible to declare victory in this game, which had no end. They were the brother and the sister, so they were called, and that stuck to them and they didn't deny it. After all their hair was somewhat similar, and maybe something in their walk was the same, and maybe all deaf people resemble each other in your eyes, such that you have no reason to be too precise. In fact, of all things, the conspicuous difference between them (she so small and he so big and heavy) proved whatever needed proving, because a connection like theirs could only have been forged through the terms of hand-bending known only among families. Dori wasn't dying to change the impression and Dima expressed no interest in what they thought or didn't think about him. On the contrary—let them be the deaf Hansel and Gretel.

In the first café, which was adorned with a decorative cornice in an imitation of some Roman ruin, and where most of the tables were out in the street, Dima hit the fingers of his right hand on his left arm, signing the rank of an undercover cop, because an inspector in civilian clothes stood next to the bar and was speaking with the owners. Dori signed that she understood. They sat down and drank coffee like two customers. Dima gave her a tiny smile, careful not to let his fingers accidentally touch her; he knew how much Dori recoiled from touch, and Dori looked at the damaged teeth she knew by heart and allowed the doubts that sprang up in her to disappear.

Those cards, written this way or that, didn't allow her to forget what the world saw in her. When she collected a card from a competitor (or colleague), setting down two coins in exchange, she would reexamine it on both sides, as if verifying that the stars were spinning on their paths and that, at least in regard to the cards, nothing had changed. Actually, when she spread out the different cards next to one another, the eye paused on a certain variety in the register and on a slight difference in the features of the three illustrated monkeys on hers (a deaf monkey, a blind monkey, and their friend, whose hands covered his mouth; he was the mute). One of the other cards, which Dori held on to and later stuck to her bulletin board next to her schedule and a lone movie ticket, featured red hearts sprouting ears that were divided in half. Because regardless of the drawings, all of the cards signed in the language "thank you" and "hello" or "please please." All of them said, in this way or that, "We are the deaf."

Here they are, pitiable, miserable, in possession of inferior social skills and perhaps even suspect personal hygiene, who knows, who would dare come close to check? Dima's clothes gave off a slight scent of wood chips and Dori herself smelled like an apple, or at least that's what she preferred to assume, considering the only perfume she had in her possession. Either way, Dori and Dima knew what whispers came from the mouths that opened and closed like fish behind aquarium glass, just as they knew that it was only with resentment that the money was given to them, those coins that landed on the table without making any sound. They knew that everyone sitting in the café redeemed their lives with a small payment. Dori and Dima were beggars at the entrance to a church, insurance salesmen of eternity, a guarantee of the spenders' good fortune or at least their fine condition.

The café patrons, all of them as one, considered themselves certain in their world. Without a doubt, compared with the deaf brother and sister who placed the cards on their table and expected recompense, fate had been kind to them. "No, not fate," nine of ten dentists would definitely say, as they considered making a toothpick out of the card before them and passing it between the crevices in their jaws. And not just them; the businessmen too, the free professionals, and even the good friends relaxing opposite a slice of pound cake that they'd be sure to share and never quite finish—all of them would agree that it wasn't at all a matter of fate but rather, how to say it, of "hard work, responsibility, a matter of moral strength." Without a doubt, the deaf siblings were lacking these qualities from the jump. No doubt they were lacking. "And why, in fact," one among them would always rise and declare as if this insight had struck him like lightning, "why don't those two kindly help themselves and go do some normal work? They're young people, after all."

The word *parasites* filtered through the teeth hidden behind the napkins stained with bright lipstick. And truly look at them, everyone agreed—look and see the utter excess, the millstone around the neck of productive society. Each one of the patrons had at least one hearing-impaired cousin who overcame difficulty with hard work and heroic efforts and became a building engineer, a private investigator, a dentist. During the story about the integrated cousin Dori would quickly gather up the cards. She wouldn't waste a moment on a closed door. But there was always one who threw a coin to them at the last moment, definitive proof of his superiority. And this coin too they would gather up.

When the inspector was about to leave the café, gesturing with his hands his desire to pay and receiving a clear sign of negation from the shift manager (at the owner's command), they decided to cross the street, as if they had better avoid the puddle of turbid light the inspector left behind. They shuffled into the café owned by a man proud of his organic, fair-trade coffee, and who pinned to the walls pictures of smiling farmers in their fields. Beneath the farmers sat poets who linked one long line to another, glued together by the word I. Sometimes they raised their heads and offered Dori a child's smile, more defiant than apologetic, a smile to say that they and only they, the wordsmiths, the wretched of spirit, could be the poorest of all.

It was a weak day, the two of them concluded with a show of indifference, comparing the piles of cards with the pile of coins, and Dori again thought that perhaps Georgia was right and the time had come to retire. It was Dori who had urged Dima to join her in this business, which from the beginning looked dubious and miserable to him. But actually because of this, as a patron of lost causes, he suddenly agreed, presenting himself beside her in his military tunic, heavyset and clumsy. And once he made up his mind, he distributed the cards aggressively, placing them on the table and looking deep into the eyes of the person seated there, and only Dori knew that the meaning of that clear, forceful look was pure contempt. Perhaps the decadence and not only the wretchedness enchanted him, so at least Dori concluded, and he agreed to serve all that he hated for the sake of a goal greater than moneymaking. Because what were they doing but driving another nail into the coffin of the society that he loathed? She knew what Lili would say, if she only knew that Dori was humiliating herself like this with strangers. And for money, no less. She could anticipate her horror. Because this was worse than anything that she and Lili ever did and anything that Lili was liable to do individually. But this time, Lili, who continued speaking in her head with a strange, nasal English accent, didn't get it. Because it wasn't only Dima who tossed the coins and bills into some drawer and forgot about them. Dori didn't do it for the money either, and she didn't resist the humiliation bound up in it. In fact, the humiliation was part of the appeal. To wear the pleated skirt each time, to put on an impenetrable expression, to be that little one who presents her limitations to the masses, who exposes the scale that is never held straight between the deaf and the hearing. So not everyone got it, so what? And anyway, even though only a few knew it, Dori made her living somewhere else.

### WHEN SHE WAS SEVENTEEN

When she was seventeen, Georgia O'Keeffe presented to her the file upon which was written "Dora (Dori) Ackerman," as if to say, "We have nothing to hide." Her calm cat eyes looked directly at Dori, who held the file in her hands. For a moment, as she grasped the rubber band that held together the two cardboard folders, Dori seemed to consent. But the moment passed and she returned the file without reading it. From Dori's side, things looked like this: she felt Georgia's admiration for her actions like something alive, something sensual, with soft, glistening fur. When her hands stretched out and placed the file on the small table between them, she already understood that in this tiny act, in her avoidance of reading about herself, she had earned a limitless line of maturity credit.

And yet, if from Georgia's perspective she had excelled in this test, for Dori it was no challenge at all. She already understood then that at best she'd read a story about someone else, a girl from a troubled home, a girl who grew up in conditions that the establishment abhorred, until it decided to remove her from this home, from these conditions. She knew that what she'd read would miss everything. "And if I'm going to"—she'd say to Anton, lifting her chin—"if I'm going to read about abusive childhoods, I prefer literature and not the formulations of welfare officials."

In the years after, Dori wondered what would have happened had she leafed through the personal file, learned a bit more about her life's circumstances. But from the beginning Georgia had been kind to her for the wrong reasons, even though it wasn't always easy to be kind to her. Dori was a tough case, one that didn't quickly produce results. Were she a plant that was transferred from silty soil to a rich flowerpot (let's suppose), a plant that was finally cared for by a sure hand, she would have already budded and strangely bloomed. But that wasn't how it went. Dori herself knew this and in general had reservations about gardening imagery, but that moment, when she was seventeen and Georgia O'Keeffe's age was some multiple of that number, that moment, when Georgia O'Keeffe's eyes rested on her with obvious admiration and Dori was like a moon upon which the light of a great sun was finally cast: that moment the two of them would remember, as if they'd believed for a moment that the moon had shed a light of its own.

The very fact of sitting opposite G.O. at fixed times, when almost nothing changed in the room—not even Georgia's features, other than the deepening wrinkles on the sides of her mouth—was the presence of the absolute in Dori's life. And not just because of the décor or the time of day. In fact, the things that Georgia refused to understand, and what Dori didn't consider telling her, these actually preserved this relationship and sustained it anew each time she knocked on the door and went inside. The frequency of the meetings lessened over the years, but by that point she was already used to sitting in the pleasant room, like she had gotten used to brushing her teeth or reading with a foot resting on the wall and her head on the pillow. It never occurred to her to miss a meeting.

Dori was unable to find a real difference between the room she visited when she was eleven and the room she visited five or ten years later. An unthreatening brightness always prevailed there, like an overexposed photograph in which the objects nevertheless don't disappear but exist in a state of pure softness (these were Dori's words, this is exactly how she thought about it). There were large pictures of feminine flowers, devouring and devoured, and Georgia O'Keeffe sat cross-legged like Buddha under the Bodhi Tree. On the writing desk, always at the same angle, stood a tiny reproduction of a flattened rabbit and a copper pot. Next to it sat a picture of a young woman with a square jaw, smoking and laughing. The picture of the rabbit, which remained a bit blurry even when the light filtered in through the blinds, created the darkest point in the bright room, like filth congealing on snow, and if Dori had to choose, it was her favorite. Even the shelves loaded with books didn't weigh down the place and instead supported the sense that it was always noon, that outside there sprawled green gardens on which the two of them might rest their eyes for a moment before the air grew too hot.

Conventional wisdom held that speaking occurred there. The sounds were cut up and divided; words were directed in a hesitant arc at the world of the hearing. In that room Dori confirmed what was already known. Even when you suspect that a continent exists, you release a sigh of relief when it truly comes into view and you can say—America. Only in that room did Georgia confirm beyond a shadow of a doubt (as she shared with all others concerned) that the girl could indeed hear and communicate with words. Miraculously, her speech was not impaired. Someone proclaimed the continent, running and calling out with a choked throat that this was indeed America, and somewhere was a deck full of excited people, holding hands, blessing the scope of the achievement and the expectations confirmed and even exceeded. But all this happened, if it happened at all, far, far away from that room.

From the perspective of Georgia O'Keeffe (or what she was called outside that room, a rather simple name, which there's no point in disclosing other than to gratify mere voyeurism), the words that emerged in their entirety from Dori's mouth were the Archimedean point from which it was possible to raise Dori like a flag waving on a flagpole. Had Dori been aware of this image, which Georgia repeated in a few of her excellent articles, she would have explained that it wasn't a flag flying on high but an actual girl who was raised on a pole, and only the shortsighted could get something like that wrong, seeing a flag instead of a girl. But even if she didn't know the exact words Georgia used to describe the size of the achievement, Dori certainly assumed that she credited the breakthrough to the special bond that formed between them. And yes, even Dori had to admit that despite all the lies, at the edge of things there grew a bluish tinge, thin as an eggshell, of truth. Georgia was the one who suggested the announcer's test. The zoo cafeteria was no longer an option, "lucky for everyone," Georgia said. She mentioned it almost in passing, not disclosing the fact that in her hand was the winning card under which the entire pile would fall.

The two of them thought about the juvenile judge and her practical proposals following the zoo incident. This judge, who, free of gavel and robe, was just a regular woman, but a woman who clearly believed in her own persuasive force, saw Dori as someone in need of clearer guidance and encouragement than Georgia's airy suggestions. And so the judge sweetly proposed to her that she follow a more certain professional path and, more precisely, become a sign language interpreter. As much as she tried to remember this woman, only a short time later, she couldn't. She remembered only her sweet perfume, which reminded her of something unseemly, at once living and dead. Georgia told Dori that she must meet with her one more time and that would be it, there was no need for more than that. Nevertheless Dori identified on her face, on her hand, suddenly busied with her amber necklace until she caught Dori looking, something that resembled fear.

"Look," Dori opened up and said to that gavel-free woman (and she didn't say "look" and not "listen" from meticulousness, but simply out of habit). "Look, I don't think so."

"It's very common in complicated families like yours," the judge pronounced slowly, and waved her hand to emphasize her surprise. The bracelets swayed on her arm and Dori looked at the way they captured the light and just nodded and said "No" as if with her the signs and the words spoke opposite languages.

But this time it wasn't merely another suggestion. She, Georgia, had a plan, she knew someone who knew someone, it was paid work, a job with convenient hours that fit Dori like a glass slipper or a leather shoe. She knew Dori couldn't refuse. So she placed a note in Dori's hand with arrival instructions and telephone numbers. Dori looked at the telephone numbers with amazement. "What I am supposed to do with this?" she asked in the language, but Georgia understood and answered her quietly, "You can call. You'll hear them and they you. Talk." Dori fixed her with that old opaque gaze that she recognized, that of a nine-year-old girl whose legs swung with an odd, stubborn rhythm, while the rest of her body was frozen and rigid. Georgia doubted it was possible; could everything really be forgotten in an instant? Was it in Dori's power to huddle up once more inside the cochlea and never emerge again? She was unable to capture her gaze and it seemed that a milky film flooded over her eyes. All the hatches were battened and the land that was discovered through so much effort again sank below the water. At that moment, for the sake of despair, even elegance abandoned Georgia. How old she looked when she repeated her name aloud, "Dori, Dori, Dori." And she called out again: "Dori." And again. "Dori, Dori, Dori." Even those in the adjacent rooms could hear her. A spoon striking a plate and doling out a single name: Doridoridori.

And Dori heard and said, "Yes."

## WHEN SHE CLOSED THE STUDIO DOOR BEHIND HER

When she closed the studio door behind her she already knew that she had been accepted. She went down the stairs to the noisy street, sealing off her ears from the tumult and waiting for Georgia's warmhearted congratulations and, following those, the position itself, which would come to her tied with a bow. And so it happened, more or less, indeed with a bit less formality than she anticipated. Dori looked at the scratched phone monitor that presented her with her new working hours and thought, yes.

All this happened as it happened not because Dori's voice was pleasant, although it is possible that it was. The main matter was that Dori's voice lacked an identifiable tone. This is one of the paradoxes characterizing the speech of extremely late learners. And this is also the paradox located in the silent underside of the announcements that people prefer to hear, announcements appropriate for the street, the weather, the flight schedule. For things of this sort. The best voice is one that conveys threatening words in an impartial tone, as if they are the truth itself. And even if the truth isn't really what the listener wants, even if what they hear is a lie, the tone of truth is the tone in which they prefer things be brought to their attention. This, at least, was Dori's conclusion.

"How wonderful," he said to her during their meeting in the recording studio, after she sent a shortened version of her résumé. "How wonderful," said the doll-like man, who identified himself as one of the studio's owners. He looked for approval from the woman whom Dori judged to be his older sister, and Dori too looked at the legs spread wide, the crossed hands, the square jaw, and the thick glasses with the metal frames. Yes, as if it had already happened before, they marveled at Dori as at a puppy standing on a ball. But since the owners of the studio themselves looked like other participants in this circus—not sword swallowers or lion tamers but two human cannonballs—Dori didn't mind. If the sister resembled a tough, downtrodden farmer, the brother was seemingly taken from a very old staged photograph, upon which someone had marked up the eyebrows and lips for emphasis. They were an inconceivable combination. She listened to the man politely, looking at his soft hands, which moved unsynchronized with his speaking mouth. The more she considered it, and she definitely considered it at that moment, she was convinced that they were brother and sister. There was an intimacy between them that couldn't be explained any other way. A realistic portrait of a farmer from the Great Depression holding a wax doll.

As if to compensate for his sister's attitude, the brother again clapped his pretty hands. He finished telling about the history of "this special place of ours" and admired Dori's résumé one more time, shook his head as if he couldn't believe it, and said, "What can we do, the time has arrived to talk business," and now he and his wife would allow her to get ready for a moment and begin the test. Dori looked at him inquisitively because she didn't know how to get ready or for what, and he quickly reassured her that he hadn't a shadow of a doubt that she was suitable, "but business is business," especially with them, in show business. Because in this studio they sometimes recorded broadcasts and ads that were carried on the airwaves. And perhaps only when they left the room, one after the other, while he waved to her—like a parent explaining to his child that he won't go far and that he'll still exist even after he leaves the room—and then sat down in the leather chairs on the other side of the glass in a room that almost resembled the room in which they sat until now, only then did she understand she was mistaken. Husband and wife, who would believe it. Dori held the book that was given to her and started to read from the spot marked.

"I'll come to one place and pray; before I have time to get used to it and love it, I'll go on. And I'll keep going until my legs give out, and I lie down and die somewhere, and come finally to that eternal, quiet haven, where there is no sorrow or sighing! . . ."

"That's it, someone who can read from *War and Peace* can read anything," the sister who'd turned out to be the wife said into the microphone. When the severe impression of her appearance faded, the woman resembled a shortsighted, well-trained mole, and instantaneously Dori's array of images sailed like a ship leaning on its side—from a farmer, armed with an agricultural implement and chasing down a mole, to the pet of the farmer's little daughter that in a moment would lie down on the studio's polished floor and ask for its fur to be stroked.

"We don't accept everyone," she warned in her warm voice, trying to preserve something of the first, severe impression, but she immediately added, "Ada, my name is Ada." And from the tone of her voice Dori understood that they would actually accept her.

The voice of her husband, the male doll, was forgotten immediately after he finished speaking, but Ada spoke with a rich, thick voice, and Dori imagined this was the explanation. That despite everything the husband had told her about "taking advantage of opportunities and understanding market forces and surviving in this tough business of ours," from the outset, they had Ada's voice. They could draw a circle in the dirt and set up the studio and the rest around it. Because the moment that Ada stopped speaking, she silently waited to hear her again.

When Dori shook their hands goodbye, in her mind's eye, she saw Georgia O'Keeffe closing up the file dedicated to Dori Ackerman with satisfaction. She always had a weakness for stories. "Dori Ackerman has a good ending," or perhaps, "Girl D finds her voice." Either way, she could now place her in the drawer of solved cases, in the cabinet painted white that was locked with a key.

And during one of those meetings, coated in satisfaction like the frosting on a cake, Georgia confirmed for her that it was thanks only to Ada's exceptional voice (which the cigarettes had somewhat scorched over the years) that her husband was able to establish the recording studio. Ada, so she said, was once a rather well-known professional who read the news, provided the voice-over for state ceremonies, and, as a hobby, read from the masterpieces of world literature at the library for the blind. Dori laughed, because once again the disabled had gathered around her like beggars at the edge of town. And when Dori laughed, Georgia smiled. Only when she left did Dori realize that Ada was the figure who appeared in the photograph in Georgia's office. That she was the woman laughing with a cigarette in one hand.

## SHE MET ANTON AGAIN

She met Anton again in Continental Philosophy. In the college's stuffy air she could forget that only an hour earlier she had been sitting opposite Georgia O'Keeffe, staring as if from habit at the tortoiseshell brooch, the painted nails, the hair gathered around her skull, knowing from experience that even if she really tried such things they wouldn't suit her and the refined headband would slide off her like water. During classes she also easily forgot the emergency instructions that she had recorded over the course of three days. The college's charmless building easily erased all that came before and after it, and its visual dullness implied that there, somehow, the main event was happening, even without the bene-fit of climbing ivy or a peaceful stream.

On that day the college looked especially colorless, and even the students themselves looked as if their hues had been drained away and they had been forced to trot out these infinitely pale versions of themselves in public. Dori found her place on the left side of the lecture hall, no less pale than the rest of her neigh-bors in the row. Through the large windows it was possible to see all that the world had to give her at that moment. Which wasn't much.

She woke up when the discussion was already at its height and on the whiteboard was written: *The present King of France is bald.* Against her will she imagined him, the exiled king, bald and red-eyed, even though she had already been told that there was no point in imagining something without a referent. Not to mention a king with no kingdom or name or likeness and whose impossible baldness shines with the colors of sunset. Yes, as if summoned, the royal family pranced about between college classes, eagerly anticipating every example: The king died and then the queen died. It was necessary to add a correction: The king died and then the queen died because of grief. Because what distinguishes an average story from a tightly drawn one is the cause. So it was already determined and explained and passed on. One might correct this and say, what distinguishes them is the grief. And this Dori actually understood. Instead of listening to the material being taught, she pondered whether or not all the kings who hovered over the young bodies bent over their books lived together in the same heavenly castle and descended each day in order to act out roles in paradoxes and examples for tired students. Are the kings too amazed anew each day that the morning star is the evening star, without simply saying: Venus, the star is Venus? In any case, with a certain mulish stubbornness, she went from class to class, grabbing the ideas by their fringes, always grasping on to an image instead of the thing itself. And in each Anton watched her like a shadow.

Now he approached, with his measured steps, in the old leather shoes that looked heavy and ancient, and she quickly straightened up and in the same motion stiffened her back and smoothed out the flowers that spread across her dress like eczema, remembering her constant tendency to slouch. This too Anton saw, saw and smiled. And instead of being insulted, Dori smiled, even if the joke was at her expense, even if he signaled to her that he saw her at her weakest. As if they had known each other forever and always, she thought, and they stood and smiled smiles that were very different from each other, but Dori mistakenly saw them as a single smile. His eyes were red, he was very skinny, his wrists were white, thinner than hers. She thought that he was wonderful, beaten and winning all at once, defeated in an enchanting, theatrical manner, like a prince who knowingly transforms into a beggar, or better, shatters his own kneecap with his father's golf club, and she didn't say a thing because she suspected that this was one of those paradoxes that evaporates when spoken aloud, and anyway it was unlikely that Anton golfed. "The coffee here is terrible," he finally said, as if continuing a conversation they'd been having for some time. "We'll go to the medical school. They have enough donors to keep from burning the coffee." And so for a moment they were the current king and queen of France, bald or adorned with hair.

When they sat at one of the tables Anton smoked and drank while Dori ate noodles with red sauce. "You really look like that girl on the box of noodles," he said to her after another long silence. He was handsome at that moment and Dori, who nervously gathered up and tossed her hair, couldn't believe that Anton was a citizen of a country like this, one with noodles in it.

She was hot. Maybe because of the noodles. Her skin turned pink and red and she didn't care. Her fingers grew weightless and the tableware itself became quite heavy. If she had put down the fork it may well have split open the table and fallen forever. When she moved the hair from her face with her hand, it was as if his hands were the ones moving the hair, confidently touching her forehead, temples, and finally gathering the hair from behind in a ponytail whose many strands broke loose from itself.

He wanted her to speak, this she understood; he acted as if she had something to say and her words had importance. But Dori doubted that he wanted to hear excerpts from *War and Peace*, because other than the words of Prince Andrei running around in her head, at that moment Dori knew only how to remain silent. Together they missed a class, two classes, an entire day. Evening had already fallen and they had smoked everything that remained in his pack and afterward he asked for and demanded a cigarette from anyone who was in the cafeteria. Anton looked only at Dori and said, "Philosophy is crippled." And because he didn't know if he had gotten all of her attention he said, "Philosophy is blind. Philosophy is deaf." He declared that the only future was in politics and money, and that the only path to true creativity lay there, and Dori, since she knew of nothing to say or why this was being said to her of all people, just nodded.

Her throat was burning and they drank coffee from mugs

containing the dregs of other people's coffee. An hour or hours later he leaned back. The cafeteria had already almost emptied out and the foreign worker cleaned the tables with a rag that was neither dry nor wet. Her eyes latched on to his movements as if at each table he cleaned he was doling out the end of the evening or perhaps his own end. Anton coughed badly and immediately afterward spread a broken smile across his lips. He said, "Actually, we know each other." Dori raised her eyebrows inquisitively and tried to understand what he meant by "know," and decided finally to mention that failed matter at the zoo and that in fact he was right.

Anton continued, "You're that little one who passes out cards in cafés. You're famous among us, only the whole time we thought you were deaf as a rock. Seems to me you already owe me more than a little money for all that impersonating." The smile again divided his face in two. She knew that she had never placed a card before him, that a coin or a bill had never passed between them, that she hadn't spread out her hand before him. But he looked at her like someone who catches a small fish and lets it go because there's no reason to bother keeping it on the hook.

Dori continued sitting across from him. Because that's how it is in life. Girl D doesn't always find her voice. Sometimes the cat steals her tongue. She sat in the chair and felt how much the narrow backrest hurt, how much it hurt her for hours or days. She was small and ugly, she understood, miserable and beyond repair. Yes, and she also understood that there was nothing to fix, not her and not what was happening in that moment. The current king of France is a liar and there's no queen. And if philosophy is blind and deaf, what is she. What-is-Dori. In a smooth motion she emptied the contents of her bag onto the table. Alongside the wallet, the book, the plugs, and the toothpaste, the cards that sat in bundles at the bottom of the bag dropped out. She lifted up one of them and placed it before him. "Don't hand out, sell," she said. "You want it? Buy it."

She lost more and more shifts at the studio, and Ada left her polite messages asking Dori to get back to her soon please, and her husband's messages were more irate, his voice failing to cover up his anger. Lili's letters arrived one after the other as if she felt something, as if all the envelopes always contained the same bunch of words: "I told you so!" But Dori knew that she hadn't told her. And even if Lili felt something, Dori herself didn't feel a thing. She was like the shards in the display cabinets in the department, the ones with the notes meant to remind visitors where it was taken from or the function of the jar or plate from which it was broken, but that no one paused to read, or if they did pause they only shrugged their shoulders and continued on their way. If Anati knew about Dori's broken shard example, she would have laughed at the drama of it. But since the reason for Dori's sadness, her criminal inaction, was a guy, just a guy, she actually left her alone.

Every morning and evening, Dori made up her eyes in black, which Anati had once said was pretty and suited her. In meetings with Georgia, she reviewed, eyes closed, the titles of the books according to their customary order on the shelves five years earlier, as over the years she'd memorized them more than once and this useless knowledge made periodic sudden appearances. Her days were filled with words that her mind struggled to absorb. The world didn't lag behind; it too became pointless, like a remote archeological exhibition. For hours she lay and stared at the flaking roses that she cut out and stuck to the wall, and she only went out to cafés. Alone and with Dima, and in fact with increased frequency, such that occasionally she went out on shifts two to three times a day, traveling to areas she hadn't visited before. Dori no longer accepted avoidance or averted gazes. She smiled a broken smile and they paid. The fraternity of the deaf and stupid named after Dori and Lili Ackerman flourished like never before.

At a café on the Upholsterers' Street, she saw him again. Dori noticed him sitting with his legs crossed and all his bad qualities prancing around him. The place sparkled with cleanliness and the white tablecloths were stretched out under the silverware, but Dori didn't retreat, and didn't even sign to Dima that he should go in this time, that her head hurt or simply that the sickly man at the round table would recognize her. Instead, with a courage that she didn't know she had, she approached the table. Anton sat next to an impressive woman, not young. The woman's lipstick was as purple as a struck blood vessel but she still looked wealthy and confident. The scarf around her neck, the leather bag, the amused expression, all these looked valuable, and the woman placed the bag on a chair of its own, like a third diner, and she rummaged through it in search of a sucking candy or some change. Dori looked at the red liquid that the two of them drank. The more sickly and flushed Anton appeared, the healthier the woman looked, and Dori too suddenly felt strong and vital. She refused to try to guess the relationship between them. Under this was the thought: a bachelor is an unmarried man. She thought: a rose is a rose is a rose and Anton is Anton. Because despite everything, she'd learned something in college. It turned out that she knew herself how to calculate the sum of zero. The woman looked at her with slight curiosity and Dori returned her gaze, even though she was definitely the kind of woman whose door swings open to reveal an exemplary apartment when she goes out for the day. Erect as a primrose, Dori placed the cards in the center of the white tablecloth, making sure to straighten the corners. When she left the café followed by Dima, her hands were empty. She left the cards and the tower of coins next to them, untouched.

A week passed, and one evening Anton appeared with them in the stairwell. She didn't know how he found the address, because the only name on the mailbox was that of a German tourist who had left the country a decade before. But he stood there, with a jacket, even, looking at a poster of *The Bride Wore Black* that they'd hung on the door on their first day in the apartment. In his hand he was carrying a circular cardboard container decorated with bearded faces. He said that he had brought her soup. "Couldn't find any flowers?" whispered Anati, who was looking at him as if she didn't recognize him, as if they had never met before, but Dori hushed her.

"You made soup?" she asked.

He hadn't made it. But Dori invited him inside all the same, so whatever she later told herself about that evening, she knew that it was she who had let him enter.

Anton sat on the only chair in the room, seeming to her ailing and fragile, like someone suffering from a severe illness. He glowed with a refined light. If Georgia had been aware of Anton's existence, Dori would have described this to her, as if people really could glow with that sort of internal light, which perhaps in a different century characterized those suffering from tuberculosis or arsenic swallowers a moment before death. She didn't intend to resist; she didn't want to be in opposition. He was beautiful like an ornamented altar on which money is burned for the gods. The beauty of someone who hides away while the earthly world slams against all his windows. Purple hollows appeared around his eyes. She saw on him the signs of her insult as if they had been drawn out in a blue line along his skin. Poor Anton, she saw. A child. An emperor who has a mother. She knew that she'd agree to anything. Whatever he'd ask and whatever he'd want and whatever he'd say or not say.

She stood with the pail of soup in which small carrots floated while he rose and wandered in the narrow space that was hers, his hands browsing the postcards tacked to the corkboard, the diagram of a missile that Dima sketched for them as a house-warming gift, the edges of which had already started to bend. His hands rested on the back of the sofa bed and finally on the pile of cards that formed miniature skyscrapers, casting shadows. Anton looked at her and smiled as if he was conspiring. "So what, you're deaf on even days and mute on odd ones?"

This time he took the cards in his hands, shuffling them as in an old, simple magic trick. She saw no sleight of hand before her, but rather heartbreaking clumsiness. It was almost possible to believe that he was really seeing the cards for the first time, that Dori hadn't dropped one in front of him only a week before. Dori finally left the soup in its container; until that moment she had still been holding it and couldn't find anywhere to put it, like a guest rather than a host. "I'll make tea," she said, happy to have something to do. When she left the room she was suddenly sorry she didn't have a cake to slice and serve, and this thought, odd and unnecessary, came and called as if Anna Ackerman herself had sat down in her ear canal and explained in a spirited, jovial soprano that "in moments like this everything must be perfect, from the cake to the blinds, and it's just a pity that Dori doesn't take care of herself." She ignored Anton's questions, Anna's erroneous advice, and Anati, who was waiting for her in the hallway, determined to clarify what Anton was doing there, especially after that one time. She especially ignored Lili, who knocked inside her head, "Really, you're letting this vampire into the house?" Even if the words didn't seem to suit her, Dori knew it was her voice, whistling like the wind.

All at once she was surrounded inside and out, and she knew

that what she really needed was to breathe and breathe until only two remained, she and Anton (and in the face of the breathing, Lili held on last, whispering to her aloud in a disembodied voice, a voice that Dori knew had to be hers, even though she had never spoken about vampires before: "So that's all you need? For them to smile at you?" And Dori thought back to her: "Maybe. Maybe that's all I need, would you believe it?"). She poured the tea into two cracked cups with thick rims that the previous tenant, the German, had left behind.

Anton asked again and Dori answered. Of course she answered. He opened the small window and hung from the peeling sill facing outside, drawing out an acute angle with the chimney visible from the window. As he smoked opposite the chimney, she thought that it was the most beautiful thing she'd ever seen. The new streetlights that had been installed as part of an effort at community improvement and development, successful on neither front, came on with surprising strength. In the play of light and shadow the chimney looked almost beautiful, or at least impressive. "It toughens us up in the event of a nuclear storm," she said. "Fixed servings of air pollution." Anton went on smoking and she could tell that he'd laughed. And even though she didn't hear what he said in return, she laughed too. When he came back inside, the top half of his body looked refreshed from the smog, and he sweetened his tea with heaping spoonfuls of sugar and this caused her to stop and waver and finally not sweeten hers at all. Before he could ask again, she said that the cards were work; he'd seen for himself. "But you're not deaf," he insisted, his gaze calling her an imposter, and only then, with burning pinkies, she removed the plugs from her ears, heard the sprinklers in the garden that was planted at the foot of the chimney, Anton's hand rubbing against the jeans she wore under the dress, she heard all that breathing and said, "I was once."

## YOU'RE FAKING IT

"You're faking it," the girl who slept in the bed nearby whispered to her every night, getting out of her bed in the dark to stand barefoot next to Dori. Almost touching her but no, never quite. Dori could feel the cold of the tiles climbing up the girl's legs but there was no way of knowing if she was cold. The darkness wasn't absolute, but rather brightly dappled by the rusty light that illuminated the main corridor. But it was dark enough to draw close to what one held at a distance in the daytime. They showered in the same shower (one after the other) and hung and folded their clothes in the same closet and despite this the girl gave off a scent of peaches and acetone and Dori didn't. They were ten years old. They were even born in the same month. But this was all they had in common. The girl had wonderful dresses she didn't wear and Dori saw them hanging up in the wall closet like headless dolls. At night too. "You can hear me now, right? Can you hear? And now? And now?" the girl asked with her mouth very close to the ear canal, almost resting on it. So it went night after night, her face hovering above like an airborne search squad. Dori never knew if before she had been sleeping and had suddenly woken up or perhaps she was never asleep. She suspected that now it would always be like this, until the end of days; she would lie down and this girl would float above her in a perpetual examination. Dori's gaze was turned to the low ceiling and she lay stiff with limbs tensed, eyes always opened, cottonballs stuffed into her ears, trying to understand how at first she'd thought the girl looked like Lili.

The smells of urine and bleach and the faint, peachy scent that the girl gave off carried from their room. They unrolled the checkered bed covering each night and spread it out each morning. The girl disappeared each morning and returned unexpectedly, in a noisy panic, swaying strangely. They didn't speak, as if Dori was nothing more than another bookshelf added to the room. But Dori didn't speak with anyone then.

Dori left the shared room only when they forced her, and then she would walk along the edges of the vegetable garden, measuring with her legs the artificial lawn, a gift from generous donors who waged a war against the local weather. Only at nights were the two of them peas in a pod, close and alike, until the girl would unroll her blanket and stand by her head. "Can you hear me?" she'd ask again as if verifying a fact. "Can you? Can you?" Dori didn't know if she enjoyed this, or if she had to do it, maybe she too had simply gotten used to spending nights this way. But she only thought all this afterward, because during those nights she lay with tensed limbs like a doll built out of wood with joints screwed together, the dread climbed over her and curled up in her belly and tallied up her vertebrae. They were supposed to become friends. That was how they were introduced to each other, with an emphatic promise, a promise laced with an implicit threat: Anat and Dori would be the best of friends, they had so much in common, and Dori looked at her toes in the blue sandals she had recently been given and that didn't suit her and she knew that this was a lie, and Anat ignored the counselors' words and insisted on adding the i to her name, saying, "My name is Anati, not Anat." And even Dori knew that this didn't make her name or the girl herself cute.

Despite all this, Dori preferred the night. During the days, paper bags filled with air exploded behind her back. They imitated her language with hand movements that didn't mean a thing; they imitated in a heavy, mocking voice what their ears heard as the speech of the deaf. After one of them succeeded with an imitation, the others burst out with laughter that sounded as if it had been hanging around for a long time, waiting for its chance.

When her novelty dissipated, the bullying weakened, grew

more sporadic. She learned it was best to give in a little and keep the fear inside. Give a finger and not the whole hand, so they didn't know which finger she'd given and what she'd kept. But in the institution, which Dori got used to calling a boarding school like everyone else, there was no place for secrets. Children always broke into your secrets and shook them around until everything came out, clattering and worthless. Everyone knew who didn't have a mother, who wet the bed, who was beaten, who was beaten worse, who was removed from their home with a court order and why. The children kept pictures and letters under the thin mattresses even though strange hands pulled them out and fondled them. They read one another's diaries and left comments and sometimes cut out entire pages. But Dori didn't keep a diary. She didn't write a single word. In their language too she kept silent for days and weeks. Only at night did she call for Lili. Underneath the blanket her fingers signed for her to come. She knew by heart how Lili's body felt next to her and out of habit she drew close to the wall, making space for her. An entire world had been taken from her and what was given in its place screeched like chalk on a blackboard.

And it was actually that girl, Anati, who opened and closed doors, who rattled and rustled and blew her nose in ways that Dori hadn't ever considered possible, it was actually she who gave her the first earplugs. On that day she got dressed next to her, while the door to their room was ajar. She threw on the wide purple shirt with the collar cut off, and wore a bathing suit without a drop of embarrassment. Dori sat on the bed and stared at her. Without wanting to, she heard the electricity moving in the walls on its way to light up the many rooms, just how many she didn't know, the water moving in the pipe with its uneven flow, the window banging in its frame in the dining hall without a person stopping to close its latch. The world was always too noisy.

With incredible dexterity, the girl they called Anati tied a shrunken turquoise and blue and gold bikini behind her back and with another smooth motion inserted into her ears two lumps of gray material. "I have water in my ears," she said, almost apologetically. "They make me." After a moment, she stopped, opened up the dresser drawer, and threw a small bag at Dori. "I have spare plugs in the drawer, try them yourself, you can't hear almost anything."

Dori inserted the two strange lumps of material into the auricles of her ears. In her hands the plugs were repulsive; they looked like something bodily, like something alien, like a part left over from someone or something. But inside the auricle it wasn't unpleasant. The material quickly sealed her up, like sealing cracks in a broken jar. Because for those moments the plugs caused the creaks of the window to sound as if they were coming from the adjacent room and not inside of her, the buzzing whisper of the electricity to fall silent, Anati's steady rustling to quiet. Dori hunched and froze under the summer blanket in her stained shirt, and Anati looked at her with renewed interest. "You can't even pity that girl," as one teacher said to another and Dori, unfortunately, overheard. But Dori lifted up her eyes and looked into Anati's as if she were looking into a mirror. To the few pieces of furniture in the room (two metal beds, a closet, a carpet with a homey weave) the proper shadow was finally added, the purple edges that things had in the past returned to their places. The world stopped for a moment and was reset with the proper color and texture, and it seemed to Dori that the always, the familiar always, which had left her behind, had suddenly returned. And Anat-Anati looked at her as if she was going to scream "can you hear me" into her ears, but that question finally had no meaning then, and instead she said, with eyebrows raised in amazement, "Yeah, I knew it! You're crazy, I knew it!" This Dori heard, and she nodded as if to agree.

When she sat in Georgia's office, her hands under her knees, disposable plugs were stuffed into her ears, the yellow kind that come packaged in pairs at the drugstore. Dori had adjusted to the feel of them, less spongy and stringy than the wads of cotton from childhood and also less irritating than the plugs from her elementary school years. Anati had supplied her with them without reserve, even though she had nothing to give in exchange. Suddenly they were friends. "You know that you always could hear," Georgia told her again with the uncompromising gentleness that Dori already knew well. Delicate white gladioli in a new vase quivered from the breeze of the air conditioner, while Georgia stressed every vowel and consonant, knowing that Dori couldn't keep from lip reading, all still supplemented with incomplete, mistake-ridden gestures in the language. "There are those who hear and those who don't. It's that simple." This wasn't the first time that this was said to her, but each time it sounded more baseless than before. "They did you an injustice. They raised you in opposition to your abilities."

Sometimes she wanted to be seduced by the smooth, clean explanations that Georgia gave her. The clean and clear explanations about the world and about Dori herself that drew in the air between them a bright, vivid map of the stars. But even she couldn't convince Dori that she could hear. At least she knew that once, she was their girl, belonging to them completely.

"You turned yourself off," Georgia O'Keeffe said to her.

"I'm not an electronic device," she quickly objected. "Can you imagine that? Nice to meet you, Dori the Toaster."

"But all the same," said Georgia, Dori's joke passing by her like a paper airplane.

Dori was silent; what was there for her to say?

"Hearing isn't a voluntary sense, but apparently you were a very strong girl. You succeeded in closing it off, sealing it up. You succeeded in telling your brain that you couldn't hear, that with you the sounds were stopped at the threshold." As she spoke, Dori recalled those sailors who fell off the edge of the earth because they believed the earth was flat.

She focused with her gaze on the letter *E* and discovered seven books on the shelf whose titles included the word *End* in a variety of configurations. Recently Georgia had changed the internal order of the library and the books were classified according to the name of the book and not the author. Dori read the names aloud and stopped. She knew that Georgia was listening to her. That she had time and wouldn't rush her. In any case, Georgia's theory was lacking. Even with her unique key wrench, which had proven itself more than once, she couldn't turn all the screws. "What you need is a skeleton key," Dori said aloud, and Georgia asked, "What do you mean?" and Dori shrugged her shoulders and said, "Whatever." But she knew that only by stealing would it be possible to find a trace of what once was, only by coming with impure intentions and a great, overwhelming will. But she wasn't sure who she was supposed to steal from.

And perhaps the truth was only what was recorded in their books, only what happened afterward, in the world of sounds. She knew that they had forced her to accept the voices' weight inside her. Dori was the first woman and therefore was required to give a name to every noise and rustle in the world. When she tried, she discovered that even this was impossible, because the sounds had names from time immemorial and people and animals and even objects had voices, and things made noises. They raged and clattered and squeaked, even more vulgar than the bodily odors that were masked by perfumes and nevertheless always reached Dori first, tiny particles floating to her to be quickly absorbed.

Even then, in the first years outside the house, in days that had no floor or ceiling, as much as they asked and speculated (and at that time Dori didn't know just how interesting she was, from a research perspective, and how many researchers wasted their time on her case), they couldn't find the key. The therapists hypothesized and Dori sat silent. Closed up like a wall of bricks in a fallow field. A girl in the form of a wall. Because Dori swallowed the key, the entire key ring. At first it rested on her tongue like foreign words and then it was swallowed, plunging inward. Had they asked her, they'd have learned the only way to get it back was to shake her upside down. So many things would had fallen out of her stomach and pockets. Dori herself would have been surprised to see what fell out, but this they didn't do. Not even Georgia. Therefore they went on missing things big and small. Because she wasn't a strong girl at all, but very weak. A person without any strength of her own. Lili had more strength than her, that was clear, but look, look, all she'd done was take it and leave.

But Lili wrote her. It didn't matter where Dori lived, Lili's letters found their way to her like water and electric bills. They rested in Dori and Anati's mailbox, on which the name of the German tourist was still written. And like the bills, the very existence of Lili's letters, most of which remained sealed and silent, indicated a debt. But in fact, that year, simultaneously with her college studies, the recording studio, Anton, Dori did finally open the envelopes. At least some of them (every tenth envelope and sometimes every seventh envelope and once two in a row). When she read, her eyes skipping between the rows, she wondered when Lili became so ridiculous, desperate, so different from the brilliant, objective voice in her head. She wrote as if it was clear to her that Dori would read and read and find Lili's opinions on the weather and the death of painting interesting. She sent her fragmented sketches from an exhibition that she saw and informed her about the deaths of old female painters. Dori understood. Even if they didn't exchange a single word, she understood that Lili was writing to her about Georgia. That her sister was referring to her out of everyone. Because she again gave her a big sister's instructions, imagining that she had power over her: Do you remember? You must remember. Do you forgive me? I forgive you. Actually, she was saying: Go, leave, obey.

She read only a fraction of those letters, a fraction of a fraction maybe, but alas, the fraction that she did read she knew by heart.

Yes, the words themselves weren't worth much. Had she pinned Lili to the wall, her sister would have admitted this herself. Nevertheless she sent letters. Along with them, Lili sent small drawings of the hotel she lived in and diagrams of five ways to make a bed. She drew with quick lines a few of the guests in the hotel and the cooks, most of whom were immigrants from their own dying countries, chopping and frying and resting during cigarette breaks. Later on she drew the dogs she walked, adding their names in tiny writing to the drawing, noting who was aggressive and who was simply amazing, and who was in love with whom and who was jealous. And Dori smiled against her will and sometimes showed these illustrated letters to Dima, who looked at them with a furrowed brow. Again she pointed out the small drawings that adorned the outsides of the envelopes, an impartial tour guide, but she knew that all this was a smoke screen. Once Dori relented and wrote to her something in return, perhaps out of courtesy, perhaps from exhaustion, she mailed to her scenes from plays she borrowed almost at random from Georgia, who preferred Shakespeare, and from Anati, who had recently announced her intention to study acting and had bought all the Greek plays. But mostly she just cut out and pasted the texts she was required to read at the studio. More directions to a destination than Natasha asking, to the amusement of the entire table, what they'd get for dessert; more turn left, plaza up ahead than Ismene pleading before Antigone. But anyway, Lili didn't respond to either.

## ANTON SAID GOODBYE TO HIS MOTHER

Anton said goodbye to his mother at the entrance to the house and Dori nodded to her from a distance. She sat on one of the eight carved wooden chairs in the kitchen, dressed in a shirt with spots that didn't match anything, looking through the broad window at the movement of clouds that drifted past as if by special invitation. The wealth still stunned her and she tried to pretend as if she belonged even though she never would belong with these people, who, for instance, ate oysters. Were Anati there instead of her, she would have immediately felt at home, placing her feet on the counter and still looking incredibly appropriate. As if this sequoia-wood counter was only waiting for that talented-but-disturbed girl to come home. Dori's feet swayed a few centimeters from the floor and Dori, who refused to feel like a girl, moved to the opposite chair, which actually was identical to the chair she'd sat on a moment before. Around then, the two of them nodded to each other, as if mimicking each other's movement, but the similarity between them ended there. And the mother said, "Don't let him drive you crazy. My boy, he drives people crazy." Dori nodded again, for the second or third time, and reflected on the tone of explicit pride that accompanied these words. Dori wrung her hands and the mother clutched the silk scarf tied around her neck and tightened her grip on the keys in her other hand. Her short, fair curls waved around thanks to the blowing of an unseen breeze dedicated only to her. She looked like a graceful, courageous pilot who was about to cross the ocean. Hard to believe that she gave birth to Anton at the age of thirty. Hard to believe that she gave birth to anyone at all. Dori thought, there's no need for such camouflage, for sentences made of words that contradict what they seem to mean, because when it came to Anton she and his mother were of one mind. In their eyes, every fault of his looked like evidence of his unique soul. So it happened that Dori suddenly remembered what she'd found written in a book by one poetess, dedicated to a different poet. The dedication said that she and his mother were proud of him and loved him. How strange these things were in her eyes then. It's almost unnecessary to point out that the mother was the woman from the café. The one whom Anton sat next to silently, the one before whom Dori danced her little scene with the cards. Dori assumed that she didn't recognize her; usually they didn't recognize her. But Dori immediately identified the expensive bag and the purple lipstick, purple as a bruise, and the inquisitive eyes.

After she visited one of their three homes for the first time, Dori concluded that there was indeed a place that was called the mother's house, and there was the son's apartment and the additional apartment as well, but in fact the division of the spaces between the mother and her son were rather fluid. They shared the places they owned with impressive generosity, like twenty-year-old roommates in a leaky apartment. There were always too many cartons of milk or none at all and the pantry was incredibly well stocked until suddenly they were missing something and they'd decide it was possible, it was certainly possible, to live without sugar, lemons, or flowers. So they lived together with the same modernist works, with open spaces, covered in glass and metal. The apartments and the house (the "properties," Anton would correct her) were all listed under Anton's name for some reason. When she encountered his mother again (indeed less frequently than it seemed likely they would meet, and even this was hasty, like a superficial kiss on a cheek), Dori still couldn't figure out why she and Anton tended to move through space together and each time settle down together in one place and abandon their other homes. Whether or not this moving, according to which they locked one apartment behind them and moved on to another, happened out of loneliness, whether or not they desired each other's presence or whether they acted like this out of convenience only—Dori felt for the mother. Because she was able to find a good explanation for each and every motive, even if she herself remained a guest among them for a limited time. There was no one to blame other than herself. She herself doled out the time. She stayed as long as she could give it.

Only in the old house, which was called the mother's house, was Anton sometimes alone or alone with Dori. Because the mother couldn't stand the house in which Anton was raised and complained about the automobile traffic that ran too close, likewise about the color of the walls. Yet only there did Anton's boredom disappear, like clothing he could roll up, under which Dori saw a boy, just a boy. A passionate boy who wanted exactly the same stories that everyone wants, and when the newness threatened to evaporate he'd close his eyes across from Dori's moving mouth. Dori couldn't shake the image of a chain of hearers clinging one to the other, asking one after the other to hear about Lili. Sometimes it seemed to her that she was trying to go forward but forcefully stuck to her back was a funny line of listeners, judges and social workers who held on to one another's hips, coveting the golden goose that she held in her hands. And now Anton as well. But very quickly he found his place at the head of the chain and the hips he held were hers. Each time he asked her to speak she plucked another feather from Lili's tail, and if Anton hadn't been so skinny, it would have been even easier to imagine that he intended to swallow the entire goose—beak, feathers, deafness, and all.

But no one was twisting her arm to speak. Not even Anton, and no, she really didn't have to. At certain moments it seemed to her that an arrow long since released had finally struck the target. And even if she wasn't the one who shot the arrow, the target was nevertheless struck. Because finally she spoke about Lili. When this happened she didn't feel relief, but the guilt didn't bother her either. Because what she said and what she didn't were the same to everyone. What lives is what dies, like the king, like the queen. Wherever they are, they die one after the other, or one following the other. One could go on endlessly enumerating the royal chain of the dead (the king died and then the queen died and the princes died and the guards died and the cook died and the gardeners died and the cat died), and compared with all that, what was Lili? Almost nothing. A random collection of cells, unfocused thought, air particles, memory on top of memory, voice in the head, hole in the head.

And it's not nice to say this, but there wasn't enough in just the two of them together. Because there was no "Dori and Anton"; such a thing didn't exist except as a phrase with no foothold in the world. The rooms they sat in were quite empty, when she bent toward him, almost leaning into him, it was as if she were leaning into a wall or a closet. When they slept together the body was elsewhere. No one reached out a hand. This was so different from what Dori had hoped for, the suffocation grabbed her from inside, saying to the limbs, move, continue without a heart, without lungs, press on, and Dori, because she had no choice, pressed on. He came to her because she wanted him, because the desire was valid and strong. But from the time he stayed she had to give something, something else besides the desire itself, which was pure and somehow so embarrassing (for example: she'd collapse into his arms and he'd lift up her dress. She no longer wore almost any dresses). Dori tried to be daring and thoughtless. She tried to act like she thought women were acting in other rooms at the exact same time. She did what it seemed to her had to be done, but it always looked stupid. She couldn't keep from seeing herself from the side and shaking her head in amazement. What exactly are you doing? When she took her shirt off facing him, with a clumsy motion that seemed to her to convey defiance or sophistication, she only put it back on quickly. Even at age ten Anati had taken off shirts better than her.

Yet when he didn't come to her she counted the hours. Immediately after midnight she'd set down her book and call him. She always chose the same words. Like a child, like someone whose sleep is very important: "Come to me, I can't sleep." Face-to-face this wouldn't be said; what are you talking about? Face-to-face she said only what he wanted to hear. The first time he said, "I'm coming," and she thought he'd have a plan, but they only walked for hours. He didn't believe in public transportation, he threw up in taxis, and his Citroën was up on cinder blocks for an unknown reason. Afterward she would discover he had set routes. She walked with him on a commercial street full of garbage. On a jewelers' street emptied of its gold at night. Among prostitutes and pimps. In a small club hidden under a restaurant Dori clung to the crimson wall and Anton caressed the face of someone he knew. She didn't protest, as if such tribulations were necessary. Suddenly they were like one body, for an instant, smoking the same cigarette, sticking a hand under a shirt, the same hand, the same shirt. She didn't like to be touched, but Anton had such familiar hands, hands of a prince from ancient legends, a marble statue made of flesh and blood. And when he placed his palm on her stomach the entire world couldn't touch her.

## THERE WERE OTHER NIGHTS TOO

There were other nights too. On those nights she spread blue eye shadow under her eyes, unintentionally creating for herself the look of an ill person. She wore clothes taken straight from Anati's closet, the fineness of its clothing unequaled since its owner was ten. Dresses with sculpted collars that buttoned down her back, patterned stockings without a run. She still wore the same tattered boots that were buckled with a snap of the copper clasp, like gnome's shoes. The boots stepped on Anton's leather shoes more than once and each time she apologized and received confirmation of her excessive physicality against the solid wind, the frozen milk that was Anton. On those nights only the stories ruled the roost and she was the one who told them. After some thought Dori painted her nails peach-orange.

Afterward he apparently loved her more and she hated herself a bit more. "I prefer to be your mistress rather than the emperor's wife." She memorized words that she never had the opportunity to use. Anton still caressed other girls' cheeks. He still loved his mother more than her (What did you think? Lili and Anati, who never met, said to her. What exactly did you think? they sang as a chorus). But what was hers was hers by law. Anton saw in her a coding machine with ten thousand combinations. His hands wandered over her. Grasping, so blind, clumsier than you might guess. But she taught him what he asked to learn, and sometimes what she wanted too, signing the word "breathe" like lungs rising and falling above her chest and each time Anton looked on, spell-bound anew.

After they finished she would try out the selection of lipsticks that his mother left in the bathroom, spraying perfumes on herself as if at a department store, smelling like a shopgirl who spent eight or nine hours behind a counter perfumed until it stank. Traces of the perfume were hard to cover up, but the lipstick she always wiped off afterward with the back of her hand, leaving only remnants on the edges of her lips. When they were in one of his homes she wore his mother's clothes, which were beautiful and expensive, and by chance, as it were, they found themselves in her double bed. "Queen size," he said, and Dori laughed. There she spoke again and there he listened and there she signed stripes and dots and before his eyes she slowly, so very slowly, demonstrated how to sign "dream" and "house" and "youth" and "desire" and "go fuck yourself." And sometimes those words that existed in their language only and in no other. At long last she had something to give to someone who seemed the intended customer for those strange stores selling brain teasers, metallic marbles knocking into one another and wooden cubes fitting inside three-dimensional puzzles. Presents for someone who has everything. She told him about the boy in the basement, about Mother's garden, about looking for metal in the fields. She told him about Lili.

Little by little Anton understood that it wasn't her father and mother but rather Lili who signed the whole world to her. And she'd taught her well, even though she detested the role of the teacher, one given to her only because she was born before Dori. After all, the two of them knew so little about what happened outside of them, they caught specks of dust and thought, here's a star, here's the whole world.

It always came back to Lili. Fairly soon it became clear that Anton and Dori had a need for a third. Who would be with them in the room, to describe what she did and how she did it and sometimes why as well. Who would be like the air surrounding them. A third was required there, even though the third didn't grow together with them, but instead remained a twelve-year-old girl in green boots. Maybe because Dori knew Lili's age twelve completely. She remembered the color of the sky and the touch of Lili's skin on hers. He asked to see pictures, but she didn't have pictures. They weren't a family that took pictures. She had her words and this would have to do.

But despite all her stories and all the chains of words that issued from her mouth, holding hands like paper dolls, she felt empty. She was a rattling barrel with only a single coin banging against its insides over and over. Had Dori told her everything, perhaps Georgia would have revealed to Dori that she was in great distress. That she signed "love" and "I love" erroneously and compulsively. That she'd gone and lost herself. But Georgia was only Georgia, and in any case Dori told her even less than she had in the past, because everything she said about him faded away in her mouth. Despite this the words wouldn't stop and the precise lines evaporated like smoke. She no longer knew how to describe the light or the smell, the fear, what she wanted or didn't want. Not even the sensation of balancing on one hand the blue fish the uncles made for them.

Maybe only one of the uncles made the fish, and not both of them. And it might be that they weren't fish but dolphins or even mermaids instead. And maybe she never had any uncles but only her father's geese who gathered around him, fat and idiotic. Who could say. Ever since she spoke about them, the uncles had faded as if they were never anything but a story. And when they lay breathless between the duvet and mattress, and everything but them was white and pure, Anton asked her again, "And what else." Her hair cast a shadow on her face and the glow of the nightlight washed over her, making her features coarse and thick. Again they appeared there, just like before, Pocahontas and Captain John Smith, who in this version was even more handsome and tired and weak until he woke up from a fresh shower of blood and words, whereas Pocahontas was clumsy and not attractive at all and completely forgot the name she was born with. She told more, despite the spoiled taste that stood on her tongue, even though when the tongue met the palate and the teeth out of the need for pronunciation and speech she realized the teeth had loosened and had possibly begun to crumble in her mouth. She continued the story in her language, in their language, but she no longer knew who it was she was talking about.

She lay on the bedcovers, spreading out her toes and closing her eyes. She knew that she was mimicking something. Some other presence, some other woman, more mysterious than her, talking sweetly about herself. But she didn't care at all, even though she knew that the two of them appeared to him as two sisters in a marginal, low-budget tragedy. She still wanted to tell. To say almost everything, to say too much, to say what no one would want to hear.

One night they stayed together. And instead of just heading out, as always, going in and out of places without signs, without her understanding the rules, why there of all places and why are we leaving now, on this night they had an actual address and destination. Anton said the name of one of the clubs of which Anati claimed he was a silent partner and Dori nodded as if she were a regular at the place, as if she knew herself. She put on makeup in the small bathroom and in the mirror saw the same little Dori, only in color, and quickly put on the lipstick that was too dark and turned off the light because there was no point dwelling on it. Even when she switched one dress for another she still couldn't decide if this was a real date or just an imitation of a date and just to be safe she dragged Anati with her. Anati looked at her as if she being kind to her, for agreeing to go from dragging to dragged, and with an exaggerated gesture she tossed the Racine play she was reading onto the bed. "God, I don't have the strength for those French," she said, and wrapped the balding feather boa around her neck. Dori knew Anati had decided to act superior to everyone that evening and, perhaps under the influence of the "cursed playwright," as she called Racine, by the time they reached the stairwell she was already speaking with a fake French accent.

And what was always charming became a bit disgusting when the two of them switched roles. Dori tried to tell Anati, enough, maybe she was getting carried away with the drinking, even though it was Dori who drank glass after glass. The floor at the club looked as if dozens of wineglasses had been shattered on it and ground to a glassy dust. Anati took off her heels and danced alone on the open floor, and Dori prepared herself to see one of those moments when Anati was beautiful and unstoppable. But when she danced there, barefoot, her wet hair falling in damp strips onto her back, she looked miserable, ugly even, from trying too hard. Her jaw looked angular and sharp and her skin turned green and Dori thought, what does it matter if she's pretty, why does it have to matter if she's pretty, and just a tiny happiness lit up inside her because the seesaw had for a moment tipped in her favor.

The noise was terrible, jarring and repetitive, like a hospital respirator turned up high. "Welcome to the world, they call this music," Anati had said to her once, long ago, the first time they went to a club. "Get used to it." And Dori really did get used to it, because you get used to everything. She now saw Anton's derisive gaze as he looked at Anati and she hated him and hated herself for not doing anything, for not saving her, for continuing to sit next to him as if nothing was happening. Then they kissed. So many other people were kissing there, so many mouths were caught by exposed skin, that even Dori and Anton managed to kiss without adding another single word about Lili, but a moment later she threw up into a tall metal ashtray and Anati threw up too but each was late in grabbing the other's hair in that moment, which was humiliating. Anton escorted them to their apartment and Anati fell asleep in her clothes in Dori's bed, as would sometimes happen when they were little.

Anton washed her hair under the faucet of the sink. He used an apple shampoo that was still left from the German tenant. His hands were extremely gentle, as if she were very fragile. Her head was bent over the sink, pulsing with pain, the water rinsed and the sound rang in her ears as she told him about the game that she and Lili had. She spoke as if it was in the water's power to mask every sound, as if she spoke only to herself, but when her voice sounded she knew that Anton was listening attentively. "What strange girls we were, honestly," Dori said like someone unfamiliar, external, because in fact there was nothing strange about it. If anything it was amazing. At those times, when the small house became a black sky and they ran breathless through the rooms, crashing into crates and furniture, all the limitations were forgotten, extraneous forces of gravity were finally eliminated. Like pictures in *The Complete Encyclopedia for Young Adults*, the two of them were beautiful objects and hovered voiceless in the place you reach after the numbers end and words turn into a floating nothingness.

Anton wrapped her hair in a hand towel and she understood that this was it, now she really had given everything. The joy that whirled around them when they danced like stars dying out and being born, illuminated like planets, this was the last thing to give. Dori realized that the pain was easier to give by far, but she gave it all anyway. This time Dori Ackerman was the one emptied from the outside in, turned inside out like a sock, and nothing remained of her.

At the end of that night, when the light already rose pale in the windows, and the first birds sang, as if checking with the sound of their voice to see if they were still alive, Dori pulled out the shoebox from under the bed. She tossed it in his direction so that the lid fell off and the contents scattered like confetti. Like letters. Because that's what they were. She said aloud, "Here's Lili, these are her words." And for a moment it seemed that her sister was folded up there in the envelopes, eyes closed like a fetus.

Until that moment Anton didn't know that Lili still wrote to her little sister, still played that old game of writer and reader. Dori saw the boredom pass by and disappear from his face as if in an accelerated motion, leaving in its place an expression of desire and thirst, but not for her, definitely not for her. When she stood up and dried her hair she knew that she'd bought herself more time opposite Anton, but she didn't know why or what she'd do with all this purchased time. Because Anton truly looked fascinated, ardent even, in those moments, again wearing the expression of the innocent boy, but Dori knew him and understood that when the newness passed, the boredom would return and Anton would close his eyes.

Anton turned on another light in the room, ignoring Anati sleeping in Dori's bed, and searched through the sealed and opened envelopes with his long fingers. Like a simple voyeur. Like someone there's no point in approaching, like the weakest finger in the hand. No, not like, but identical to. And her fingers moved on their own, signing the worker, the soldier, the merchant, the king. Signing the artist who chose an idiot, a greedy one, a thief for herself, and she said to herself in a voice that sounded very familiar, "Here's one that doesn't even have his own finger." And that was Anton, Anton who washed her hair with the smell of apples and Anton whom she watched from a distance in college, brilliant and exalted, and Anton who left them with beautiful, measured steps as they faced the gate to the zoo. He was the one she thought that she couldn't live without, but she could. Dori looked at him and was unable to rekindle any of what she felt, anything of what she knew she'd felt until that very moment. No, it wasn't a short-term stupor but the end; it gnawed and arrived. The feeling died. It died in an instant.

And as for the letters, it didn't matter how many of the envelopes Dori never opened and how many lines she skipped over, and if the letters that she already read were quickly stained with grease and ink, becoming illegible, forgotten in every corner, wrinkled and tossed aside. It didn't even matter that most of the envelopes remained sealed (until Anton opened them) and that in some of them not a thing waited for her. In any case, Lili sent her nothing more than locks of hair, clipped nails, scraps. Not the truth, not the truth and nothing but the truth, and the two of them knew it.

***Dori wrote to Lili:***

Once there was a calf that walked through the meadow and a small boy walked in front of him. Above them a star twinkled. Once we lived in an apartment littler than little with Dad and Mom. Do you remember that, Lili? Because I actually remember. It was possible to count all of us on the fingers of one hand but there would be something left over, a small, pink little finger for signing "cat" or "dog." We didn't have a dog. Sometimes the little finger signed just us, joining the hand that signed a full circle around us, here we are. Once there was a single hand that struck a knee but no one heard the slap of the fingers. Once we learned to speak word after word. Here my hand stretches forward. Look, my hand is mute but the fingers are as pink as dawn. I remember the smell of oranges. Do you remember?

***Dori wrote to Lili:***

Once upon a time, definitely once, there was a calf that leapt giddy-up giddy-up up and up on Ireland's green meadows. There was a boy who ran in front of him, not me, I read it in a book. Once there was a boy who taught himself to read from writings on the empty cartons of coffee and laundry detergent. Not me. Someone polished the old kettle until our faces sparkled and smiled when we smiled. The whole world was reflected in our white teeth. We were so happy, weren't we?

***Afterward Lili answered Dori:***

Sometimes we were.

*Dori sent Lili a letter with letters cut out from the newspaper. The letters spelled a single word repeating.*

*Afterward Anton read everything he could find.*

## PART FOUR

## THE KINGDOM

*I want to write about the good life.*
*Even if it's somebody else's.*
—SHIRLEY KAUFMAN

It's a wonderful place, I wrote to them. I live in a wonderful place and my job is wonderful. My friends are wonderful; I even adopted a dog. That's what I wrote, roughly. That is, more or less. Not necessarily in that order. And only after the words were sent, by the good graces of an underwater or underground cable, a signal that was thrown into space and reached the mailbox on which was written ACKERMANALEX, only then did I recall that I'd chosen the word that Alex hated. One of them, anyhow. When I wrote to them I covered myself up in self-pity and immediately laughed at myself. Because with the same wide mouth I cried and then immediately laughed aloud at my wailing.

It's impossible not to praise modern technology. There's no need for a singer on an imaginary street corner, singing under a fake set's lone streetlight. There's not even any need for the fucking Red Army Choir. When I was the miserable Lili whom no one loved, I played "Lili Marlene" on repeat. I heard the song and sighed with great emotion, until finally it was reduced to a series of actions like this: hearing and sighing.

In a rare moment of candor Anna once told me that she named me after that song. She signed: "That was my inspiration," and I pretended I didn't see. Maybe something got in my eye. Maybe the whole world. So pathetic and miserable is Lili. So delicate, like a rose's petals. And it wasn't even strange to me, that her favorite song was as beloved by the Nazis as it was by the Allies. I didn't find anything strange in her naming me after a chorus, a song people hum, a song you need working ears in order to hear. Yes, that's what our life was like, a hole on top of a hole. In the face of that hole, what was there left to do? One could be a mouse and one could, very belatedly, say: How wonderful. How wonderful the world is. How wonderful my life is, in the present and in the past.

Whenever I recalled another lie that was told to us, a lie we swallowed like poisoned fish tossed to seals, I felt sorry for myself all over again. Sometimes I drank. How ridiculous Lili is. Unconnected, unaffiliated, no kin, no acquaintances, no one who cares. Nor anyone who will call her to come back. Ha! I felt sorry for myself for being raised among them and I felt no less sorry for being far away. Believe me, I had enough pity for both this and that. Overflowing with self-concern. At those moments my hands pretended to be dead and only my feet smacked against each other, like someone trying to swim on dry land.

Because the past didn't stay in the past. It's an air pocket that drifts through the blood and all at once bursts open. It's an ancient pain that petrifies the muscle and suddenly in midstride, decades later, the muscle tears and you fall. With all the self-pity (which at least for the most part I kept to myself and didn't exhaust my surroundings with) and despite the self-rebuke ("Lili, enough already," I said to myself in all my languages, and my fingers said it quite firmly, like someone unfamiliar and authoritative, someone you can believe), with all this dramatic extravagance (which it turned out I had great talent for), there was something to it. The past advanced. It came. Sometimes you go toward it. What does it mean, leaping like a mindless colt? An idiotic Bambi.

And what did I do all this time? Why, the time passed, accumulated. Something happened to me. It couldn't be that I continued working at the same prestigious hotel, cleaning rooms and putting on sheets, honoring the standard furniture with a duster. It's inconceivable that I still walk dogs through the streets of New

York, handling them without fear after I acquired the miserable tricks designed to get them to obey. But that's really not so important. They always want to know, "Where are you from? Your accent's strange" ("I'm deaf," I answer them if I want. "I came from the Land of the Deaf") and "What do you do?" And I feel like saying to them: nothing. I'm not doing a thing. Every day I read *Walden* at the edge of a calm pond, not in New England, true, but there's no reason to insist on such technicalities. Perhaps I don't read *Walden* either. After all, I'm not from here.

Sometimes I wake up with a burning desire to understand the locals. On those mornings it seems to me there's a point in researching and understanding what causes them to tick like clocks that never stop, like squirrels that rush to the top of a tree only in order to climb back down again. But usually this effort seems pointless to me. Still, the view here is as lovely as a Disney movie. This I don't deny and yes, these are my images. I don't look around and think, hmm, the pond here is like Thoreau's Walden. The experience of American solitude and the clear soul don't pass before my eyes. My consciousness is attracted to baby-faced heroes who are meant to be sewn onto blankets and socks, stamped onto glasses and engine covers. Animated characters whose likenesses will appear on banknotes someday. When I studied at the regional high school I watched them in infinite sequences, movie after movie. Before my eyes they would sing and joke, dance and fall in love, learn and teach a lesson. And I, like the last of the gullible geese, found myself extracting moral standards from them. Ladies and gentlemen, this is the entirety of Lili Ackerman's ethical code. So too is my soul, I say to all who can't hear me, a superficial, colorful soul. As flexible as a singing crab or a dancing candlestick.

Again and again I remember a lone sentence from Uriel's mother; she said to me, "Why, you grew up with nature, you were raised in a village." Even then it was hard for me to believe that she meant my parents' one-story house, where the rooms were so cramped and crowded together that the refrigerator was kept on the porch. Maybe because she never paid a visit. Maybe because she had no idea that Anna's most complicated technical achievement was to break the refrigerator's short legs with hammer blows so that the cats couldn't jump onto it and swarm into the pantry for an all-you-can-eat-buffet. That's what nature was like. That's what the village was like. The longed-for pastoral. *Fauna* and *flora* were words that didn't grasp on to anything. I could spread my hands wide and the fingers would touch only air, and opinions were divided over whether the air was good or bad. Our nature was barrenness from horizon to horizon, electric lines and streets that were paved alongside dirt roads, neighborhoods in the distance and occasional visits from stray cats and mongooses emerging as night fell. There were a few fields that were watered for some governmental reasons and there was the puddle that only Dori could find any beauty in. But that was all.

Of course I never said a thing about this to Uriel's mother. When she spoke I felt that I had won something, a trickle of stolen water. From her ability to see in me a nature girl who skips after friendly animals in the meadow or rides on the backs of horses, I too, for a few fragile moments, saw myself in that image.

But most days the outdoors terrified me. With all my hatred of Anna and Alex, I preferred not to leave the house. I remained in the house and saw them. They passed quickly from hot to cold, conducting extreme temperatures like metals, and next to them I was as cold as an ax cleaving a glacier. Maybe Anna was scared of me. I felt something of this even without the commentary from Alex, who scolded and explained how bad I'd been, how delicate Anna was and how ill-suited to the half-wild life we led. I saw that she looked at me with the eyes of a hunted animal, big and frightened and made-up, waiting for me to tear apart the main artery in her neck with my teeth. But all this obvious suffering was called upon for a purpose. We were performing for an unseen audience. Not only Anna behaved as if her movements were concealing a secret, a fixed object meant for interpretation and hidden reflections. Both Dori and I behaved like that too.

We specialized in subtle and extreme mimicry, we were quick-handed. All the excitement over her mannerisms was intended for those who see but don't hear. Who looked at us through the holes in the doors, through ourselves. Someone, somewhere, sat and wouldn't take his eyes off of us.

Dori practiced fainting and Anna revealed her many injuries, which were as attractive as the wounds of Christ. But no one knew a thing about us. Anna was as determined as a warhorse and even I was never as delicate as a raindrop, a finger, or a rose's petal. We were no more sensitive than metal forged in fire. And nevertheless we carried on. The crowd needed to understand that I was the villain, that I, with evil looks, with shoulder shrugs, with my ostentatious introversion, I was the source of all evil, the cause of Anna's injury and all the injuries still to come.

And beneath all this the fear still pecked away at me that no one was looking, that no one saw, that all this could continue until the end of time without anyone noticing, the same stained couch, the same air that was hard to walk in, us. Me.

In light of this one might imagine that I would be an incredible actress, that my career in the theater would last longer than a single high school production. But that's not how it went. So yes, Ms. Savyon, I'm answering you a bit late, with the assistance of the cleanest vodka I could find in the area, because there are things a lady doesn't compromise on even though the cup stays full. Do you understand yet, Ms. Uriel's-Mother Savyon? This is the nature in which I was raised. No connection to the green abundance I'm now immersed in. I live in a house that isn't mine, in which every piece of furniture and every object appears to be a paragon of its kind. Look at the glass in my hand, the rug under my feet, how they point in the proper direction: restrained good taste. Even the fauna and the flora here are endowed with the owners' tranquility. It's easy to be impressed by the velvety green of the trees' leaves and the silky green of the soft grass. The picture is rich in details, as if a level-headed architect with a slight tendency for the rococo designed it. And amid all this, only the foreignness suits me.

Eventually I did indeed do a few things that piled up one on top of the other; I took a few steps along a path that could hesitantly be called a career. I left school and returned to it. There's some diploma you can hang on some wall and my name is written on it in Latin letters. My failure is not necessarily obvious. But beneath all this I'm still Lili. Lili who sits on the green couch with Dori's flowery fabric, the thick fabric that wrinkles whenever limbs stretch out, that resists the possibility of ever being comfortable. These are Dori's printed flowers that grow unsightly tendrils and climbing branches nonstop. When Dori first spread out the fabric, and with considerable effort at that, I told her it looked like someone had puked a meadow onto our couch. She tried to hide her humiliation. Dori was proud of this extravagant, itchy fabric. I hadn't suspected that a decade later I'd see that hideous covering each time I so much as closed my eyes. Yes, on that couch, on the printed fabric meant to hide its many imperfections, there still sits some half-transparent Lili, Lili who despises lies and holds up facts, Lili who looks into the emptiness without hearing, leaning on her right elbow, writing and composing. And that same Lili looks at me with a narrowed gaze. She's surprised, and not pleasantly, by who I've become. I know that this is exactly how things are; there's no need to console me.

Sometimes I want to say to her, we're the same, but each time I turn away.

Even I didn't believe that I had a chance. Just like them, I knew that the moment I passed beyond their reach I'd disappear altogether. Much like them I didn't believe that there would be a Lili without them. Bridges of words stretch out between Dori and me. The words cover the sea but it's impossible to walk along these bridges, the water won't bear us. There isn't enough, in stories there isn't enough. "I sank beneath the water, Dori," I sign out of habit, facing an open window and not even the squirrels on the tree grant me a look. But my little sister won't save me. Not her. Look at me and see who I have become.

I'm Lili Ackerman. And you?

## DORI

There's a limit to what you can expect from people, as perhaps Dori especially understood. She sat facing the camera and fixed her collar. Not that it did much good, because the wrinkle was set deep into the fabric and a slight smell of sweat still came from her despite all the hand-washing that she had almost gotten used to. And that wasn't the only thing she'd been forced to get used to in the non-technological universe where she'd voluntarily settled down.

But these were trifles, so everyone said, trifles that are easy to adjust to following a certain effort. Slowly the body recovers, the stiff relaxes, the heavy lightens, the worthless takes on value. Many described the calm that took hold of them from the moment they dedicated themselves to the place, since they disconnected from the oppressive, monotonous buzz of electricity and electrons. Everyone signed the same words, "rest," "calm," "relaxation," and "quiet," and Dori nodded distractedly, even though it was all the same to them whether she nodded or not.

She turned on the webcam herself. No, technology wasn't desirable, was contaminating even, but two cameras were the exception. The camera in front of which Dori sat was located in a locked room outside the complex, a nonidentical twin of the other camera, which was hidden in an old mailbox and filmed a field where only weeds grew. Mostly she sat there together with Alex, on two unassuming wooden chairs that folded easily. Lotti spread out an embroidered tablecloth over the school table and set down a vase with flowers; Alex refused any more than this. But the vase was usually empty, and Alex and Dori agreed that neither of them was interested in flowers.

He signed to her and she looked at him, and when it was her turn, she would sign or speak according to the sign he had given her, according to the spirit that had moved him. Recently she had taken to calling him Alex and not Father, and ignored the honorary titles that were attached to him in the complex, whereas he called her Dori and this name, which was signed with the first letter, seemed strange on his fingers. The camera showed only her, although there were a few broadcasts that transmitted the tips of Alex's fingers. They were extremely rare and there were those who said that they had already become a collector's item. But of course they were exaggerating. In any case, Alex claimed that their broadcast had many fans, all willing to watch the empty field that the additional camera filmed for days on end, waiting for his word. There was even someone who watched them in China, as Alex had discovered a few days earlier, even though Dori was certain that the viewer was a bored diplomat or at best an exiled goods importer who'd gone out to make his fortune and actually meant to visit a lingerie website with a name similar to that of their own. But Alex imagined a Chinese farmer blinking toward the horizon, fleeing from the infinite rice fields to the sight of their very finite field.

Dori's camera, as they had gotten used to calling it, recorded and broadcasted once or at most twice a week. If Alex was absent for unknown reasons, Dori read the simple messages that he wrote to her on wrinkled lined paper. She mostly preferred to read them aloud, expecting each time that her voice would sound strange and alien in her ears, but each time the voice sounded clean as in the past, as in the studio, where Ada was her mirror. She read without skipping over a single comma. She reported to the empty space on the jewelry and organic fruit featured for sale, on the dedicated girl who salvaged dolls and toys, restored their painted faces, and gave birth to clean, unblemished plastic girls and boys without uniforms or makeup. When she was required to speak aloud, Dori read all this with a blank expression. But mostly she went back to her mother tongue and signed. Sometimes in his messages Alex emphasized the Western world's dependence on technology and discussed the blessed return to simplicity and silence. Once, in another life, he'd explained to Lili and Dori that the deaf were merely deaf to the vanities of this world, deaf to its numerous flaws. With absolute seriousness he signed that were the world to make a perfect sound of goodness and kindness, they would certainly hear it. As much as she searched between the lines, there wasn't a trace of those old messages in the new. In their place came new words, shadowless sentences, explanations that struck her as stupid. But she knew that deafness was a great virtue, and the rustles she nevertheless sometimes perceived, the sounds she tried not to hear but that infiltrated her defenses, she mercilessly drowned inside her.

Dori remembered the first time she understood that what she was hearing was music. The chills, the knowledge that her bones could play it. This was one of the uncles' tiny birds, inside of which, as she understood only when she told Anton about it later, Uncle Noah had hidden a music box's simple mechanism. She thought that the bird had played something banal, an ice cream man's song. She tried to repeat it into Anton's ears but fell silent. She tried to repeat it to her own ears. Dori held it between her two hands in their old room, as if she could crush it accidentally, as if it could fly away, as if it could sing again. She hoped that it would sing again. This bird disappeared quicker than the others even though Dori hid it. Whereas now she no longer knew how to banish the sounds as she once had, they insisted on clinging to her like crabs to a rock.

Again she heard sounds from the outside, children and a dog. On the farm there was no need for plugs, and when a noise sounded she wasn't ready for it and again, like a novice, she tensed up. The few noises were created by children, who never tired of building improvised vehicles that made dull noises. Most of them were confiscated, since, despite everything, there was someone to hear them, someone whose quiet was very much disturbed. Mostly everything was so quiet, perhaps like in space, as she sometimes thought. The few rustlings that were made were gentle and natural, whereas the sounds that she had gotten used to hopping over like obstacles—cars rattling, the exhalations of buses' heavy engines, horns and motorcycles, someone braking with a screech, leaf blowers, noises of air conditioners, personal computers, loud televisions, and cell phones making varied sounds and amplifying the human voice searching for a response, planes breaking the speed of sound—all these were utterly absent. As if all the world's sounds had sunk into the sea, were swimming in a bathtub emptied of its water.

She said to him in the bathtub, "We are eternal," and he laughed and she knew nevertheless that their love was deep and ancient, like an apple that always recalls the previous apple that was eaten, an infinite chain of apples, even if she didn't know who was the apple and who the eater in her parable, and she just observed that miracle, how her leg wrapped around his leg beneath the sparse foam and the light hair on his bare legs moved slowly in the water. But instead of continuing to look or to kiss or to be, Dori just spoke about eternity.

In her mind, the two of them were gods who ate anything but apples. But it wasn't so. In fact, Dori desperately wanted that moment that already had been, that transformed before her eyes from present to past. Already then she felt robbed of him, she knew how it would end, and she listened to the music that was being played from somewhere, coming in through windows that were always opened wider at night, a guitar solo that went on endlessly and lacked any special beauty, but at that moment it was beautiful and they too, despite her efforts to ruin things, were beautiful. Anton, who was also immersed in the music, announced, "It's impossible to imagine that once, when you didn't hear it, you truly didn't hear." And for a moment that guitar sounded incredibly beautiful, perhaps from the force of his words, and Dori shrugged her shoulders. "Truly."

"Sit straight, Dori," Alex signed, and Dori blushed. Again she remembered Anton, who told her to lie on her back and she obeyed. When was that, weeks or months ago? It seemed that years covered over that past, the college, the piles of cards. Despite this she could instantly see her naked body in his eyes, as if each blue eye reflected one of her breasts. Dori undoubtedly reddened and the heat spread even to the shirt's neckline and along with it the redness. Even if her father missed the chameleon-like change in colors on her body and her face, the camera was likely to capture this too. She tugged again at her shirt and recoiled from herself even though the camera didn't transmit smells.

When she sees the edited broadcast she'll be convinced that she looks exactly like she always does in these broadcasts, relaxed, serious, and almost sweet. A portrait from another century set in an ornamental pin. The only daughter of Alex Ackerman, known by many as Father. And also the daughter of Anna Ackerman, about whom they no longer speak.

The children burst into the improvised studio. Someone, that is, Dori, again had forgotten, that is, forgot, to lock the door. And Dori gazed at the two boys and the girl who was a head taller than them and at their beautiful dog, a brushed-out collie who was better groomed than the three of them put together. She looked at them with an affection in which there was also envy. They were as naked and tan as savages except for the underwear with drawings of angry birds. All of them proudly petted the body of the well-groomed collie, which smiled a canine smile at Dori. She knew that these kids had tried previously to raise a guide dog but the loud spoken commands had disturbed many residents of the farm and this came to an end. The children had quickly and with aptitude grasped the signs and the language, as each of them demonstrated, but nevertheless more than once dropped off into speaking and even shouting. Dori asked them if they wanted chocolate and they signed, "Yes." She opened the drawer of the green table and extended a package to the girl. "Share equally but don't give to the collie," she said, and the girl exposed a mouth with especially small teeth and offered a smile that looked like a perfect imitation of the dog's and ran off laughing almost silently with the others following after her. "You didn't have to do that," signed Alex, who reprimanded the children for the noise they had made. Dori shrugged her shoulders, but all the same when she looked at him she signed, "Sorry."

## LILI

I still watch them as the dead watch the living, if indeed they can, if they're desperate to return in whatever body and role, be it as beggars, as thieves, as the world's fools. I look at them with all the lenses that technology has convened for me, observing how their kingdom is built every day. I want to believe that it's because of them. That only because of them I'm unable to avert my gaze. But what do you know, it's my independent behavior. Free will. Enough years now I've wandered without them, a satellite drifting in space. Stop blaming the parents, oh Lili Marlene. I look at them the way you look at a school of sharks that was left behind in an abandoned center underwater, only the cameras serving as company. I look at them as I look at my few patients, miserable and scratching and waiting on my word. I can't help any of them and nevertheless I am what they need, a pair of eyes to look at them without filling up with tears.

This house is strange to me. In this house I'm forever a guest praising the décor. Sentenced to good manners even though I'm here alone. Between two and four I arrange tours of the big house for myself, a guide gesturing with her hands at a host of lovely spots, practicing foreign accents as if I were again a seventeen-year-old with fleeting aspirations of becoming an actress; here's the rustic kitchen, the family room, the guest wing, I behave again as I did in those days when I believed what they said about me. Sometimes Jenna arrives and rolls around from laughter and the two of us pretend that she doesn't own the house, or is actually the owner's beloved niece who put this house at my disposal. She no longer asks me when I'll return to the city, no longer pretends that my miserable therapist career is worth a thing, just brings sweet desserts, loaded with berries I can't bear to eat. We speak

English. Lili talks about herself in third person, immigrated to the world of the hearing.

Only in Alex and Anna's house did I know every lump of plaster. Every cracked tile in our room, every stain that would never be removed from the doorpost, but would instead be joined by additional stains. My disappearances, as Dori called them, began by chance. It started the time I was locked out of the house. The hours passed. Who knows where everyone was. I never asked. Once I got sick of waiting in the doorway, driving out the cats that gathered by the refrigerator, I got up and left. When I reached the old cultural center I was as surprised as someone who discovers a palace in a fairy tale: grandeur in the heart of the wilderness, a mostly demolished palace, plastered in gray, true, but even then it was without a doubt the most beautiful structure I'd seen in my life. The damage caused by time only emphasized its natural splendor, the elongated windows, the carved lion's head set on the roof. The lion's eyes were painted in an opaque, phosphorescent, sloppy orange. The lion saw nothing and the structure itself was scribbled with writings and drawings that, I understood, were meant to be vulgar, but even then I saw in them something exciting and even touching. That the quickly drawn anatomical sketches just wanted to be applauded, to be worthy of eternity like that peculiar blinded lion. The letters that joined into words in a language I didn't know enchanted me. Yes, my first impulse was to bring Dori there. We shared everything, whether or not we wanted to. But that evening, and maybe it was pure coincidence, I didn't tell her a thing about it. That's how it was and that's how it remained.

I wasn't the only one who encountered that structure. Plans were made for it, hidden plans; there were other interested parties beyond me. I discovered that some of Alex's ducks had a habit of going there, but when we ran into each other we acted like strangers, satellites momentarily separated from the fathership. They informed me that the structure existed on borrowed time, that the climbing plants and raspberry bushes would grow there for a limited time only. That the moment the money passed from one pocket to another all this would likely disappear altogether. I assume that since then the land has been flattened and sold, that something was probably erected on it. But at that time it was a kind of demilitarized zone that no one claimed ownership of other than us, and couples momentarily looking for a place far from everything; kids with cap guns; wanderers; a few emaciated homeless people who came and went. Once I even saw a herd of goats grazing there. Maybe I went there only so I'd have somewhere to go. But both there and on the way there I was never without an awareness that caught me by the back of the neck like a mother cat grasping kittens. I always knew: Here I am. I'm Lili Ackerman. I'm here. Now I'm walking, now I'm sitting down on the rounded cement steps, now I'm breathing, now time isn't moving. Now.

After the land rest, I went there almost every day. Such that after I met Uriel I called him to come there with me. To this day I can't say why him, because truthfully it would have been better to ask Dima to come with me, without acting as if I was lighthearted and as full of mischief as the spring wind. That day I wore a long skirt and the thistles got stuck on it. With the back of my hand I wiped away Anna's clear lip gloss that I'd found. My gesture was more than he was ready to accept. It would have been better to let things go, to let him woo and myself be wooed, but I said to him: come.

The air was blazing and embers stood in it, proclaiming a future fire that would spread through the great many thistles. Uriel complained about an annoying pain in his leg; I laughed when he imagined bloodsucking parasites and ticks among the thorns.

Very quickly he grew impatient, and even when he tried to joke around I saw that he was dying to leave, that this rickety structure I'd presented to him seemed to him out of a nightmare. I ignored his discomfort. I drew away the spiderwebs and pointed at the view. One after another I presented to him the old notices, full of exclamation marks, that remained from the time when bands still performed there, the illustrated coulisses I found stored in one of the rooms with the rot climbing over them. The more he looked at it with scorn the more I insisted, sure, they hadn't been drawn with great skill, but with considerable investment. Love, even.

Finally I said to him, "Look up," and showed him the lion's head, the stone mane and the mouth open in a mute roar. Almost against his will a whistle escaped; he loved to whistle, but then he said, "That's fake, you know." I spread my hands out to the sides, the fingers grasped air and closed, my arms joined each other, hugging just me. Uriel kicked at the cigarette butts left on the ground and a bag full of rotting oranges. With the third kick the bag ripped open and a foul juice covered his white gym shoes. He looked at me as if I had put the bag there. When he said, "I'm going," I walked a step behind him. I didn't look back at the lion with the eyes pecked out. I had hoped he would see what I saw, that he would suggest we put on a production there, a play, *A Midsummer Night's Dream* or *A Winter's Tale*, but he didn't and so neither did I.

Uriel, of course, started investigations and inquiries. Two days later he arrived smiling and explained to me that it was a drug den and if I didn't want to fall into the hands of a local gang or a druggie going through withdrawal then it was best to take myself elsewhere. It was clear he was proud of the terms he tossed out into the air with a showy nonchalance that didn't suit him. I knew the druggies he was talking about. I heard their words enunciated slowly, trudging along, mangled from the first syllable. But I was certain that at the least they didn't constantly think: Now I'm getting up, now I'm scratching my right cheek, flinging my hair and gathering it back up, now my neck is stiff and wooden. Now I'm imagining that I'm somewhere else, living a different life, now I'm still here here here.

After the conversation with Uriel I didn't return there. The taste faded and ever since I've barely thought about the place. Uriel, for his part, told me about Europe, about the beauty of the Old World, about cities where carved lions can be seen all over, where fountains spray water onto Poseidon's barefoot sons, standing among sculpted coral and fish, and on every gable you can see angels peeking over the back of a tired, naked boy made of stone. We'll travel there together, he said. But those stone lads and maidens remained misty, dust-clad, all of them bearing Uriel's smiling visage.

When I watch the broadcasts from the farm, which is nothing but the old house bloated and renamed, officially and in complete earnestness, "Tranquility," I discover that the broadcasts themselves take place in that old cultural center. I recognize the color of the walls, the straight angles, and something else that the camera somehow manages to capture. After hours of viewing it becomes clear to me that what was for me a secret never really was one. Even this was revealed and exposed to everyone's eyes. She's frozen in her stiff clothing, collar buttoned, hair skewed to the side, extended over the right ear, and when she reads aloud or signs, her eyes look almost transparent. "Can you hear, Little One?" I turn up the voice of Dori suddenly erupting through the computer speakers. "Can you hear?" Her ears are already developed enough by the twentieth week and I know that she can also hear the world that exists beyond the beating of my heart. "Can you hear that voice? That's your aunt."

## DORI

It all started accidentally. Dori didn't plan on returning home, certainly not like heroes return, their bodies adorned with battle scars. It's actually the first scar carved into their flesh that enables identification; the years have passed and the countenance stiffened, but someone will nevertheless recognize them with surprise. Dori bore no scars and her skin didn't say a thing about her. She didn't even return as girls or women return in their bad years, wretched and familiar with suffering, their backs bent, their hair gathered in a flimsy ponytail. Women forced to pay the price. She still looked, at least from a certain distance, like a child. In fact, she almost looked like she always had.

When they reached the farm at noon, Anati, who until then had driven in silence, began to sing. In a jovial voice she sang that song from *The Sound of Music* when the children say goodbye to the guests in song and with sweet mannerisms. Dori laughed at the imitation of the Von Trapp family and said to her, as if she didn't know, "I always hated that movie too." Over her shoulder she slung the nylon bag, which contained mostly sweaters and books, and said goodbye with a kiss on Anati's cheek, to her friend's amazement and pleasure. When she started walking she knew without looking back that Anati still stood there proudly, supported by her new crutches next to the shiny car that she'd bought with the settlement money from the zoo. Anati shouted to her heartily, "Dori, you lunatic," and launched a kiss into the air, and Dori, with cramped shoulders, nevertheless turned around and sent a kiss as well.

But only when she was walking on the paved path that once was firm sand and gravel did she realize that she was still wearing the phosphorescent purple exercise shoes that belonged to Anati, who hadn't commented on this even once. The pairs of eyes followed her until she stood on the doorstep of the house, which thanks only to its location was she able to identify as the house of then. It seemed no one had a doubt about who she was. If any of them wondered and asked with a quick sign, who's this, they learned without delay that it was the daughter.

Dori ignored the crowd that escorted her along with more friendliness than expected and stood there like a student before an important test, waiting for some clear feeling to direct her, an inner compass pointing to nausea or dizziness, or a dread rising up in her throat because she was once again in this place, in the house that was almost only the stuff of proverbs. She stood at the edge of the black hole that was always present in conversations and silences with Georgia O'Keeffe, in the stories she told Anton. Georgia certainly would see in these latest events the consequences of her recklessness. To be again, without any defense, in this place, which wasn't proverbial at all. She was as irresponsible as someone handing a girl a box of matches. And to continue with this simile, Dori was, without a doubt, less the responsible adult than she was, still, the girl.

No fire was lit there. The uprightness she'd adopted switched within moments to her permanently lowered stature. But even so, her wandering eyes met the rhymed blessing that Lotti, or some creature resembling Lotti, had embroidered and hung on a nail. When they were still four and she was the littlest among them, they undoubtedly would have mocked such domestic idolatry. But Dori stood and read the lines embroidered in red stitching. THROUGH THIS DOOR, SORROW NO MORE; IN THIS HOME, SICKNESS WON'T ROAM. The writing was decorated with angels wearing loincloths, which were nothing more than tied-up diaper fabric that would definitely fall off during the first flight, if their chubby bodies could lift off at all. THROUGH THIS DOORWAY SHALL COME NO DISMAY. And out of the most ancient of habits she wanted to raise her eyebrows, as if searching for a partner for her feelings. Almost involuntarily she looked for Anton, who at that moment must have been far away, in some cathedral of money or knowledge, buried in a computer screen. But the one who raised his eyebrow in front of her was actually her father. Not even his thick beard could cover up the playful expression that flashed across his face, and in that tiny moment, Dori understood that her brief visit would be extended. She was back home.

Afterward, when she detailed her experiences, skipping over the period of the institution, focusing on academia of all things, asking for his approval after everything, she was surprised to realize just how little her father knew of what she had done. Only then did she realize that she had always suspected that someone was reporting to him about her life, that her father was indeed far away from her for legal and political reasons, but his disguised emissaries were informing him about everything she did, writing letters to him that he would eagerly read.

Dori looked at him in confusion as he patiently asked her a few questions that had nothing to do with anything. He asked her about the old bank branch, if she knew how to write a check. Dori signed yes but stuck to the facts. The facts and only the facts and nothing but them: she had been lost to them for years. She knew this clearly. And she pushed their grief away, deflected it from herself, and the very act of pushing away proved that there was something concrete that she had to prevent from getting in. She knew that the two of them had inflicted heavy damage on her and therefore she continuously pushed away pictures of her mother weeping and her father standing over her, helpless. But this diligent labor, "years of work," as Georgia called it, crumbled easily. Fact: Dori saw her father for the first time in more than a decade and a half, and without him speaking about it she knew that the exhaustion and age that had creeped up on him were nothing but a different dress for sorrow, another name for the sadness that enveloped him because she'd disappeared as she had. Because she hadn't returned when she could have. And he mourned that she remained beyond the field of his supervision until the mourning transformed into a better day and a blessed time and the new life he established on the farm.

The indifference that would characterize her father in the coming days would also be but an expression of the confidence that always nested inside him. He always knew his daughter would return to him just as Dori now had, in borrowed shoes, without a clear future and trained in a dubious profession that was nothing but the human version of a mimicking parrot. A stupid parrot on a ship of fools. Dori pictured what was about to happen, how for her too the world beyond the farm would gradually lose its shine and she'd remember that everything around her was all that really mattered. She waited patiently for her father to sign things resembling her thoughts. How with a few decisive sentences he'd separate the wheat from the chaff, the pinky from the rest of the feeble fingers. She already started to nod, intending like the others to raise her open palms and move them in mute applause. But her father patted his thigh with his heavy hand and with the other signed, "Good, good." The conversation quickly returned to the house, which was called, according to rules that Dori was unable to get to the bottom of, at times "The Farm," and at times "Tranquility." Either way, it became clear to her, the place had blossomed. They enjoyed not insignificant successes. An organic farm. Volunteers and advanced instruction in the language. They were a refuge for those upon whom the noise of the world took an unimaginable toll. "We went through the front door," he signed proudly, and pointed at the framed newspaper clipping about the farm and the community achievement award. The photograph that claimed most of the article's allotted columns showed her father shaking hands with a heavily bearded man. The two of them appeared quite pleased.

"Where's Mom," she asked suddenly, without a question mark. As if only at that moment had she noticed her absence. Her father clapped his hands and replied, "Here, there, she's without a doubt somewhere," and to reinforce matters he pointed in opposite directions. How old he looked at that moment, old, frail, and kindhearted, an old man harming no one, a friend of the flies, bees, and ants, not the man who raised her to work her way in by taking advantage of the stupidity of the masses.

Lotti glanced gloomily at him, wringing her hands together before signing again. Only now did Dori notice how much she had swelled up. She had always been chubby, but now she bore her weight as a kind of honor. Her hair had been trimmed and gone gray, bracelets covered her wrists, and her dress offered surplus fabric to any who might ask. You could clothe an entire family in that dress with a sail to spare, she thought, not knowing why she hated her so, her round face, her crude hands, and her thick ankles. She remembered her tendency, which had something heartbreaking about it, to concern herself with life's trifles, with cleaning faucets and folding napkins, as well as with her father's health. And indeed, her black eyes narrowed in their holes and her freckled, heavily wrinkled face now expressed admonishing concern. She signed that there was a problem with her father's blood pressure, so why annoy him for nothing? She'd had enough of Dori's unnecessary questions; there was chicken in the oven. Dori knew that she'd be unable to eat a thing served to her there and smiled with great effort. At least someone fulfilled their desire to the end, she thought, and imagined Lotti cracking young chicken bones in her teeth that were, as far as she could tell, as strong as ever. Lotti had finally found her longed-for place beside her father, like a cat beside the hearth.

Days later she would try to understand if her father's raised eyebrow was an expression of deep insight or a moment of conspiring between old allies. The father and the daughter, a fearless duo. She told herself that this was exactly what it was, a flicker of clarity among all the embroidered pillows and organic squashes piled up on all sides. Perhaps Dori forgot those times, the precious ones, that they'd spent together in perfect harmony. Indeed, she was the first one he told about his childhood in the cellar. Indeed, there were the Wednesday trips in the metal truck when her father decreed that Dori had a sense of smell for finding metal, and Dori carried this praise close to her heart like an old decoration that shone brightly again when given the slightest rub.

She had no pity for her mother at all. When she thought about her, she seemed like an elegant watercolor painted on a silk canvas, fluttering in the distance, a canvas no one would ever wrap himself up in or use to sew anything useful. Neither the efforts of Georgia O'Keeffe nor the inquiries of Anton, whose mother was the steadiest element in his world, changed her mind. Despite her familiar sobbing, the tears that flowed down her face almost constantly, her mother never gave herself over to them completely; parts of her were always kept beyond the reach of Lili's and Dori's little hands. Sometimes Dori forgot the color or shape of her eyes or the way she looked at Dori with utter hopelessness. But how could she forget? It was pointless, considering that for more than a third of her life she saw her anguished face morning and night. Lili would say to her, "What do you want, she looks like you." But their mother, for all her flaws and tears, was beautiful.

Dori still stood in her spot, a few steps away from the blessed entry, even though Lotti again suggested she sit down. Almost nothing remained as it had been, but nevertheless this was the house, in which there were now many places to sit. Their old

room had been turned into a room for thinking, which was des-
ignated not only for her father, Lotti pointed out, but rather for
the entire community that sought to consult with Father. And
when Dori stared at her she signed, "Father, your father." All
these years later her sign language was still awful. A young girl
with a wise gaze, who later on they explained was Lotti's niece,
stuck a glass of lemonade in her hand. She drank the flavorless
juice and didn't know what to do with the empty glass until the
girl returned and took it from her. Her father began dozing off
in his chair and Dori recalled the story about the man who had
mice living in his beard and thought about telling it to the girl
with the serious face. She laughed, a laugh that seemed to die out
before it made a sound, because she was the only clear witness to
its existence. As she quickly discovered, even the hearing in this
place preferred to ignore superfluous sounds.

"We kept your dolls," Lotti signed to her as if Dori were still
a girl, and sent the niece to bring her a cardboard box decorated
with faded drawings of mermaids. Dori rummaged among the
painted smiles, the plastic and porcelain limbs. Beneath these she
saw a few of Uncle Noah's creations that had remained whole despite the years. She suddenly recognized something dandyish in
his design, in the initials "N.A.," Noah Ackerman, which were also
signed on the tiny bottoms of the toys. She removed two children
from matchbooks and a pink fish, which were covered in a layer of
dust that wasn't typical of this house, like a kind of projection from
the previous house, which one couldn't even long for. Dori swore
that the fish now resting in her palm was once blue. Green, perhaps. "These are all my sister's," she said. When she encountered a
blank stare she emphasized again, "They're Lili's, I lost mine some
time ago." But Lotti pretended not to notice and plumped up a few
pillows that required no plumping, while her father was already in

a deep sleep. Only the girl looked at her with interest, as if learning for the first time of Lili Ackerman's existence.

## LILI

Almost against my will I'm counting the weeks until you're born. In the workroom that I insist on not entering, bundles of towels, sheets, cloth diapers, and tiny baby clothes pile up. Jenna and Mikala bring them. Jenna, thanks to whom I live here, even though she still pretends that I'm doing her a favor, mainly brings me gifts of dubious utility, rattles of pure silver, embroidered designer baby socks. Mikala worries about more practical things, insists on going over the birth plan with me again and again. She's also the one who reminds me that I have a life to get back to, referring to the tiny clinic in which I rented space as if it were a valid career and life option. She reminds me of our shared studies, even though I survived them thanks mainly to her. It was our deafness that connected us, three students in a full hall, even if to the world we seem like we hear or half-hear. But what kept us connected to one another couldn't be seen or touched.

While they arrange the bundles, compare lists, look at each other with worried faces, I look at the field. Not at the view outside the house, but rather at the empty field the webcam films from their stupid farm. It's not the field that we sat in during our childhood, trying to respond to Alex's delusions of grandeur, seeing flames on the horizon, taking an active part in the prophecy. Had they asked me then, I would have said I saw them. Every natural disaster that Alex envisioned, I saw too. But the current camera films a different field. Sometimes people appear in it, not farmers, God forbid, rather those who come in private to sit alone with nature. I don't recognize most of them, but from time to time Lotti arrives. It's impossible to mistake her even though she's heavier than in the past, wearing a printed dress, her hair trimmed close to her scalp, and like a seasoned farmer she sits down among the stubble with an expression of almost embarrassingly intimate relief. She closes her eyes, her face, ruined from a lifetime of injuries, still conveying pleasure. There's no doubt she's aware of the camera's existence, but I doubt if anyone watches the broadcast other than me.

Jenna is busy with the question of whether or not the girl will hear. She's equipped with statistics attesting to a high probability of the baby having at most partial hearing. After all, both of my parents are deaf from birth. Yes, I answer, even though I'm not at all certain about even that. I've been presented more than once with contradictory evidence regarding their mysterious pasts. Nevertheless I mostly preferred to retell only what was told to me. Even if the cellar never existed, I find myself reporting on it like a family memory, like a line engraved on one's palm. It was there and that's that. Enough with the stories I know. On the basis of those stories, I've moved on. On the basis of those stories, I told my few clients that it's possible to live with contradictions, with lies. But to Jenna and Mikala I've mainly told the truth. And the truth is that I don't know. There's not one thing I could say that I know without a doubt about the two people who raised us, the two who had the labels *father* and *mother* attached to them. Despite everything, I don't know either of them.

## DORI

Ogden was chopping trees behind the house. The years were visible on him, in the hair that had gone entirely gray but still rested in a kind of emperor haircut around his face, which resembled the face of a mastiff, in the hands full of bulging veins. He wasn't harmful, Dori knew; he was never harmful. But suddenly the name *duck*, which came to mind when she saw him for the first time in years, in the tall grass (because after all she thought *Here's a duck* well before she thought *Here's Ogden*), seemed meaningless to her. The swinging of the ax was strong and rhythmic. These were the motions of a young man, even though Dori remembered him as an older man back then too. Ogden himself didn't appear surprised by Dori's presence in the place; the ax continued to strike at the same rhythm, as if a small girl hadn't left there, accompanied by flashing lights and sirens that perhaps none of them had heard, and now returned. She had already noticed that this was how almost everyone who knew her from the past was treating her. Warmly but without excitement. One might think that Dori had been absent for only an hour or two, that she had returned from a brief visit to a nearby town, that she stopped to buy gum or knee socks. But she was no longer one of them. Only the new ones still looked at her with eyes wide with wonder and amazement, as if in a moment she'd turn water into wine. "This is for the tourists," he signed to her about the ax, "your father's idea." And indeed Dori saw a not-so-young couple in bright clothes on a straw swing nearby. With expressions of intent seriousness, the two of them gently swung, gripping identical mugs of tea and watching Ogden formally. "Welcome," he signed, and out of habit she translated aloud. It seemed to her that she recognized irony in the expression of his face, but when he finished signing he went back to chopping the wood.

Facing Ogden's orderly pile of wood, she finally understood the essence of the change that had taken place at home. Everything in the area was meticulously built from natural materials or at least covered in them as if due to a categorical local imperative, an emergency regulation that left no trace of any visible metal object in the region. The Iron Age was rejected entirely in favor of a rounder, wooden time, blooming slightly, a perfect setting for Lotti's awful cakes and even her father's white beard, if not for he who lived beneath it. To the naked eye it appeared that the farm and all its inhabitants had neglected no cranny in a meticulous weave of naturalness. The house as well as the few structures she could see were built as uniform facades of wood and raffia, products of simple craftsmanship, straw, and homey embroidery. The farm never stopped affirming village life, a simple life that shunned toxins and stood on the threshold of tranquility. It looked like the tourists, at least, understood this, and perhaps it was all really intended for them. Dori doubted it all. Her father hadn't abandoned metal for their sake, not he, who collected it almost as if on a mission, never mind that he later sold it for a hefty price. Like metal, he knew how to escape and blend into the ordinary alloy just as he always went back to his glittering self, and like every metal expert he knew how to run hot and cold and hide the valuable under a cheap veneer. This entire return to nature couldn't have been to his liking. At most he must have grudgingly gotten used to it. Because even then it was their mother who insisted on growing her ridiculous garden.

Dori thought sadly about the beautiful metals they left behind, as if the years hadn't passed and a mountain of iron intended just for her stood a touch away. And now it suddenly vanished and was gone. Her fingers could still sense the cool touch of the steel, caress the brass rods, skip over the dark taste the lead stored, tarry with the impure alloys she actually liked for being complex and composite, with a low market value. Lines stubbornly stuck in her head, as if she had no words of her own at all: "And last of all the ruthless and hard Age of Iron prevailed, from which malignant vein great evil sprung; and modest and faith and truth took flight," she mumbled, a bit proud in spite of herself that she'd remembered the lines even if she couldn't remember when and how she read them. What was more, this time she didn't have Georgia O'Keeffe's eyes to defy with words, words, words.

Because the words were Dori's and as such there was no one to doubt her. Not in a place where words didn't change a thing. Signed words, words spoken aloud, words read in a book or on a bill with a bottom line. They were attributed to her out of habit or proximity or error, like a feature of her features, and it didn't matter to anyone if Dori's pages were entirely blank. Perhaps she wrote words only because no one wanted them other than her, and in Lotti's book everyone must do something, even write. She had forgotten that Dori knew how to be Alex's voice and hands, that Dori knew many things (at least she herself believed this) and not just one. But by virtue of that same mistake Dori was rechristened as "Alex's daughter who writes." It was only natural that she was introduced like that to Idit, who was herself given the description "dear friend."

If Lotti hadn't been Lotti and Dori hadn't been Dori, the latter would have been liable to be confused and think that Lotti was proud of her, that she was making this introduction to Dori out of some impression of her character. But everything was utterly clear to Dori. When Lotti introduced Idit to her, in the courtyard of her and Alex's house, in the place that was once a vegetable garden, she interlaced her arm with Idit's sturdy arm and hopped back a step. All her movements, which Dori recognized and knew to be authentic, communicated that this was a splendid honor. The neck of her dear friend was adorned in stiff brown and golden necklaces, her body was wrapped in muslin fabrics like a giant diaper, and on her feet were crude wooden clogs. From her hand hung a large basket full of binders. Her entire appearance rang of

poetry. Idit, as it turned out, oversaw the farm for the local council, but with time had become Lotti's confidante and a dear friend
of the whole farm.

All this became clear to her. At first Dori didn't know if Idit
was very naive like Lotti, or very evil and very fervent like Lotti,
and only afterward did she understand that this woman was an
egg sitting on a stone wall, singing her songs and never falling
down. Because in addition to the lines of poetry she recited for
ears that were deaf due to volition, effort, or necessity, it seemed
there were a few official budgets mixed up in the matter.

Idit looked at Dori with a secretive smile. "So you're the sinful
daughter!" she announced in a raised voice that sounded like the
ringing of a school bell, decisive and cheerful and violent. Weeks
had passed since Dori heard a voice speak other than her own,
when she translated Alex's speech into enunciated words, such
that she almost didn't pay attention to the content of the words.
"Sinful!" the dear friend Idit repeated, scattering exclamation
marks around, and Dori thought about Hester Prynne and the
fiery letter that she sewed onto her dress. She had always been
dramatic, and here was someone even more dramatic than her.

"The sin of writing!" she declared again with overt bliss when
she understood that Dori had missed the point, and her necklaces
accompanied her with a rattling sound.

"I mainly read," Dori said after some time, even though she
didn't know if this was true.

Idit looked at her the way one looks at a strange animal, say,
a three-legged cat. "I myself am beyond reading," she explained
calmly. "I read and I read and I read until that was it. Enough for
me. I discovered that there were too many books in the world."
Her Roman nose fluttered aggressively but her hands were
crossed under her chest, as though she intended to sing an aria.
Pleasure shone from her, full and round. Her skin went pink like

the skin of a well-pampered baby. "And in general," she added, "if I read, I prefer not to understand. Isn't it more pleasant not to understand?" Lotti nodded vigorously as if hearing words of extreme wisdom, forgetting for a moment the pact of the deaf, and Dori wondered how Lotti's loyalties were divided between Alex and the philosopher facing her. No way can Alex stand her, she thought. No way.

"I prefer to understand," Dori said. With a smooth motion, as if her hand had extended greatly and became a swaying, eel-like arm, Idit grabbed the book Dori was holding, a book that Dori had grown used to carrying around like an umbrella, even though it didn't rain. Idit opened it at random, reached out a finger, and came to rest on a line of text. She read with emphasis, breathing between the words, "The French have already come and gone." Then she closed the book with a kiss and gazed victoriously at Dori. Her watery eyes sparkled, the makeup shining below them.

"Why, that's wonderful," she said. "That's absolutely enough. I could wander around that line for many days."

No, thought Dori, no and no, but her thoughts were unreadable on her face. Not when she thought, you cow, and not when she thought, idiot. And in her rage she wondered why Idit of all people had aroused her anger. Suddenly it was clear to her that it was actually this heavy woman, with the wooden and amber jewelry and the authority that flowed from her, authority that had no basis at all, she was the woman whom Alex needed. She was the woman he was supposed to marry. But instead of embracing her and calling her Mom, she thought what a shame that Anton wasn't there to laugh with her about this, and what a shame Lili wasn't. And what a shame about all those who were gone and what a shame that no ammunition was given to her against that carefree expression, which called on her to let go of meaning, of the flimsy rope connecting form to content. Only the buzzing of the flies could be heard clearly and it competed with the distant whisper of generators.

Now Idit walked proudly in the apple orchard, her wooden clogs almost sinking in the muddy earth. Dori saw her upright figure hidden and disappearing among the trunks and Lotti panting a step behind her. Ogden rose above the ax and looked at the two of them and then shrugged his shoulders. Sweat gathered on the nape of his reddened neck. Instead of wiping it off he turned to Dori. "Your mother's house," he signed, "it's in a development area, on the other side."

"Is it far?" she asked, and he signed the distance.

"And is she there?" Dori took her time when asking a trick question.

"She's there," he confirmed. "I brought her apples this morning."

Her parents lived separately. That's how they were, not Alex and Anna Ackerman, not a single, monolithic unit. She had understood this even before she stood across from her father's white beard and Lotti's sovereign gaze.

Dori had made sure not to know a thing about them, nothing following the moment she was removed from them, as if a period was marked at the end of a sentence, after the word *end*. Because what happened afterward, to Dori and definitely to them, occurred in another life in which it was possible to divorce and marry, to die and to give birth. In that order, actually. There was no past, rich and fertile like a plant that never stopped climbing and winding around the walls of an abandoned heart. She knew what she knew, this couldn't be uprooted from her. But it was healthier to remain separate from what happened afterward. Not every pain must be scraped with a shard.

During the first years Dori thought about them as pillars of sand. Her parents were frozen in time like Lot's wife, since they couldn't help but look toward her with longing. But Lili would never turn into a statue, this she knew. She began picturing them as two, a father made of salt, a mother of sparkling crystal. Afterward Lili wrote to her and the address on the envelope indicated another place, not the village, not the house. The address indicated that Lili had gone away and left her behind. And maybe Dori would have completely forgotten that image, which floated before her eyes just then, no longer a home cut from paper but instead a father and a mother who were frozen face-to-face, if she hadn't now made her way to what was called the development zone. A silent yellow tractor, a technological wonder seemingly landed from another planet, signaled the place with its presence. She touched the hood of the engine that was cold and motionless. The driver had definitely fled for his life so that the locals, lovers of tranquility and pine paneling, didn't pelt him with stones.

During her final years at the school, the pillars of salt ceded their place in her thoughts to a decorated porcelain plate that hung in the office of the boarding school's principal, a souvenir from a trip to Holland. On the plate a father and mother were painted with a paintbrush. Every time she arrived at the office she complimented the principal on the plate and asked to study the details. When she left the boarding school she thought that she'd give it to her as a parting gift. But that didn't happen. Maybe the principal forgot that she promised it to her; maybe it was unpleasant for Dori to ask. Anyway, her blue parents, painted against a country backdrop made in Delft, were left hanging on the wall until the principal was replaced and a bright circle was left in the spot where the plate had once hung.

But anyone looking closely at the plate, as Dori had done more than once or twice, would see that the face of the mother was turned to the ornamented edges, not to the father. She pulled on the straps of her hat and a strange wind stirred. Yes, even with a quick glance at the illustration, one might guess that at the moment he let her, Anna herself would undo the knots and the straps and fly off like a groundsel. She was always willing, like a nomad, like a prostitute, to be taken in by another land. Dori just hadn't supposed that she'd land so close.

"Ackerman" was written on the door. At least there's that, she thought, and felt an inexplicable satisfaction that her mother hadn't gone back to her maiden name. But if the eight letters hadn't appeared there, gold on green, she could have guessed by the garden that the house with the green door was hers. Before she entered the courtyard she set down on the fence the book she was still carrying in her hands.

## LILI

These days are empty and thus good for thinking. Nevertheless they slip away from me one after another. All that is spread out before me is the past, and in an indulgent gesture I read it like tea leaves. Look there, in the upper left corner of the mug—a pentagon shape, a star shape. It's natural that we'd remember we were two dancing stars. It's natural that this is how you remember the game of the disturbed girls that echoed in that house, which had more corners than windows. Look closely at your mug. It's not a star.

We weren't comets, we were satellites, a cluster of metal in space. Look and you'll see clumsy, man-made celestial bodies. True, in the beginning we were the big bang and the little bang, and afterward a black hole and a white dwarf. Sometimes we were glaciers like the icy centaurs orbiting the sun, the first of which was discovered exactly in the year I was born. We didn't have clear rules for the game, but we never got it wrong. You remember, Dori, there was just running around, there were hands and feet hurled at one another, vast amounts of air that swept around as if a gust of wind had come through the window and threatened to carry the house away. You would say that we were the wind, that we were the running, sisters storm and whirlwind. I'll tell you we were hurt during that running and days later it was possible to see yellow, purple, and black marks on our hands and feet. It really was, but no one looked.

Perhaps I'm lying. That's how we are, fortune-tellers, give me whatever you'll give me and I'll read it, lines and dots, stars and stripes, dry blows and motherships, letters and the absence of mothers. And as for the actual mother, our dear Anna, beautiful, sad Anna, it would only be natural for me to reflect on her now. But I don't think about her at all.

DORI

In the small garden no vegetables or herbs grew that would be of any use. The vertiginous height of the flowers that reached past Dori's waist indicated that this was the residence of the mother with the green thumb. The small garden was filled with birds of paradise and in its middle an upright, fleshy cactus grew. "That's the queen of the night. You're lucky, it's about to bloom one of these nights." Dori heard the voice that had to be that voice. Because Dori could indeed tell herself stories that would last one thousand and one nights; she could dissolve the pillar of salt, decorate and break piles of ornamental plates, bring to life and kill a thousand mermaids with gills and lungs in her imagination, stupid amphibians with an algae's brain, she could do all this; at least, once she could; at least, who she once was could, but her mother's voice she recognized.

They hugged. They hugged as is acceptable after years, when one comes from the cold and the other from the heat, when the east, for instance, meets the west. Even though there was no warmth in the hug. As if two trees were trying to hug—and this is less exciting or pleasant than one might imagine, it's mainly rigid. The quiet tree will move its top without a sound. Mainly it was impossible.

Her mother wore a pink kimono and her hair was gathered up over her head in a high bun. Her eyelids were covered in the blue eye shadow she always liked. Dori didn't know if she woke up just now or was on her way to bed. Either way she was even more beautiful than in the past, although a fine network of capillaries covered her face. The queen of the night in person. She just barely resembled that weeping willow who raised her. "You smoke?" she asked in a hoarse voice and added, "Don't smoke, it ruins your vocal cords." From an oblong pack she removed a cigarette of the brand that teenagers smoke, and nevertheless offered one of them to Dori, who took it and didn't smoke. She knew that they were supposed to talk about Lili, who seemed to be sitting there next to them on the old sofa that the two of them were sure not to sit on, stretching forward her blue boots. Dori didn't sit on the old sofa, which was like a final monument to that old house. She skipped over the questions of what had changed and if her mother was surprised to see her and if she had been searching for her all these years. Someone else might have asked, but not Dori. When she saw her there, thin and ornamental like a candlestick, she understood that her mother really was imprisoned inside a porcelain plate. And perhaps her soul resided in one of Uncle Noah's complex mechanical toys, which to her surprise claimed an entire, glass-encased cabinet there. Because those toys, which were made with the hands of an artist, actually weren't meant for children at all, and perhaps were never meant for her and Lili.

"He continued to visit me," Anna said, "for years. Always

bringing his offerings. Do you remember how you used to break them?"

"Two left hands," Dori said, and Anna Ackerman confirmed, "Yes, exactly." She looked at Dori's hands, which had nevertheless lengthened since and no longer knocked everything over. The toys themselves were spectacular and it appeared that Noah had improved over the years. Dori got up from her seat, placed the cigarette wherever she placed it, and stood facing the display case. There were mermaids with beautiful tails next to two children playing with a ball, the ball moving between them on a metal rail the moment you turned the key on the side of the blue child, and there was a goose. Dori couldn't control herself; she opened the glass cabinet and picked it up with her left hands. When she caressed the tail feathers, the toy stirred in her hand. The goose dropped a golden ball, an egg. "The gold didn't come out like he wanted," Anna noted, "but he was proud of it."

Between two fingers she held the tiny golden egg, on which the teeth of time could be seen. Despite everything, it was perfect. Dori wouldn't have been surprised had an even tinier gosling hatched from it. But there was no gosling.

Then she searched for the birds, the well-known birds that he always made for her and Lili, the last of which was sent to her when she graduated college, the one that revealed the voice buried inside it. But there was no bird. On the top shelf stood a tiny choir with mouths open and Anna was pleased that Dori gave it her attention. All the girls had black braided hair and bright, thin faces. "That's me," Anna said, "all of them are me." But she didn't need to say so, because Dori knew immediately that this was her mother, duplicated as in a hall of mirrors. She remembered the photograph she wasn't supposed to see. Her mother who once heard and sang, who now had an amazingly elegant white device connected to her left ear like a piece of futuristic jewelry. Without touching the choir, she left it in its place, and her eyes met a small bed with a checked blanket, a masterpiece of weaving. This was perhaps the most beautiful of the creations in Anna's cabinet. Even more beautiful than the goose, but she didn't want to touch it. Two girls lay in the bed. Similar and not similar, because one had red hair and the other brown, and the two of them had narrow eyes, almost slits. They looked as if they were scared of the dark, of the wolf, of Little Red Riding Hood. "Are those Lili and me?" she asked.

Anna shrugged her shoulders. "I always thought that they resembled you a bit. But who knows, you aren't the only sisters in the world."

"No," Dori said, still getting used to speaking with her mother aloud, "we definitely aren't."

"Don't break anything," she said again, and Dori wanted to bring the entire cabinet down to the floor, with all the terrible inventions inside it. "He was strange, Noah, I know, such a character. Always coughing. Well, you knew him. He had bad eyes from all the magnifying glasses he looked through for his hobby. Yes," she said theatrically, and Dori noticed how much her mother enjoyed speaking aloud, how her pronunciation was rich and didn't resemble her own at all, "but he was a gentleman." Her pupils looked as if they were floating from all that pleasure.

"He didn't reach your father's ankles," she stated casually. "Your father is a great man, that bastard. We did very great things together. Look, you have nothing to complain about, you didn't come out so bad," and she studied Dori slowly, the shorts, the short hair, the short stature, and her gaze said very different things than did her lips. It's likely that without this gaze the conversation wouldn't have lasted as long as it lasted. It's likely that Dori would have said goodbye to her mother for another ten or twenty years, exiting the green door as she had entered, the same Dori, the same river. But that gaze, there was enough in it nevertheless for Dori to speak, as if Georgia sat on one shoulder and Anati on the other, as if the two of them said: C'mon, now, speak now. As if Anton stood on the side and watched the two of them like an amusing spectacle, a drama of ignorant villagers. And in front of him, out of all of them, she couldn't humiliate herself. "Mother," she said, as if inside the address itself the rest was folded as well. "Mother, why did you do it? Why didn't you let me hear?"

The aging spots that climbed over her mother's hand created a complicated pattern, as if she had drawn them herself. Her mother opened her mouth wide for a moment and inhaled through it and Dori realized that she wasn't missing a single tooth. When she closed her mouth she no longer looked like someone who was about to cry, and only then did Dori wonder where the flood of tears had gone to. She didn't look frightened or angry either. As a matter of fact, it seemed that she had waited quite some time for this question, and the answer calmly rolled off her tongue as well.

"It was you who chose to be like us," she said. "It was your choice. You chose freely." Her mother looked at her defiantly and Dori knew that she saw the army behind her, maybe not Anati and Georgia and Ada, maybe not Dima or Anton who watched all this from the side, but she certainly saw the dozens of policemen and social workers, the investigators who stood up to her to eliminate her, who doubted her maternal sense of duty and threatened her with prison, who mocked her parenting skills and cautioned her with sticks and stones when it came to her ongoing possession of Lili.

They'd had an excellent lawyer, Anna and Alex Ackerman had, a lawyer who specialized in minority rights and was enlisted in their cause. The seasoned lawyer showed that every story can be unraveled in another way, a story is more holes than woven fabric, and as such can surprise he who holds a needle or a pen. Yet even when the honorable attorney positioned himself next to her, with his fluttering jacket and mane of hair and dizzying intelligence, a collection of features that Anna Ackerman very much admired, nevertheless that army was a humiliation that her raised chin struggled to bear.

Did Dori know this? She knew some of it. She read the press about her, deciphering microfilm in an old machine, opening volumes that bound old newspapers together, her hand sliding over the page until the place where the shocking story of the girl D was written, the family under close inspection, the consequences not yet known. She read the professional articles and the chapter in Georgia's book. She even read the novel that Arad wrote, at the center of which is a brilliant and handsome social worker who saves a deaf and mute girl. His book, which was put out by an independent publisher with a shiny cover, was Anati's favorite reading material (other than her plays) and she never tired of reading to Dori the treasure trove of erotic allusions. "You were nine years old!" Anati would shout at her each time with feigned shock. "The man's a pervert!" And Dori would gather up the book that Anati threw at her and remind her that she was ten or eleven whereas Isadora, the beautiful deaf girl in the book, had just reached the age of consent. But despite all that, Arad the idiot actually remembered a few things that Dori had forgotten.

So she did know something about all that, even if she preferred to forget. But Anna Ackerman's advantage was that she understood what Dori had come for, with much greater clarity than Dori herself. Indeed she had prepared herself for this visit over many long years. She'd come not for a plate of cookies or a basket of wormy apples for maximum health or tea in tall glasses, and not in order to finally piece together what was broken. She knew Dori had come to hurl accusations, just as she knew that Dori was soon to discover she was standing opposite a mirror and looking only at herself. Anna Ackerman was a Zen artist of blamelessness.

"Everything changes, everything is suffering," she said, "other than what isn't. Why does your generation think that only it mustn't suffer? You don't always have to be happy. Free yourself, Dori, you didn't eat from the bread of affliction." When she spoke this way, Dori didn't know how deep was the source of this mockery that accompanied her calm words. Mockery for a daughter who came like all satiated children to complain about an ancient hunger, about an empty plate. "All in all, the two of you ate what I made for you," that woman said. And at that moment the words sounded pure and innocent, as if she was really talking about three plates of rice.

### LILI

A goose floats along the water of a lake. I recognize her child's face only when it's reflected in the black water. On those other nights extinct whales float on their belly from continent to continent. The blue whales sing a long and complicated song, but I don't hear a thing. The goose floats in circles. Every night I wake up from my shrieking, because I hear only that.

### DORI

If he wanted complete accuracy, he could have done it himself. For instance, combing his beard in front of the camera, and signing fluently, or choosing a more obedient parrot for himself.

Clearly she didn't say this to him, not explicitly, but her look gave it away—you didn't have to choose me of all people. A moment later she had already lowered her eyes back to the written text, which on that day had no use. When Dori signed in front of the camera her face was full of expression and her movements were soft and round but it's hard to say that she was precise, and here her father, or one of his minions, is again clarifying that this audacity, presuming to be the master of the words, was out of place. It was forbidden for her to belittle in this way the responsibility that was given to her. Dori was an additional pair of hands for her father. The only pair of hands that remained from the inner circle that had abandoned him. She was the only one other than him who knew how to be a pinky, even if they pretended they were a full hand or ingratiated themselves with the other fingers. But only outwardly. As her time passed on the farm, Dori became convinced that Alex Ackerman had built only a facade, elaborate indeed, which concealed many tunnels that had been dug right under the feet of the bourgeoisie. Because she knew her father through and through. And if that wasn't the case, then why would Dima have up and joined him?

Her father again signed the content, making sure to choose the same signs, using them at intervals like the time before, and Dori watched and this time signed as she was instructed, being precise with each and every sign. Her motions were absolutely clear, like the hands of a talking clock. As he did every week, Alex Ackerman described the pastoral life of the farm like a scenic postcard. And she, like a miniaturized and adorable mirror of her father, signed in front of the camera. At times she spoke aloud, although less and less. Thus she described the flourishing of the apple orchard that overcame the cold and yielded a perfect crop. And when she spoke about the German researchers who were conducting pathbreaking research on the farm, research that would make great contributions to the community as well, she didn't mention that they were long-legged and clumsy as young giraffes, and she didn't even contort her face when she described the healthy cake competition that was held two days earlier. She did only what was asked of her and Alex watched her with approval.

She could be even less precise; she actually could sign what she felt like, children's songs or masterpieces, she could translate into sign language book excerpts like Lili and she once would, when the boredom got the best of them, because few deaf people watched the broadcast, if any. She was certain that the absolute majority of their viewers—wherever her father gathered them, Abu Dhabi or upstate New York—could hear, and watched them as an exotic phenomenon, like amateur birdwatchers who catch with their binoculars a rare bird that's also liable to carry contagious diseases. For them the content was more or less extraneous. They were impressed by Dori as if she didn't speak a real language but instead only executed a type of regimented dance, beautiful but meaningless. In their eyes her hands performed a strange, expressive act, which gave rise in them to all sorts of subtle aesthetic feelings. In this matter Dori and her father were of one mind: those who could hear preferred not to understand. At first the use of the language surely astonished them; they were angry to be left outside, in the cold, the rain, the silence, where who knew if they were talking about bats or crumbs, or perhaps they were showing them complete gibberish, but in the end they'd end up pleased. Sometimes they identified a lone sign that they could understand, a very intuitive sign, connected to eating or drinking, for instance, and then they'd sit back with the feeling that they'd acquired real knowledge.

Other than those foolish broadcasts, they left her alone. She wandered for long hours in the farmland, emanating restlessness even though she tried hard to smile at everyone she saw, local or stranger. But there was a purpose to this wandering, because it wasn't wandering at all, but a search. Without saying it explicitly, not even to herself, she searched for him. Dori stuck her hands in all the holes and openings (the very existence of which scared her when she was a girl, to the point that Lili, who knew that her snake-fearing sister walked on tiptoes in fear of a scaly head bursting forth from wherever, found half a sack of plaster and sealed up the many holes in their old room). Sometimes it seemed to her that she recognized his scarf, worn despite the summer, or his heavy gait. They met in another world, which from day to day she struggled to believe ever existed, and if it had, that it was meant for her too.

During the first days on the farm they stopped her every few steps, kissed her on the forehead, patted her shoulders. She tried hard to tolerate it, all that extra touching, as soft lips rested on her forehead and hardworking mouths kissed and moist palms drew near and the smells of many bodies threatened to be absorbed by hers. Then she again weighed whether to inform them that she had come only for a limited time and for a certain purpose, however vague. She meant to explain, but there was no value in this anyway. They saw in her what they wanted to see. As the days passed, the pats and the kisses turned mainly into abundantly warm nods, and those who knew her as a girl were satisfied with a quick hello.

On that afternoon, when she left the improvised studio, saying goodbye to the white plaster lion's head, she wasn't looking forward to meeting the snotty, clear-eyed band of children who set out each and every day on their adventures. They were so different from the children that the two of them had been, with bare tummies and tanned limbs and dirty faces, with the running and the trampling. She searched for Dima among them as well, as if he had shrunken down to a child again. As if she could identify him from among all the children.

The children looked at her, checking if she was one of them or not. The girl whom she met at the studio, her hair straw and a baseball cap with an image of a cat on her head, laughed at Dori and Dori laughed at her. Also at the other children, who looked at the two of them with clear admiration; it was clear that they were sharing some joke, maybe because of that chocolate, maybe because the girl was Lotti's second niece, the younger of the two. Blonde as wheat, deaf as plywood, like Lotti would never be.

She turned to the girl and spelled out the name "Dima," checking if he had made it there and, if he had, when he left. Because he'd explicitly specified the aim of his trip (to the farm, to Dori's father) in the letter he left for her, as if he had caught from her and Lili the letter-writing disease. And if he wrote that he went, then that was what happened; Dima didn't tend to lie. He said that at the farm there was the clarity he needed, he wrote that he had good reasons, he invited her to come visit and lay down the past wherever it was. Buried. Obviously he wrote this with other words. Shorter. Simple. But that was what Dori read on the morning after that night.

But Dima hadn't followed her in the evenings, Anton had. Even then, Anton didn't follow her every time. Not always. Only sometimes. Only when they agreed on it in advance. And when she saw him sitting alone in a café that was included in her excursion, she turned around and left. This was the agreement between them, the main method of compromise: a journey of cafés with Dori in exchange for all the journeys with Anton, a liter of deafness for all the nocturnal sojourns that cut through her flesh, when he loved others, when he forgot for a moment that she was there, forays that she hated but never intended giving up on. It was clear he wanted them to hand out the cards together. He and she, as she had done with Dima.

"Anyway, you're pretending," he said, as if his cuspid-revealing smile could make this sound like a joke.

"No," she said, and not for the first time. "I'm not."

But Anton refused to understand and in fact Dori never explained to him her permanent need for humiliation, the compulsion to be that girl she despised with all her heart, the one who acknowledges deafness not as a strength but rather as a disability and defect, who offers up her deaf ears on a platter, who puts herself on display. Time after time she absorbed those stolen glances, the pity and the criticism. Anton didn't know how much this pain overwhelmed her, lifted her up and degraded her, how much then of all times she felt like Dori Ackerman, flesh and blood, as if who she was meant to be was truly resurrected in these moments. From his perspective this was a small, sweet sting operation. He thought it was sweet, like picking flowers from the neighbors' garden, and mischievous, like selling them in the town square afterward. He liked this streak in her personality, even though in his opinion it was too restrained. She could have added a slight limp, an eye patch. A deformity that would only have made her beautiful, and if not beautiful, then interesting.

He, who appreciated free enterprise and business thinking, didn't understand why Dori amassed jars full of coins and bills on her writing table but he couldn't touch them and she wouldn't take from them even when she was short on money. Dori described Anton's thought process to herself. From his perspective, cooperation between the two of them would only help, certainly from an economic point of view. Anton, who knew how to elicit trust and interest, would certainly bring about an increase in profits by his very presence. What was preventing him from joining, other than Dori's stubbornness? He could be deaf like anyone. Like her. He already tried Dori's plugs, the yellow ones, the pink ones, the green ones, her noise-canceling earplugs, the way certain men try on their lovers' undergarments. This excited him, but he wanted more.

With Anton's eyes fixed on the back of her neck she went to distant cafés, carrying with her a pile of cheap toys to pass out in exchange. Rag-doll monkeys with googly eyes, smiling rubber balls, hair bands, and clothespins. She always hated the pseudo-bartering, as if they were actually buying the cheap lighters from her, as if fair business was being conducted, a transaction between equals and not panhandling. But it was better when Anton was behind her. She hoped that his eyes would focus on the worthless merchandise and not her.

At the start of that evening Anton walked behind her like a shadow, and whoever saw them knew that the shadow was much more successful than the source. His supple gait appeared to be imbued with purpose and interest, whereas Dori walked quickly and bent over, the bag banging against her back, her hands in the pockets of her pants.

She stopped in a café with a branching tree standing at its center and tiny lights hanging from it. The tree, under which the round tables took refuge, was meant to cause the café patrons to forget that the place wasn't a small, independent business but rather part of a thriving chain of coffeehouses. Next to one of the tables a grandfather in the presence of his young grandson pointed at the artificial tree and said, "It's an almond tree," and the boy raised his eyes in amazement and Dori smiled. The second time Dori smiled that evening was when she stood opposite a young woman, almost a girl, with a white scar stretched across the length of her right cheek. Strange, but what Dori thought was that this was apparently one of those flaws that Anton had mentioned, one that made the woman beautiful or at least interesting. And perhaps the woman appeared interesting because she actually looked familiar to her, even though she couldn't determine from where or when. She smiled at Dori with very white teeth and Dori smiled as well, a smile she never smiled when the cards were in her hand. With her finger the girl drew a line from ear to mouth, asking if she was deaf, and Dori, to whom the question was presented with such directness, was dumbstruck. The rest didn't surprise her. She had long expected it. She thought it would be much more violent than that air horn the girl lifted up and pointed at her left ear. The girl's movements were slow and formal and Dori could have simply ducked down and left, but she stayed.

The fist that crushed her stomach was nothing but the pure sound, the thundering, shrieking noise, not music, no, the opposite of it, the sound that sheds blood from the eyes of horses and their riders, under whose auspices all sorts of calamities occur. The girl continued pulling on the trigger even once Dori shrieked from pain and perhaps sang from pain because sometimes the singing and the shrieking took turns, no, not music, something else and Dori folded over, her legs under her chest, until she slackened and lay on the ground, until she was silent, until someone from the café intervened, removing his hands from his ears and standing up to them, because the noise was terrible for everyone, even for those who didn't have the siren pointing straight into their eardrum. And that same someone grabbed the girl, who didn't resist at all, and warned her not to come back. Dori didn't know who it was, maybe Anton, it had to be Anton, who in fact took her home afterward and waited until Anati got her into bed before leaving.

Before Dori fell asleep in her bed, Anati and Anton argued in the doorway to the entrance about the identity of the girl with the air horn. Anati said that it was definitely one of Dori's father's psychos and that when she met them back then at the zoo she already could see that they'd be trouble, and Anton said that Dori must have invaded someone else's territory and that it was an economic conflict, pure and simple. Only Dima, who knew to come to her even though no one called him, placed his hand on her forehead. Dori usually shrank away from contact like this, as if ants were marching across her skin, but there was relief in that heavy hand. Still in that fog, when the blood still hadn't quieted in her veins, she knew that she hadn't paid the full price. Then Dima squeezed out of her a promise that she would never, absolutely never, go back there again.

She left the house early in the morning. Her ears still rang, but she could walk without swaying. Dima sat on a bench in the street and looked at the sparkling chimney, at the smoke that was rising beautifully like in an English mining town, and Dori didn't know if he was waiting for her, even though of course he was waiting for her; after all, it wasn't possible that he was there just because. He had a home somewhere, he didn't live on the street. Her bag was very heavy and she held it in her hands like a baby and he took it from her in silence. They walked on the paved path and Dori recalled her and Anati's old joke about the cat heads and recalled that night when they got drunk together and it suddenly became clear to her that these weren't paving stones but actual cats instead she was stepping on, squashing them with each step, and she refused to continue walking until Anati promised her that the cats were already dead and there was nothing to fear. Dima and Dori walked to the fountain in the small square with the broken mosaic, not far from the main street where kids get drunk and pass out during those dark hours when the filth isn't yet visible in the sunlight and anything can happen.

When they arrived Dori took the bag from him, undid the

laces, and took out nine jars packed with coins and bills. She stood them side by side on the edge of the fountain. Without looking she took out a silver coin and tossed it into the water. The sound of it striking the bottom could be heard clear and faint against the background of the sleeping street. "Now you'll have to come back here," Dima signed, a sentence that didn't suit him, as if he had suddenly begun to believe in destiny instead of sticking to impartial Marxist thinking, but Dori just shrugged her shoulders. She removed the top and spilled the contents of the first jar into the water. Perhaps it was the proximity to the main street, perhaps it was the homeless who lay on benches there and woke up from the noise of the coins, but by the time the contents of the third jar were emptied into the water a crowd of curious people had gathered. At first they just stood and looked until one of those kids who arrived from the main street with wasted eyes interrupted the magic and jumped into the water, gathering up coins in his hands, trampling in the cold water with cries of joy, his hands sailing after bills. The others didn't lag far behind. Dori paused between jars, giving everyone an equal chance, and they understood that these were the rules, and each time only once the coins splashed into the foul water did they begin the hunt. When the ninth jar was emptied Dori stood up and said, "That's it, that's everything," and Dima looked at her as if asking for another promise that this chapter was over for them, that she'd agree with him that almost anything was preferable to this transgressive begging, and Dori again shrugged her shoulders as if that was the only movement she remembered. Dima escorted her home and was already on his way to the farm the next day.

"He's on a mission," the girl signed to her with a look of importance.

"When's he coming back?" Dori asked, and the girl only

shrugged her shoulder and added, as if speaking on behalf of many others, "We don't know."

## ANTON

We're walking in the street. It could be any street, but it's a particular street in a particular neighborhood. A neighborhood that fell from greatness. A neighborhood that people pass through quickly, hands in pockets, a neighborhood that gets poor results on measures of air pollution and hate crimes. She cuts through the old commercial quarter, the nails in the soles of her boots tapping against the paving stones, tick-tick-tick, on the way to a better neighborhood. Recognizable music emerges from the cafés, a calming beat that was composed in countries poorer than ours. This melody could be a soundtrack for anything, accompaniment for attack planes or a company manufacturing soft drinks. And for her too. She walks before me, at a precise distance of five steps, her back a little bent. Her face is tilted downward as if she's looking for a dropped coin. Someone like her should walk upright, like a book is resting on her head. But in her case it wouldn't matter. She would never straighten up; she'd stop and read the book. You understand, I know her. Perhaps I even like her.

The way she cuts across streets, staring at headlights with frightened eyes, like cats and old people do—this way still pleases me. It's a sign that she hasn't given up, that she still fears an unnatural death. I, by the way, cut across streets with eyes closed. Nothing ever happens to me.

A man follows your sister in the street like someone who pants on the phone, who breathes heavily down your neck. Maybe even worse than that. You understand who this man is. Amen, I tell you, Lili. Amen and amen. From any distance I could recognize the back of her neck and the hair resting on it in dark strands. She knows that I'm there but only throws me a glance from time to time, hoping that I've given up and left. And despite what's clear to you now, I'm not crazy; I need you to pay attention. I've already learned that with you only anger cuts through the numb feelings, raises the dead. So you can start getting angry at the pervert clinging to your little sister. Get angry and get up. Hold on, we're not done.

In the first café there are nine tables. Human beings sit around six of them and drink coffee. Someone eats a pastry. Someone is eating his heart out, Dori would say and would maybe be right too, but at these moments she doesn't talk to me. Three couples, an additional table with three, and two loners, one of whom is me. She leaves a handwritten card for everyone and places on top of it a stitched doll for banishing bad dreams, a doll stitched in a rising third-world country to resemble folk art from the sinking third world. The stupid doll reaches us by way of these worlds, landing on the coffee table. At two of the tables they take a finger-sized doll and leave money without looking at her.

Imagine me, if you can, and maybe you can't. From your perspective I probably never existed, but imagine me. Not as the one who follows her from café to café, but me with fingers crossed, bent over a pile of letters you sent. Imagine that I'm the writer and the addressee. That I sit in all the seats, drinking the last sip of coffee in the cup, wearing the hats you left empty. Just imagine. But I'm no one, a ghost, a devil wearing a jacket. Nevertheless, imagine me and do it slowly, with pleasure, even. I'm the one writing you.

You're completely awake now; your skin is trembling. You didn't know that this is what your little sister does and you certainly didn't know that someone is following her. You would call the police, but you're on the other side of the globe, beyond the zipper. I know that too. I even know about the fake globe that you learned geography from, the zipper that cut through the Americas, the place where her finger would rub against the defective edges. Maybe it would be better if you felt some sympathy for me. We'll start over, maybe I'm a boy who lives in the forest, picks berries, sees angels going up and down a ladder, grows wings. Yes, I'm trying hard now, getting carried away. You won't even think that I inspire confidence or empathy, you'll puke from all this. And that's okay. Just keep reading. Nod your head and say, "Total psychopath." I accept it. No problem.

Love is the only point. Your sister said this to me before morning came. She sat on a tall chair, upright and serious with a mixture of expectation and acceptance. I saw her and it was as if the night itself was a thick substance that was about to drip down onto her, as if night was all that there was and the word *love* was the only word in the world.

She didn't expect me to say it to her myself. She's not one whom love would slap in the face without reservations. Look at me, I who love neither man nor woman. I who call out "who's there" just to hear the echo. This is Dori's version of my life, I understand. But sometimes she's certain, with a kind of cold desperation, that I'm in love not just with myself but with everyone except her. With her friend, with my mother, with you. But you and I, we haven't met, we're shadows passing through each other's life. Only outlines.

I read your letters, but I don't believe you. Don't believe a single word. Dori says you have the scent of milk. But she's the one who smells of chalk and milk. Maybe she was mistaken. Maybe she was always smelling only herself.

Once we traveled together, I had an American car for a couple of days. It was like a ship with a massive prow, so your sister said, but she didn't ask anything about it. It was a holiday and she looked like herself, like always, dressed a bit wretchedly, wearing a headband with the ears of a mouse. After an hour we stopped at a commercial center on the side of the highway. Dori went inside to get us coffee and I looked through the windshield. All the cashiers in the place had identical ears, the same mouse ears from the movies. I saw everything. I thought she'd notice and remove her ears, holiday or no holiday, anyone would do that, but she began laughing. She became quite happy over the fact that at any moment she could have replaced one of the cashiers.

Perhaps I love her, but I had the good sense not to tell her. I've never in my life seen someone who is gripped by non-love like her. Since then, your sister has closed the door, and I'll admit that closed doors fascinate me more than wide-open windows. But I don't pass through. Not through the window and not through the door.

In her eyes I'm Anton, a spoiled child. Someone whom she's better without. Someone whose departure they applaud when she says goodbye to him. After all, my mother and I are rich and lonely, swimming the breaststroke through stocks and bonds. Did she write you? We own homes and she's homeless. There's no reason to tell her that it's because of the creditors that we move among the apartments that were once in our possession. There was money and there were debts and only the latter expanded. Simply, we have nothing. The bank owns the apartments and we reside in them for the present, thanks to a kindness that someone at the bank has extended to my mother and a clause that could be nullified at any moment. If they need an apartment for hosting, we're out with a suitcase. In another era they would bury me in the potter's field.

Even as an extremely poor person, I'm not an innocent or honest man. My acts until now don't testify in my favor. So be it.

I don't save my mother either, letting her bite her lips, allowing the two of us to be impoverished until the end of time. No, I'm not lifting a finger. But I'm writing to you because after everything it has become clear that it's my task to tell you the truth. Apparently I'm the only one who remembers you and I'm also adequately honest to write to you—Lili Ackerman, who turned invisible. The world has forgotten you. Impossible not to envy you for this.

Anyone with eyes in his head would understand everything from the beginning, would see how things developed and not be surprised the day your sister left and went to your father. This person would know that your father's nonsense still has power over her. Odd that you didn't arrive there before her. Odd that you didn't see. Yes, it may be that I couldn't watch Dori until the end; I was voluntarily blind before her. But you I know. I may be the last who still differentiates between the two of you. I'm doubtful you can do that yourself. You remember, we already met before. Blue boots but you didn't have a coat. The air was cold. You looked to the other side when someone kissed my hand, my neck. Now too my neck is often kissed. You understand, I'm never alone for long.

Bye, Lili. I'm not bursting into your life but rather saying farewell to the two of you. The door is already open, but I don't intend on staying. She indeed left me, but nevertheless it was me who let her go. She left me, I admit, but only because she left you first.

Anton

## ALEX

At this time no one causes him injustice, voluntarily or involuntarily, anymore. At this time injustice is caused because the world is waiting for its tiny prey that in truth looks like an old exalted man who lies in his bed but in fact isn't so old, in fact this is a small boy teetering on his toes, a boy who's about to fall off the edge of the world. There are many mothers, big and small, they are like soft columns surrounding him and the bed is very white because worried hands stretched over it the whitest of sheets, like his beard that now appears to his blurry, swollen eyes like a disguise and he wants to tear it out but the belated pain arrives at once and a hand hushes him the way one hushes a child, enough now enough already. They gather around him and he wants to get up and escape and play with a ball outside, he once had a wonderful ball a splendid ball with strong seams where is it? No one knew how to kick hard like Alex, throughout the neighborhood they were amazed by Alex's kick and someone whistled and called out Alexander the Great and he kept on kicking with a massive smile on his face and yes he still heard then he heard. This was before he met Anna this was before the school for the deaf that came to him after the diving accident that took his ears from him, angry mad and irate and he discovered how easy it is for him to establish a monarchy, ugh where's that ball dammit it seems to him that he's swallowing it now a soft and sticky ball a ball that fills his whole mouth it's impossible to breathe impossible to swallow impossible not to vomit, out with it here's Alex my good boy it's only the fever puke it up here's a mother hen cluck cluck cluck she cackles she's looking for grain for her children the—doesn't matter, the hand cleaning his mouth is unfamiliar to him, a stranger's hand wipes his mouth, it was good to hurl it to throw it into the air poof like a balloon or an airplane, high up in the sky, tears fall onto the sheet, pigs, only pigs cry like that, he looks up and the room is too full give him air he wants air the hands spread out and round heads burst forth like balls and rest under his hands and someone draws out a sign, bless them and Alex blesses. Blessed may you be. Here's Ogden. Good Ogden. Here's Lotti. Good Lotti. Here they are the good people scarecrows children of scarecrows stinking from so much good, he needs his mother now he wants to drink. I'm Dima someone says, signing his name slowly as if Alex is a fool trust me he says but Alex doesn't trust why would he trust maybe he actually has the ball bloated chicken that he is, phooey, phooey Dima, but the hands are like demons signing alone blessed may you be and Dima returns to shadow. Like at the theater he thinks and enjoys it because who doesn't love the theater, someone stands at the edge of the room the light falls on her in a straight beam her clothes are pink like a sunset her hair, what's this, it falls from her head like a snake, impossible to see her face but it's his Anna who isn't good but she's his, he waits for her to caress him on the neck and feed him a small raisin cake, no, he needs water to drink water or tea or cherries in water, he once tasted cherries but he can no longer recall their taste, blessed may you be his hands draw out. Anna doesn't come to him. Someone signs saint, Anna also signs saint and cries, he wants to turn his head and see the holy man but he can't. The holy man should come and sit next to him, what doesn't he see that little Alex is sick? Here are his hands. A man's strong hands. Not an old man's. Whose hands are these? Strange. There are many hands in the world. He'd count the hands if only they'd give him time. Two women at his side. This one from here and this one from there. A smell of milk and smoke. A smell of chalk and a flower whose name it's impossible to recall but he remembers. Maybe it's his mother why his mother is very late when will she return already, the anticipation flows over the tongue like a candy, yes it's Mother, twice it's Mother, he doesn't hear her but he actually knows what she's saying, his mother calls him Father, the second mother is silent, funny, so funny to call a child Father, it's from the metal, one mother signs, it's his heart says the second one. He knows it's not the first time they signed to each other, his dear mothers, the world is white like sugar like a pillowcase like snow like a blanket, go forth Alex Ackerman fly away already heavy white bird fat dove that you are, fly over the living lands and all the best to you Alex to the Ackerman home who was once Alexander the Great.

Once upon a time there was a girl who walked opposite a calf and the calf mooed. Once there were two girls. Like a pair of mismatched shoes. Once upon a time they grew and were young women. Perhaps this happened many times. Not so educated. Not so successful. But here they are. Once upon a time Dori signed to her sister in the weekly broadcast, "Come home, Father is sick," and she didn't know it was already too late for this because Lili carrying her oversized belly is already on the plane, counting the hours, hurrying home, saying the word "home" in a few languages and in all of them it sounds strange and familiar to her. Their father was about to die. They had nothing to do but wait together for the death pangs.

Their holy father lay in his white bed, covered in pillows. Lotti surprised them with her good taste, with the complete and pure majesty that suited all the ritual's rules. She sat stooped next to him, seizing a dominant corner but adequately remote in the picture. Opposite them stood dozens of plastic chairs and in them were people crying bitterly. Anna leaned on a wall and rubbed her eyes emphatically. Her shoulders shook. His face was red but his white beard still pointed toward the ceiling like a flagpole.

"These are the daughters." Lotti signed the obvious. "Let them approach." At the foot of the bed were gathered toys the children had brought, offerings before a sacred tree. Lotti's nieces sorted the toys with great care, moving a broken train car from here to there. Lili and Dori didn't grant them even a glance. The faces of those present wore true suffering, as if head- and stomachaches, shriveled intestines, and constricted lungs had attacked them all at once. But this was their father's power; they felt it in their flesh. Heartbreak and body-break were one. Dori and Lili stood across from each other in summer dresses. Lili's belly protruded and Dori was thin as ever. They didn't look like sisters. Not exactly.

Lotti declared to the two of them with mournful solemnity, without distinguishing between Lili and Dori, "He's on borrowed time. He was waiting only for you." Revulsion spread across her face but maybe it was just a twitch. In fact, Alex Ackerman's daughters seemed to be gangly and budding as if the years had fallen from them and the two stood as teens, holding hands before the whole world, before a bright future, but they didn't hold hands and each one of them could only speculate about her sister's youth.

Dori was the first to approach the white bed and Lili caught up to her and stood on his other side. One of them carefully caressed his face and her sister signed, "Hello, Father," even though what she meant to say was "Hello, Sir King," and in response her father will raise himself up on his elbows and that same glimmer of scorn will appear in his eyes while his hands will say, "Hello, my dear daughters, where have you been and what have you done?" and perhaps she wanted to hurl harsher words than those at him. Even with the pregnant stomach it was hard to distinguish her, even from the plastic chairs arranged in a U shape, and in any case Lotti had no intention of looking at them. "There was never a cellar," Lili finally said, signing the made-up cellar opposite the face of the boy from the cellar and perhaps opposite her sister's face. Dori looked at them alternately but the father was silent as he had been silent up to that moment and blessed them with his heavy hands, blessed may you be.

And they were truly blessed. "He left you everything," Dima said. "I saw to it. All the papers are with me. This farm is yours."

"I don't want it," Dori said, such that Lili didn't even have to say a thing. Indeed the two of them only wanted to say how good it was to have Dima here, how they had missed him.

"You lost weight, Dima," Lili said, laughing, and Dori agreed. He'd lost weight and grown taller. He'd grown a mustache. But despite the heat that prevailed there, he still went about with a scarf wrapped around his neck. It wasn't foppish. It suited him. The three of them trod through a puddle outside the cultural center that had almost dried up, stealing glances as if they had just met for the first time. "First we'll destroy it," one says, and gestures with her hand at the old structure, and the other recoils, "Not the lion," and her sister understands and approves.

"But what's with your child?" Dima tried again, and looked at Lili's belly only in order to quickly remove his gaze as if it were improper. "In any case," he added seriously, "you have to worry about him, Lili, you'll be a mother." Dima looked at her with admiration, as if the coming motherhood infused her with holiness. Everyone became holy there, in the Ackerman family, even though holiness was the last thing one would think to attribute to any of them.

And Lili, who didn't think that it was time to remind Dima about his beliefs about abolishing inheritance laws and justice for all, raised her chin and pointed at her belly. "In any case, this one here's a girl."

Evening had already fallen. At noon the two of them blinked at the sun that flooded the land in a white light. The sisters sat, hands in laps, without adding clods to the soil that had been gathered onto the dead body, without touching. They sat on a knoll of dirt beyond the short brick wall, beyond the city of dead that had grown and grown since they were small and scared each other with ghost stories. They gazed beyond the wall, looked back without really seeing Lotti and Anna spar over the role of the grieving widow. Lili's belly was solid as a rock. As a house. Dori rested her hand on the belly for a moment and her sister let her. She extended her legs over the dirt and looked at the flowers of the dress clinging to her. Soon she won't have anything to wear. Soon she'll have a little girl, quite tiny, who'll look only at her, who will demand from her pure love. Dori said that the original plan was for Alex to be buried in the cultural center. Lotti wanted to transform it into a mausoleum; after all, Alex Ackerman was already a public figure, she claimed, and in fact much more than that. She was already envisioning the pilgrims and their offerings. But in the end the Ministry of Health intervened. "The long arm of the establishment," said Lili, as if right then they weren't burying their father, the man who taught them everything.

It was a well-attended ceremony. Many of the mourners never met the deceased during his life but this didn't lessen their grief. Some of them arrived because of Dori's broadcasts, but when they saw her face-to-face, a young woman sitting, a bit disinterested, far from the entrance to the cemetery, they didn't recognize her. The cemetery was so full of people that the number of living was greater than that of the dead and some of them could only find a place beyond the fence, where they gathered in groups and Dori and Lili could count the hair follicles of the curious. Other than the words of the head of the council, which were spoken aloud and focused on his involvement in the community, and the long, rhyming poem that the dear friend Idit read, the handful of eulogies were carried out in their language and aroused a combination of wonder and admiration among those in attendance. It seemed to Dori that she saw Georgia and Ada standing next to each other. Anton's there, she thought for a moment, even though this wasn't at all possible, but in truth it seemed that he was glancing at her, his face covered in a beard as if he was one of the pious, wearing a leather jacket, his face defiantly calm. Lili's strange friend Uriel Savyon arrived as well. At least one person in the crowd recalled the boy he was, the boy she knew not only from Lili's letters, but from his coming to visit her once in the boarding school. They spoke about stars; this she remembered although she didn't know why he was so interested in the solar system. Without a doubt Dori was getting carried away, she was putting every person she knew in the village cemetery. She was even able to recognize among the guests a few of the tigers or waterfowl that had arrived from the zoo.

Dori looked at all those present because she was still waiting for Anati to come and swing open the cemetery gates, scream at someone and swear, smash someone's car, even though that same morning Dori had begged her not to come. "It's not a wedding, Dori," Lili said to her with reproach, guessing her thoughts as before. "You don't have to welcome the guests." But she wasn't insulted. She was no longer a letter whose contents her sister could guess without opening the envelope. After all, Lili spoke with Lili and Dori spoke with Dori, and that was it. What was spoken between them, very very little, was as minuscule as the edge of a fingernail. But even if these words were a bad bit of business, the world still whispered blue letters, like the notes teenage girls write on their wrists and backs of their hands and middle fingers so they won't forget and then immediately forget anyway.

When they sat next to each other on the knoll they now saw that their hands were very similar, the same long fingers, the same reddish roughness in the palm. In fact both their hands perfectly resembled the hands of Anna Ackerman. Something they got from her, this was certain. "Until mine swell up," Lili said. "Next month I'll be as big as a balloon."

"Like a ball," Dori suggested.

"That too," Lili agreed.

The strangers who arrived heard that the great father, Alex Ackerman, had two deaf daughters. At the end of a brief uncertainty, those present understood that the great man's daughters were none other than the two serious girls in the brown dresses who stood by the grave. No one bothered to correct this impression and announce that the deaf girls who on that day were combed and dressed with a sure hand were related to Lotti, who stood over them, stroking and patting their combed heads.

"Come, see the documents," Dima said, almost pulling them by the hands out of eagerness. His small room was extremely neat. There was little furniture in it and many books, which were arranged in straight, attractive rows. There wasn't a single picture. One could fall asleep on his low bed and dream of nothing. There was a cabinet. And inside the cabinet (Dima showed them when he swung open its doors) there was a chest. Not a treasure chest but rather a rectangular metal chest, closed with a lock. Lili recalled the story about the goose who swallowed a key that opened every door. When after much effort the key was removed and the door was finally opened, behind it there was just another goose, made of gold and precious stone, true, but a goose is a goose. And she tried to remember if she told this story to Dori or Dori to her. Actually, in Dori's story, she remembered, the hidden goose was made of shiny metal, but for God's sake how many geese can glide like this back and forth in her memory, beating their feathers, spewing out keys.

Dima opened the chest that was filled with clear binders, and in them were files of accounting pages and bills of ownership, proof of what he was giving to the two of them. They looked silently at the notary's signature and Alex's signature, under each of which appeared Dima's simple signature. "I told you, it's yours. Everything is computerized. But you," he added, and signed carefully, with a thin smile, "always loved paper." Dori looked into the neatly ordered cabinet and saw that Lili's old notebooks, or notebooks that looked very similar to them, were arranged there in stacks, even though they disappeared some time ago, were destroyed, got wet or were burned, were exposed to winds that blew page after page, word after word, from them, and they knew that neither one of them would read from them again. Dima, who followed Dori's gaze, stuck a folded-up sheet of lined paper into her hand and she closed her fist around it. "Read this afterward," he signed. "If you want." Even with a closed hand Dori understood that it was an ancient note, which had been folded up and straightened out many times. A note in a girl's handwriting, handwriting more familiar to her than her own. But there's a time for everything. A time to mourn and a time to dance, and the note was slid into her pocket.

"I kept these for you too," he added, and Dori saw the missing birds that Anna didn't have. Dima was like a magician whose tricks were no longer of any use. Once there were many more, a whole flock, but only two remain. Blue and green. The birds that Uncle Noah, who died too, long ago, built for them. Lili takes one of them and stands it on her palm. They still work if you turn the keys or move the small handle. They're like two clocks that display another, distant time. The mechanical birds sing simple songs that are buried in the bellies, single-toned songs that now sound hoarse, songs that Lili and Dori haven't heard for years and years. Once, one of them heard and the other didn't. And now both hear. "I remember them," the one says, and the other doesn't deny it. Because sometimes that's all there is. The facts and only the facts and nothing else besides.

Dear Establishment,

My name is Lili. My sister's name is Dori. Our father is deaf. I'm deaf too. Our mother is hard of hearing. Dori and I go to school at home. Sometimes we sleep in one bed. People think that Dori is deaf but she's not. You need to teach her to speak and hear even if she doesn't want to.

Sincerely,

Lili Ackerman

# ACKNOWLEDGMENTS

*Aquarium* is a work of fiction and the Ackerman family doesn't represent the diverse deaf community in any way. That being said, in the course of researching for this book, alongside the professional literature, I received help from people and organizations who generously shared their knowledge with me. I want to offer special thanks to some of them.

First among them is Tamar Halutzi, sign language interpreter, who kindly taught me the nuances and subtleties of Israeli sign language.

I'm also grateful to the Institute for the Advancement of the Deaf in Israel and my sign language teacher, Amit Elbaz, who graciously taught me basic terms in this rich language. Additional thanks to Riki Bitton, director of social services at the Deaf Association, who opened the doors of the association to me and shared her knowledge with me.

It is with great pleasure that I thank my brilliant editor, Oded Wolkstein. I hope that there will be some more strange ships for us to steer. I thank Keter Books, which provided *Aquarium* its first welcoming home. I'd like to express my gratitude to Todd Hasak-Lowy, who dared to travel to unknown territory and ingeniously echoed words, music, and spaces inhabited by tunes keyboards do not play. I am also grateful to Maayan Eitan for her enchanting attention.

It is an extremely pleasant obligation to thank my agent, Paul Lucas, whose genuine love for books is only comparable to his love for human beings.

My FSG editor, Julia Ringo, is an absolute marvel—I don't have enough words to thank her for her wisdom and generosity. And finally, I am happily indebted to the whole wonderful team at Farrar, Straus and Giroux—a publishing house I was secretly dreaming about ever since its name loomed on my horizon.

If errors and mistakes made their way into the book, they are my responsibility alone.

## A Note About the Author

Yaara Shehori is an Israeli novelist and poet. She has been an editor of Hebrew literature at Keter Books since 2013. In 2015, Shehori was awarded the Prime Minister's Prize for Hebrew Literary Works and the Ministry of Culture's award for upcoming writers. She holds a PhD in Hebrew literature from the Hebrew University of Jerusalem and was awarded a Fulbright scholarship and a fellowship from the University of Iowa International Writing Program. In 2017, *Aquarium* was recognized with the Bernstein Prize for the best original Hebrew-language novel.

## A Note About the Translator

Todd Hasak-Lowy is an American writer and translator, and a professor of creative writing and literature at the School of the Art Institute of Chicago. He is the author of *The Task of This Translator*, a short-story collection; *Captives*, a novel; a narrative memoir for young adults, *Somewhere There Is Still a Sun*, cowritten with the Holocaust survivor Michael Gruenbaum; and three books for younger readers. Hasak-Lowy lives in Evanston, Illinois, with his wife and two daughters.